An excerpt from
Under A Duke's Hand

Tilda squeezed her hands. "Goodness, you're going to marry a *duke* in two days. How can you stand the anticipation? What shall you do until it's time?"

"I'm going to ride Effie to some pretty meadow and smell the flowers, and enjoy my last afternoon of freedom. I'm sure once I'm wed, the ghastly duke will expect me to sit about in his ghastly castle and act like a ghastly duchess in a ghastly ruffled gown."

Tilda, who loved ghastly ruffled gowns, sighed and hugged herself. "Becoming a duchess is so exciting though, isn't it?"

"Would you like to do it? Marry some stranger you've never met, and go with him to London where it's crowded and dirty, and everyone speaks with a funny accent?" A wave of nerves fluttered in Gwen's stomach. "Papa says I may have to attend an audience with the king."

"A duke is practically a king," said Tilda. "And you'll be *married* to him. I wonder what he'll be like."

"I'm certain he'll be intolerably haughty and probably very ugly. He'll have crooked teeth and a big belly pouring over the front of his trousers. All those old aristocrats do."

"Not all, Gwennie. None of your brothers look like that."

"They aren't that old." Elrick was the eldest of the seven, and he had no belly at all. "Maybe the duke won't have a belly. I don't know. But something will be wrong with him." She sat to pull on her scuffed riding boots. "Otherwise he could have taken some wife in England, some fine lady with a royal pedigree."

"It's because of your father," Tilda reminded her. "He asked the king to..."

To order some poor man to marry you. It stung her pride, that it had come to that. Gwen was twenty-two, long past an age to be married, but she had never managed to attract any acceptable candidates. Not one suitor had asked for her hand.

And the Duke of Arlington hadn't either...

Under A Duke's Hand

by

Annabel Joseph

Other books by Annabel Joseph

Mercy
Cait and the Devil
Firebird
Owning Wednesday
Lily Mine
Disciplining the Duchess
The Edge of the Earth (as Molly Joseph)
Pawn (as Molly Joseph)

Fortune series:
Deep in the Woods
Fortune

Comfort series:
Comfort Object
Caressa's Knees
Odalisque
Command Performance

Cirque Masters series:
Cirque de Minuit
Bound in Blue
Master's Flame

Mephisto series:
Club Mephisto
Molly's Lips: Club Mephisto Retold
Burn For You

BDSM Ballet series:
Waking Kiss
Fever Dream

Properly Spanked series:
Training Lady Townsend
To Tame A Countess
My Naughty Minette

Chapter One:
A Handsome Stranger

Wales, 1794

"I don't think this is a good idea." Her cousin Tilda tucked a bit of ebony hair beneath Gwen's weathered bonnet. "If your father sees you sneaking out in these dreadful clothes, he'll lock you in your room."

"They're not dreadful clothes. They're riding clothes, my most comfortable ones." Gwen twitched at her faded skirts. "And Papa can't lock me in my room if I'm to be married the day after tomorrow. I'm just taking Effie for one last ride around the village."

"And how will you get home when that ragged old nag keels over dead?"

"Don't say such things, not when I'll miss her so. You promised you'd come feed her apples at least twice a week."

Her cousin's eyes softened. "I will, I promise."

"Even when you aren't sweet on Drustan anymore?" Tilda's love interest looked after the horses on Gwen's father's estate.

"Even when Dru and I are married," said Tilda with a grin. "I swear to you, old Effie shall have all the apples she desires."

Gwen pulled at her gown's ill-fitting bodice. Since her betrothal to the Duke of Arlington, all Papa's money had gone to wedding and court finery, and she dared not wear those sorts of clothes while she rode along dusty paths. "Thanks for helping me steal away, Tilly. If I must be given in marriage to some horrid English aristocrat I've never laid eyes on, I would like one last afternoon all to myself." She thought a moment. "Perhaps, while I'm away, a handsome stranger will befriend me and fall deeply in love with me, and secret me to his hilltop castle so I needn't marry the duke after all."

Tilda giggled. "You and your romantic dreams." She turned Gwen around to adjust her stays. "You'd better not run off with any strangers, or Uncle Alwyn will have my head for abetting you. I wish you'd take at least one other person along. Drustan will escort you if you ask."

"Drustan would rather stay behind with you."

Her buxom cousin blushed a furious shade of red, and her eyes got that glazed, enamored look.

"Why, the two of you intend to steal away for the afternoon," Gwen accused. "And here you've been scolding me for going out to ride."

"Drustan's officially courting me, you realize. Papa allows us to spend time together."

Gwen was so jealous of her cousin. Drustan was a kind, brawny man, with twinkling eyes and a great laugh. When he looked at Tilda, anyone could see that he adored her. "Does he kiss you when you're together?" Gwen asked shyly.

"You're a silly girl."

"Silly girl? I'm older than you."

"And far more innocent. As you should be, since you're a fine lady, and I'm only a common relation." Tilda squeezed her hands. "Goodness, you're going to marry a *duke* in two days. How can you stand the anticipation? What shall you do until it's time?"

"I'm going to ride Effie to some pretty meadow and smell the flowers, and enjoy my last afternoon of freedom. I'm sure once I'm wed, the ghastly duke will expect me to sit about in his ghastly castle and act like a ghastly duchess in a ghastly ruffled gown."

Tilda, who loved ghastly ruffled gowns, sighed and hugged herself. "Becoming a duchess is so exciting though, isn't it?"

"Would you like to do it? Marry some stranger you've never met, and go with him to London where it's crowded and dirty, and everyone speaks with a funny accent?" A wave of nerves fluttered in Gwen's stomach. "Papa says I may have to attend an audience with the king."

"A duke is practically a king," said Tilda. "And you'll be *married* to him. I wonder what he'll be like."

"I'm certain he'll be intolerably haughty and probably very ugly. He'll have crooked teeth and a big belly pouring over the front of his trousers. All those old aristocrats do."

"Not all, Gwennie. None of your brothers look like that."

"They aren't that old." Elrick was the eldest of the seven, and he had no belly at all. "Maybe the duke won't have a belly. I don't know. But something will be wrong with him." She sat to pull on her scuffed riding boots. "Otherwise he could have taken some wife in England, some fine lady with a royal pedigree."

"It's because of your father," Tilda reminded her. "He asked the king to..."

To order some poor man to marry you. It stung her pride, that it had come to that. Gwen was twenty-two, long past an age to be married, but she had never managed to attract any acceptable candidates. Not one suitor had asked for her hand.

And the Duke of Arlington hadn't either.

"He's probably no more excited to marry me," she said. "What a disaster for everyone."

She walked with Tilda toward the stables, wondering why she was so repellent to men. She was tall, it was true, but not shockingly so. She had a bit of a temper, but she mostly kept it in check. She did not whine, or wilt, or put on airs like some of the other gentry's daughters. Perhaps it was her unusual green eyes that unsettled them. But she'd inherited those pale eyes from her mother, who was considered a great beauty before the fever took her.

If only her mama was still here. She would never have allowed her daughter to be married to an Englishman, and a stranger. "I'm terrified the duke won't be kind," Gwen said. "That's my greatest fear."

Her cousin took her hand. "I'm sure he's a very kind man. In a couple of days you'll be on your way to a grand adventure, experiencing all sorts of majestic things."

Gwen and Tilda parted as Drustan sauntered over to greet his beloved. Gwen bid them farewell and climbed onto Effie's swayed back. It was a beautiful October day, warm and bright, with barely a chill in the air. Gwen skirted around the village, leading Effie through the open field beyond the miller's property. The leaves were turning orange, brown, and gold, and rustled underfoot as they plodded along the path. They cut through a copse of trees and around an overgrown hedge, and followed a crumbling stone wall until it opened into a half-shaded clearing. The nag took up her usual spot in the shade, and immediately set to grazing.

Gwen climbed down from the saddle and walked into the meadow with a sigh. If this wasn't the most picturesque, bewitching place in the world, she'd like to see its better. She couldn't remember when she'd first found this place. She'd stumbled upon it in her wanderings and been struck at once by its beauty. It was private and fragrant with wildflowers, bordered by a shady spot of lake. There was a peaceful feeling here, like one was in a dream or fairy tale.

I've come to say goodbye to this meadow, she thought. *Just as I must say goodbye to everything else.*

She pulled off her bonnet and turned her face to the sun. Her hair tumbled down her back, blowing in the breeze. She'd miss the Welsh countryside, even if she was only moving a couple days' journey east. She'd be leaving her entire life, her father and brothers and sisters-in-law, and nieces and nephews and cousins.

Gwen had always wished to be married, so she ought to be happy, but she hadn't expected to be married quite like this. Elrick and Papa had argued for some time about the betrothal. Elrick shouted that Papa was using her as a pawn, but in the end, it was her father's choice. It was her father's war heroics that had earned this opportunity from the king, and he chose to sign the contracts which sealed her fate.

Aidan Francis Samuel Drake, His Grace the Duke of Arlington. Gwen felt misgivings about marrying a stranger with ten words in his name. She had no idea if she would make him a good wife, or how she would cope with the intimacies of marriage. Unlike Tilda, Gwen knew nothing of love. She'd never been courted or kissed. Now it appeared her first kiss would come from some aged blueblood with the longest name in Christendom. Maybe the duke wouldn't even kiss her. Perhaps he would think a Welsh baron's daughter too common, too far beneath him. He'd certainly think so if he saw her now, in her faded riding gown.

Gwen picked her way through the flowers to the line of ancient boulders bordering the lake, and kicked off her boots. Her stockings went next, tossed upon the grass alongside her bonnet. She climbed atop her favorite rock and dangled her feet down into the water, and wondered how it could feel so chilly when the air was so warm. She closed her eyes and clasped her hands in her lap, and began to pray, something her mother had taught her to do when she was a young child. *Ask the heavens for what your heart wants*, she would say. *Ask the flowers and wind and sky. You are never alone; the earth knows your prayers.*

"Please," she whispered. "Please let him be at least a little bit handsome. And patient, and gentle." Often when she prayed like this, she pictured her mother's face, smiling and nodding at her. It brought her comfort, even if she was whispering to nothing but the wind. "Please let him have an understanding heart, and a kind manner." She thought a moment. "If I had to make a choice between the handsomeness and the kindness, I suppose I would prefer to have kindness, although a middling dose of both qualities would be best. And if it's not too much to ask, I wish...perhaps...someday he might come to love me, if he's the sort of duke who's not too lofty to fall in love."

"Am I in Wales, or am I in Paradise? An angel has flown into my wood."

The deep voice drew her from her whispered prayers. Someone had discovered her secret meadow! Gwen turned to find the source of the voice, and nearly fell off her rock.

It was her handsome stranger, not twenty yards away.

The gorgeous man sat upon a stump, one leg crossed lazily over the other. He was older than her, but still fit and vital. His long, golden hair framed a starkly attractive face. Not a pretty face. He was no pretty man with those gold locks, but more like a Viking, with a strong jawline and prominent features. Just like a Viking, he was sun-bronzed and able-bodied. She could not remember knowing any man with such wide shoulders, or such a muscular chest. Despite his showy physique, he was dressed plainly in doeskins and a buff vest. He balanced a sketch book on his knee, and a smudge of charcoal sullied his cheek.

This Viking had called her an angel, which was perhaps not entirely proper of him. In fact, he gazed at her so intently her cheeks began to flush.

"You aren't in Paradise," she said. "You're in Wales, a very pretty corner of it."

"Indeed," he replied.

He said only that one word, but the way he said it made her slide down from her rock and go for her stockings and boots. She knew she ought to leave without saying another word, but he was so appealing to look at, and his eyes seemed kind.

"Where have you come from?" she asked, which seemed a very safe and polite question to occupy him while she readied herself to go.

He made a gesture toward the north. "I've traveled down from Cheltenham."

That explained his English accent. "Were you there to take the baths?"

"Yes, and then I continued in search of picturesque Welsh villages." He held up his book. "I'm an artist, and what a lovely subject I've stumbled upon. Will you allow me to sketch you?"

She grimaced as she stuffed her feet into her too-small boots. "I'm sure you could find a better subject than me." She picked up her bonnet, meaning to tuck her hair beneath it.

He leaned forward. "Don't."

The authority in his tone made her go still.

He smiled then, a rakish, disarming smile that was so beautiful. "I wish you wouldn't hide your lovely face beneath that brim and run away from me. Please, let me sketch you. It will only take a short while."

Goodness, the way he looked at her. *Perhaps a handsome stranger will befriend me and fall deeply in love with me, and secret me to his hilltop castle.* She wondered if this man had a hilltop castle. Why, he was so masculine and charming, she'd settle for a cabin in the woods.

Gwen decided she would let him sketch her even though it was not quite proper, because he was her handsome stranger and because she could amuse Tilda with the story later. And here, at last, was a man who seemed to find her appealing. She certainly admired *his* comely attributes. His steady gaze, his broad shoulders, his lips...

Guinevere Vaughn, you want him to kiss you.

Of course she would never let him, but there was something exciting about a man finally wanting to kiss her. Probably wanting to kiss her. Perhaps he only wished to draw her. He certainly made a fuss about seating her in the best light, and angling her chin just so, and arranging her hair so it fell over her shoulders in just the perfect way.

As he did this, she thrilled to his nearness and his uncommon size. He smelled wonderful, like soap and sandalwood, and his eyes were a beautiful deep blue. He met her gaze for a moment as he composed her hair. His regard was so intense that she looked away. She stared instead at his lips, pursed in concentration. My goodness, did all men have such attractive lips, or had she fallen under some spell? Perhaps *he* was the angel in this meadow, come down from heaven to tempt her chastity mere hours before she was to wed.

"Can you sit very still?" he asked. "And hold this pose for me?"

"I'll try."

She wondered if he was a famous sort of artist. His clothes were common, but his sketch book looked exceedingly fine. She had heard of artists so obsessed with their craft that they cared nothing for manners or appearance, and went about looking almost as hermits, with dirty clothes and disheveled hair. Not that this man was dirty or disheveled. He was exactly the opposite, clean and attractive, and strong, and fine to look upon.

Gwen, you goose. You're to meet your betrothed on the morrow. She couldn't lose her head over this handsome stranger. He was not really going to fall in love with her, and he was not going to take her to his hilltop castle, as sweet as the fantasy was.

"How pretty you are," he said, as his charcoal scratched over the paper. "You have remarkable eyes."

"They are like my mother's."

"She must be a beautiful woman."

"She is...beautiful." Gwen had almost said she was dead, but then she thought, *there is no need for truth here.* If he was only traveling through the area, he couldn't know she was Miss Guinevere Vaughn, daughter of a Welsh baron, especially with the way she was dressed. She could be a village girl who could be named anything, and who could have a beautiful mother who still lived. "What is your name?" she asked, partly because she wished to know the name of this handsomest of all men, and partly so she could make up a name of her own.

"I'm called Jack," he said. "And you?"

"Rose," she said proudly. She had always loved simple flower names, probably because she'd been named Guinevere, which was long and cumbersome.

"Ah, a fitting name for a lady in bloom. It's very nice to meet you, Rose," said the man. "Please sit still."

Again, she heard that resonance of authority in his voice. She supposed he must be very serious about his art. She studied him as he went back to scritching and scratching at his book. He drew very confidently, as if it were easy for him to do it. It felt strange to be scrutinized so closely by someone—especially someone so blatantly virile. She tried not to blush and flutter when their eyes met.

"Have you a sweetheart, Rose?" he asked the next time he looked up from his book. "I imagine a pretty girl like you has many suitors. Or perhaps..." He paused in his sketching. "You are already wed to some fortunate fellow?"

"No," she said, feeling embarrassed that she had neither suitor nor husband. Then she remembered, *No need for truth*. "I'm not yet wed, but I am being courted by a wonderful young man named...Thomas." It was as good a name as any.

"Lucky chap. Will you be married soon?"

"I don't know. Yes. Perhaps. We have become ever so fond of one another. We're so much in love that I call him Tommy instead of Thomas." She was painfully aware that she must sound like an idiot.

"And what does he call you?"

Gwen blinked. It was a consuming task to make up all these lies. "I... I would rather not say."

"It must be something scandalous then. *Precious*, or *darling*, or *honeycake*."

Honeycake? This talk of marriage and suitors was growing uncomfortable. His charcoal pencil had gone still on the page.

"Are you almost finished with your sketch?" she asked.

"For the most part." He leaned back and examined his work. "Why don't you come have a look?"

When she arrived in his vicinity, he pulled her right down on his lap. She knew she ought to protest, but he wasn't being rude or rough. On the contrary, his arms encircled her very gently as he held the book before them. His cheek touched hers. He was so large, so warm.

She tried to concentrate on his sketch, which was quite impressive for the short amount of time he'd taken to draw it. It was mainly her face and shoulders, and breasts. Oh, she didn't know why she should feel this sketch was all about her breasts, except that her nipples had gone alarmingly taut now that he was near. Was this how Tilda felt when Drustan held her? When Drustan kissed her?

"Do you like it?" Jack asked. His soft hair brushed against her cheek. "It's only a quick study. I could draw you for hours and not capture all your bewitching charm."

Such flattery, and his gaze was *so intense*. He must be falling in love with her, to look at her that way. She wished Tilda had come with her, because Tilda would have known how to flirt and play along with this man.

"Would you like to see some other things I've drawn?" he asked, as she gawked at him like a hooked fish.

"Yes, that would be lovely."

He shifted her in his arms. Shifted her *closer*, she noted, as he flipped back through some of the pages. She did not know much about art, but she knew the drawings had some boldness that made them attractive to her. He'd sketched elegant horses and great city buildings, and a variety of persons, both ladies and gentlemen. In the middle of the book, he skipped past a few pages. Gwen thought she saw a flash of large, round breasts and naked legs, but she wasn't sure.

"I'm especially proud of this." He showed her a sketch that covered two pages, a detailed rendering of a huge manor and courtyard, and a fountain with water spraying from the middle. It brought to mind King Arthur's Lady of the Lake.

"How beautiful," she said. "I've never seen a real fountain. Not like that."

"Haven't you? Many grand houses and parks in England have them." His arm eased closer about her waist. "They're pretty to look at, aren't they? Like you."

She turned to him with a shy smile, and he chuckled.

"You're blushing pink as a rose, Rose. How modest you are, for a wild meadow nymph."

"Oh, I am not a nymph."

She looked back at his drawings, trying—and failing—to ignore the subtle caress of his thumb beneath her breast. The blush in her cheeks seemed to be spreading to other parts of her body. "I can't believe how talented you are," she blathered, to fill the silence. "You made a lovely likeness of me in such a short time. Really, you are a commendable artist."

"It's easy to make art when one is inspired." He shifted her on his lap, so she was turned more toward him, and then he tilted up her chin. "I suppose it is shocking to say, but I would like to kiss you."

Goodness, he meant it. As much as she had craved to be kissed, she knew it wouldn't be proper to allow it. "You shouldn't, sir."

"Why not?" Their lips were almost touching. His eyes were *so blue*. "Call me Jack, won't you? We're friends, you know, sitting here together in this pretty meadow on a sun-filled day. Why not have a little kiss? Especially when you've been flirting so shamelessly."

She opened her mouth to protest this accusation, and that was the moment he took advantage, brushing his lips across hers. She went very still, shocked by the whispery warmth of contact. He made a low sound of encouragement and cupped her face before she could pull away.

Oh my. He was not just kissing her once, but many times. His lips tensed and molded to hers as his fingers wove into her hair. She'd dreamed of being kissed on countless occasions, but her dreams had never approached this heady reality. He grasped her face between his thumbs and flicked his tongue inside her mouth, at the corner and along her lip. After a moment of flailing, she tried to respond and kiss him back in the same sensual fashion. And she thought, *take me away to your castle, dear sir. Thank you, flowers and trees. Thank you, heaven and earth, and Jack, for granting me this last adventure before my wedding to the duke.*

He moved her again on his lap, setting her off balance so she was obliged to open her hands upon his chest. How hard he felt, how very solid. Her palms slid up to his shoulders as he deepened their kiss. She ought not to grope this stranger, and she certainly shouldn't allow him to kiss her this way, but she couldn't find the power to stop him. Every aspect of him compelled her, from his wild artist's hair to his manly chest, to the firm, muscled thighs that supported her. He opened a hand over her breast, and she didn't even think of telling him no. His thumb brushed across her nipple through the coarse wool of her dress, a teasing pleasure that resonated all the way down to the private place between her legs.

She should tell him not to do such a thing. She knew it was wicked, but it felt so good. He whispered something to her, some endearment, but all she could think was how excited and full her middle felt. She gave a needful little sigh, her lips trembling against his. His hand traveled down and molded around her bottom, caressing and squeezing as boldly as she'd squeezed his shoulders. She pushed back from him.

"Please, sir," she said. "You should not."

He was handsome, yes, and maybe falling in love with her, but the castle was a fantasy. Too soon, she would have to leave this meadow, and return home to prepare for her wedding to the Duke of Arlington.

Jack released her, though he did not put her off his lap. His gaze burned hot as ever as he took her hand. "I apologize if I offended you. I forgot myself for a moment."

"So did I. It's this meadow, I suppose, and the fact that you are..." She ducked her head, touching her lips. "That you are very handsome."

"Ah, Rose. There you go, flirting with me again. What a naughty girl you are, when you have a young man named Tommy in love with you. How unfaithful you've been."

She looked up sharply. "No, sir. Not unfaithful." She stared over his shoulder, thinking how to keep up the fiction and still explain how she'd lost herself in his arms. "I... I know I said he was my fellow, but the truth is... Tommy and I are only...mostly...friends."

Jack gave a gentle tsk. "Then you lied to me about having a beau. If you were my lady, I believe I'd spank you for such behavior."

It was impossible to tell if he was joking, or serious, or bemused, or actually, truly disappointed in her. "You wouldn't really?" she said. "You wouldn't spank a grown woman?"

"I have and I would. Some naughty misses require an occasional bottom-reddening to keep them in line. Nothing vicious, you understand. Just enough sting to make them feel remorseful for their misdeeds."

He moved his hand over her knee, the movement animating the muscles in his chest. A spanking? Rose, the village girl, felt her breath come faster with a squalid sort of excitement. Gwen, on the other hand, was scandalized. "I can hardly...believe..."

"Don't men spank their women in Wales, then?" he asked in surprise. "Have you never been spanked, Rose?"

She shook her head quickly. "No, never. Not since I was a child."

He tightened his hands on her waist and pressed a gentle kiss to the corner of her lips. "Do you wonder what it would feel like if I spanked you?"

Yes. No. God save me. "I suppose... Well. I wonder if I ought to go check on my horse."

"Your horse is perfectly well." He gazed at her in that authoritative manner that made her stomach flutter. "Shall I give your bottom a smack or two, since you've been naughty? Then you would know what it feels like, and head home to your Tommy duly punished, with an unburdened conscience."

Gwen couldn't imagine why she didn't run off at that point, except that his eyes and his lips held her with some invisible pull. She felt captured in a spell, so that when he lifted her and rearranged her across his lap, she didn't protest or even struggle.

"There we are," he said, as if this were some normal interaction, as if he was merely posing her for art. "I'm sure you're the type to take a spanking very bravely, with nary a complaint."

"Oh, I don't know," she said with an edge of panic.

He turned up her skirts in the same casual fashion, leaving her shift down to cover her bottom. A small mercy for a foolish girl who had definitely let things go too far. "Please, sir, I'm sure this isn't proper."

"You're probably right," he agreed, stroking his palm over her shift. She wondered how his touch would feel against her bare skin. *No. You mustn't wonder such things, Guinevere. You ought to break from him and run away home.*

He began to spank her before she could find the needed words to protest further. The impact startled her, and she squirmed beneath the powerful sting of his palm. How shocking, that he would handle her with such familiarity. How shocking, that the painful spanks made her feel rather...stimulated. She gasped when she realized this. What sort of woman was she, to become aroused at this treatment?

What sort of man was he, to do this to her in the first place?

He had said "a smack or two" but he spanked her six times, firm, resonating blows atop her linen shift. "Well," she said as he raised his hand for yet another. "I believe I know what it feels like now." *Even if I don't understand my reaction.*

When she tried to get up, he stopped her with a hand pressed to her back. "Do you feel punished enough?"

She looked up and made a conflicted sound of entreaty. She dared not speak the truth to him, and admit that she had never felt so excited and agitated in her life.

"If you don't feel entirely expiated, perhaps a bare-bottomed spanking is in order after all." He brushed up her shift, and she did nothing to impede him. "That is the most effective way to get a message across."

What message was *she* getting across to *him*? That she was a wanton village girl who enjoyed this sort of dalliance? From the start, she had realized this was an exercise in seduction, not discipline, and yet she had let him do as he willed. Now he was spanking her steadily, warming her bare, naked cheeks all over. She looked up at him over her shoulder, her emotions in a tangle of confusion. He finally left off and rested his palm beneath the curve of her bottom. "Do you feel punished now?" he asked again.

"Oh, yes, sir. Please, no more."

He gave a soft chuckle, a raw, enticing sound. As he held her gaze, he slid his palm lower, and used his fingers to part the folds of her quim.

And that went far past any dalliance she could allow.

She jerked and reached back to stay his caresses. "Oh, no. You mustn't. I'm a good girl, sir."

He stopped at once, as if he had never meant to do it in the first place. She counted herself fortunate, for she had played a dangerous game.

"Now you're a good girl," he teased, helping her up. "Now that you've learned not to flirt with strange men in hidden meadows."

"Yes, sir." Once she'd straightened her skirts, she bobbed a clumsy curtsy. She was sure her cheeks must be as red and hot as her spanked bottom. "I suppose I really ought to...to be getting back to the village."

"To see Tommy, I suppose."

"Yes, and to do my work. I'm not allowed much leisure time."

"None of us are, my dear. Life is a busy business. But I was happy to make your acquaintance this fine afternoon. I don't suppose you'll give me one last kiss?"

She took a step back, and another. "I don't think that would be wise. I must bid you goodbye."

She was afraid to look at him, afraid of her weakness, afraid of what he might see. But Gwen forced herself to meet his gaze anyway, because she knew with absolute certainty that she would never see him again. She was getting married in a couple of days to some duke she didn't know, and that duke was going to take her away to England. Jack would have his sketch of her as a memory, if he even cared. It seemed to her now that he might not. It seemed to her now that he was a commonplace rogue, the type of rogue who might have kissed a thousand women, and pretended they needed spankings.

Gwen felt embarrassed and terribly ashamed, but she forced herself to smile for Jack because he'd given her her first kiss, and done a commendable job of it. He'd made her feel soft and warm and...womanly. It had been good, and bad, and confusing, and really, very embarrassing and sad. All in all, a complicated memory to keep, and she didn't even have a sketch to remember him by.

She brushed a hand over her skirts to be sure they were modestly arranged, and then turned and hurried to mount her old horse. The last view of her precious meadow was hazy and unfocused because of her rising tears.

You ought to cry, she chided herself. *You behaved like an utter strumpet.* But she was really crying because she felt silly and used, and because it was so hard to say goodbye.

Chapter Two:
First Impressions

Aidan proceeded from the village inn to Lisburne Manor in full ducal splendor, ensconced in his best traveling coach. Not that he'd traveled here in that traveling coach. He'd come from Oxfordshire by horseback, and directed the coaches, baggage carts, and servants to trail behind for his new duchess to utilize afterward, on the journey home. He'd brought a newly hired French maid to attend her, and his favorite valet, of course. He employed four valets altogether, to manage his vast wardrobe and state uniforms, and coronets, and jewels, and all the other nonsense he had to drape himself in because he'd been born the first son of a duke.

Now he would marry this Guinevere and make children on her, and his firstborn son would be a future duke, with an abundance of wealth and property and social connections and duty and headaches to look forward to. What was the point of any of it, except to uphold tradition? He'd been bred to tradition from the cradle. Honor, title, legacy. As soon as things settled down, Aidan would hire an artist to paint their portrait in rich and formal tones: *The Eleventh Duke and Duchess of Arlington.*

Because as much as he resisted the idea of marriage, he had always looked forward to joining the parade of ancestors in the East Salon, had even practiced regal poses in a mirror, when he was not observed, of course. Taking a wife was a damned nuisance, but somewhere inside, he also craved the civilized dignity of a state marriage and family.

To that end, he had kept himself respectable, waiting for the king to recommend the most appropriate and advantageous match. At social functions, he'd often pondered which high-born daughters might suit him best as a wife. The pool of candidates, in his mind, had been small and exclusive. He and Lady Aurelia might have made an excellent pair, if she had not been promised as an infant to his friend the Marquess of Townsend. Other prospects: Lady Caroline, who was well-bred and refined, and intelligent Lady Hester, upon whom he lavished attention whenever they crossed paths. Lady Frances and Lady Arabella were both dukes' daughters, and either young lady would have made him a suitable bride.

He sighed, gazing out the window as the dark, squat Lisburne homestead rose into view. His actual bride was not an English aristocrat, or even a titled lady. She was a plain old Miss, being daughter to a common-born baron who was also, unfortunately, Welsh. Aidan tried to think of positives. She would doubtless be heathenish, if not an outright hellion. Plenty of opportunity to discipline her, a pastime he very much enjoyed. Furthermore, he imagined she would be of hardy, peasant-like stock. She'd breed well, birth lots of strong children, and bring new vigor to the Arlington line. Best of all, she would be grateful to wed him, being naturally in awe of him as a much more distinguished person.

And he must act like a distinguished person, now that he was marrying. No more dalliances with ebony-haired village girls in quiet meadows. When it came to carnal pleasures, he preferred a skilled courtesan, but there had been something so tempting about that young woman yesterday afternoon. He'd wanted her from the moment she'd drifted into the clearing and taken off her bonnet, and shaken her black hair down her back like some wild fairy queen.

Rose, his fairy queen. He thought of her this morning while his valet shaved him and dressed him in a deep bronze coat with gold embroidery, and tied his cravat just so, until Aidan could barely move his neck. It might have been a noose, the perfect metaphor for marriage. He stuck a finger inside the linen knot but then lowered his hand without loosening it.

Instead he drew on his gloves and checked to be sure his long, thick hair was tamed into its queue at the back of his neck. He often wore it down about his shoulders, his one foible of hedonism in his otherwise dutiful world.

But not today. First impressions were everything, whether one was greeting a scion of English society, or a lowborn Welsh bride.

Gwen almost tripped on her way downstairs to gather with the rest of her family. That would have wreaked havoc on everyone's agendas, having the pawn, er, bride break her neck in a fall. She stepped more carefully after that, and tried to pull her scattered thoughts together.

She'd wanted one last adventure before the bonds of marriage closed in on her, and she had gotten one. Jack: artist, Viking, traveling Englishman. Flirt. Scoundrel. He had smiled at her and drawn her close, and awakened a new awareness within her, a yearning and need she recognized as desire.

It frightened her, the lingering strength of that desire. She was passionate about many things: horses, birds, weather, gardening, most things to do with nature, but she had not realized her own earthy nature until her handsome stranger had taken her in his arms. He'd elicited powerful responses in her body, tightenings and dampness and urges that made her cry into her pillow when her maid finally left her alone. He'd overcome her reason, at the same time appealing to her basest instincts. She had let him *spank her*, and it had only made her eager for more...

You'll have nothing more, she scolded herself. The Duke of Arlington was on his way to meet her, and dine with her family and some other local gentry. She could barely breathe in the fitted constriction of her formal blue gown, and her scalp ached because her hair was so tightly braided and pinned against her head. Her lady's maid had brushed it nearly an hour to achieve the requisite shine, then placed a slim gold coronet on top which had been her mother's. Her father had brought her mama's diamond-drop necklace too, although Gwen's wrists and fingers were bare.

There was a great sense of trying to impress this duke, when they did not have the necessary affluence to do so. They'd scrimped and saved for this dinner for weeks now. The gown she wore had been procured along with four others when the marriage contract had been finalized. Shoes, gloves, fans, hats had been ordered which they could not afford. Gwen possessed these things already, in reasonable variety, but her Aunt Meredith had insisted they were not fine enough, and would humiliate them before the duke.

Because of this, Gwen had come to despise her future husband before she even met him, as she noticed her father drinking less wine, selling off horses, and quietly letting go a few servants in order to buy things fine enough to impress this kingly envoy, who would only grace their presence for a couple of days. The gown she wore this evening was the finest thing she'd ever owned, aside from her ivory and silver wedding gown, which hung upstairs for tomorrow's ceremony. Even with the effort and sacrifice, Gwen feared the duke would look upon them and sneer.

So she waited with great trepidation beside her father and her brothers and their wives, all of them dressed in unaccustomed finery. The duke's gilded, crested coach came gleaming down the rutted pathway to the courtyard. It was drawn by a team of four, all of them midnight black, in the same crested livery. She heard her brothers murmuring about fancy horseflesh and heard a few titters from her sisters-in-law.

Gwen stood rigid, hands clasped at her waist, wondering if she ought to smile or look serious, or run away screaming the way she wanted to. Her father would get money and land from this match, and a tenuous link to the monarchy. The duke too would be gifted lands in Wales, for future sons or daughters to inherit. This had all been explained to Gwen, that this fine and laudable match was important because it would secure the future of the Lisburne dynasty. So running away screaming was not an option, as much as she wished it were.

The carriage came to a stop, and a set of grooms jumped down in their gilded uniforms to let down the gilded stairs and open the gilded door. When the duke emerged in his gold-embroidered coat and breeches, she thought, *my word, he is gilded too.* The man was uncommonly tall, with formal buckled shoes and a gleaming black hat, and a gold-tipped cane. She noted these first details quickly, that he did not appear old or stooped, or fat about the belly. Finally, she summoned the courage to look at his face.

The handsome stranger of the meadow—the artist and rogue—stared back at her.

Gwen felt a flailing sense of disequilibrium. They could not be the same man. They were not dressed the same. They did not have the same hair, or clothes, or the same manner. She would not have believed they were the same man if she had not noted the shocked recognition in his gaze. He quickly shuttered his expression to one of polite hauteur.

"Lord Lisburne, I presume," he said to her father. The men shook hands and exchanged formal greetings. All Gwen heard was the rush of panic in her ears. Were they to pretend not to know one another, then? Because this man—this duke!—had flirted with her, and kissed her, and handled her in a most inappropriate fashion. And she had let him, because he was charming and beautiful, and because she knew she must be married to some stodgy old aristocrat soon.

She could barely raise her face when he approached. His Viking hair was tied back, which granted him a more dignified appearance. She saw a muscle twitch in his jaw as her father led him over.

"I'm honored to introduce my daughter, Miss Guinevere Vaughn."

"Miss Vaughn." The duke bowed over her hand. "How pleased I am to make your acquaintance."

He looked up and his eyes bored into hers. He was so close she could smell the scent of his shaving soap and starched linen, but all she could think of was the meadow, the smell of the flowers, and the lake, and his lips upon hers. She lowered her gaze and sank into a curtsy. *Please, oh, please don't say anything.* Humiliation made her flush with agonizing heat.

She prayed everyone would think it nervousness, or shyness. Must he stare at her so? He was every bit as guilty as she. He was the one who had asked to sketch her, and then pulled her into his lap in that carelessly flirtatious manner. Oh yes, she was aware what sort of man he was, and he knew it.

But he knew her secrets too. God help her, she had spouted lies and behaved like a common harlot, even allowing him to spank her bare bottom. Would she be the ruination of all her father's plans? Would the duke reject her? She thought she might faint, waiting to hear his next words. *I don't think I want her after all,* or some other more subtle and political words that would invalidate their betrothal. It seemed an hour before he raised her from her curtsy and released her hand.

Then he smiled at her, a smile that said a thousand things. A smile that said *no, I won't tell*, at the same time it said, *you ought to be ashamed of yourself.*

And oh, she was mortally ashamed.

Aidan offered Miss Guinevere Vaughn his arm as Lord Lisburne invited the company in to dinner, the company being the brawny old war hero and his seven hulking, dark-haired sons with their plump country wives. And Rose, of course, his luscious village maiden.

She trembled, perhaps afraid of some reprisal, even though he was the one who had seduced her in the meadow. Who had preyed upon her, to put a finer point on it. He was ashamed to have done so, now that he knew who she was, then more ashamed that he thought it all right to do such things to a nobody with pretty hair and an alluring figure, but not all right to do to his future wife.

I'm a good girl, she had cried. Thank God he'd taken her at her word, and not tupped her on the grass the way he'd wanted to. When he glanced down, he could still see the blush upon her chest and the tops of her breasts.

Don't gawk at her breasts, you monster.

Aidan had behaved monstrously toward her in that meadow. He knew it, but it was one of those things a duke was privileged enough to forget, unless the victim in question turned out to be one's future wife. She had only to say a word of their illicit dalliance, and he'd be skewered into a thousand pieces by her hoary father and brothers for insulting her honor.

"They mustn't know," he said to her in a quiet voice.

She raised her head. Her gaze met his, those otherworldly green eyes that had haunted his dreams the night before. "Why didn't you say who you were?" she asked in her musical Welsh accent. "Why didn't you tell me your real name?"

"Why didn't you tell me *your* real name?" he retorted. "And why were you wandering about that meadow?"

"I wasn't 'wandering about.' I went there for solitude and privacy. You're the one who intruded on my peace, and accosted me."

"I hardly accosted you. You behaved like a trollop."

Her eyes narrowed. "If I did, then so did you."

Oh, to spank this Guinevere Vaughn. A real spanking, not the playful smacks he'd dealt her in the meadow. She deserved it. She had been unfaithful to him...with him... Which, come to think of it, made everything rather difficult to sort out. He had no moral high ground from which to reproach her, but he did so anyway.

"I hope it's not your general habit to dress as a servant and go about flirting with strange men," he said.

Her mouth fell open. "I wasn't dressed like a servant. Those were my riding clothes."

"You don't mean to tell me you weren't in disguise? Why, that ill-fitting bonnet, and that decrepit horse—"

"That horse is beloved to me. Do not disparage her, and do not insult me because you found my clothing too poor for your ducal sensibilities. We can't all ride about in gilded carriages."

Her sharp scolding pricked him. This was the worst possible beginning to a marriage. He would not be a henpecked husband; this snippety girl would show him respect or she'd receive a spanking in earnest, one she would be hard-pressed to forget. He looked about to see who was near, then leaned closer and spoke in her ear.

"I care nothing for your clothes, or your damned horse. I wish to know if it's your regular habit to dally with unknown men. Because if it is—"

"It's not," she said. "I had never... Before... It was your fault. You shouldn't have been there. That meadow was my special, private place to be alone, and spend time in meditation."

The heartbroken tenor of her voice confounded him. He wanted to be angry. If only this entire debacle was not his fault. If only he'd stayed silent and crept from the clearing, rather than play with the pretty toy dangled before his eyes. She'd gone straight to the lake and sat upon her rock, and he should have left her there to her musings.

He hadn't. His fault.

They exchanged no more words as they went in to dinner, both of them fuming and trying not to show it. The baron's manor seemed as shabby and old as his betrothed's pitiful horse. Was the structure fourteenth century? Thirteenth? The floor was cracked, the walls crumbling with centuries of wear. The dining room was a true medieval great hall with scorched and pocked walls from past skirmishes, probably with the English. God help him.

He and Miss Vaughn were placed next to one another at the roughhewn table, in the midst of overflowing trays and gauche candelabras. The seating was so crowded their elbows touched. The Lisburne family, whose names he could not keep straight, smiled and frowned and stared, and occasionally murmured to one another behind their fingers. Neighbors arrived in the middle of the meal, unannounced, and squeezed onto benches wherever they pleased. Aidan was introduced more times than he could remember. He finally stopped standing, as it was not a very courteous company.

Wine flowed, and noisy conversations took place in a mish-mash of English and Welsh. Whenever those around him lapsed into the unfamiliar tongue, Aidan assumed they were talking about him. Every so often, someone asked him a question about London politics, or the king's business, or some other uncomfortable topic. As soon as he answered in as vague a way as possible, they went back to bantering back and forth in Welsh. Miss Vaughn sat stiff and silent beside him, barely touching a bite of the celebratory offerings.

It was a painfully awkward dinner, but in the midst of the bedlam, a lovely thought occurred to him: *I get to marry the fairy queen.*

Crumbling castle, dripping candles, scowling brothers, rough-edged guests. So be it. At some point in the very near future, he would have the right to take her hair down from those braids and kiss her, and play with her, and turn her from a *good girl* to a bad girl. He looked down at her breasts again and, this time, he allowed his gaze to linger. Those would be his, those delectable globes, along with the rest of her body. In the meadow, she'd displayed a smoldering sensuality that he couldn't wait to explore. The way she had looked up at him as he spanked her, with that longing, and confusion—

"Your Grace?"

Her father looked at him expectantly. Blast. Had everyone at the table seen him slavering over Guinevere's breasts? "I beg your pardon," he said, to indicate he hadn't heard the question.

A few muffled guffaws drifted down the table. Lord Lisburne flashed a gap-toothed smile. "I said that you're welcome to start the toasts, sir, as our guest of honor."

The servants streamed in with more wine. Was this to devolve into a drunken rout, then? He finally understood why their wedding was to take place tomorrow afternoon, rather than the customary morning—because all these soused peasants would still be abed. He stood with his best aristocratic air and smiled down at his future bride.

"I must disagree, Lord Lisburne. I'm not the guest of honor. That title must surely go to my betrothed, who graces all of us with her purity and beauty on this happy day."

The lady in question pressed her lips together and stared up at him as if he must be daft, but he was only getting started. Public speaking was a particular talent of his. He picked up his wine and gazed for a moment into its crimson depths. "It was a long journey's ride from my holdings in England, and I spent the whole of it wondering about my bride-to-be. Would she be short or tall? Pleasant or shrewish? Would she be pock-marked, or buck-toothed?"

There was a soft rumbling of protest before the slower among them realized he made a joke. "Then I arrived..." he said. He paused and gazed down at Miss Vaughn. Guinevere. His fairy of the meadow. He made a show of touching her cheek, and perceived a tremble in her lower lip. "Then I arrived and discovered an Angel of Paradise, a Welsh rose I shall be honored to make my wife." He looked around the table and raised his glass. "I propose a toast to my future bride, and this rugged Welsh homeland which has nurtured and sheltered her until now."

The table erupted in approving shouts at this courtly speech. Her father surged to his feet and followed with rambling toasts to his daughter, his late wife, his homeland, his king, and numerous other entities, until the table was adrift in wine and Welsh exclamations. Aidan ought to have made a study of Welsh language as soon as he knew his fate, as soon as the king told him about his border bride. Too late now. Perhaps Guinevere could tutor him in the most important words, words like *pretty* and *obedient* and *mine*.

He reached under the table to take her hand. Before she could pull away, his fingers curled about hers. *Mine. You're mine now, or you soon will be.* A duke could do worse than a fairy queen, he reasoned. While their acquaintance had not begun in the most traditional fashion, he had high hopes for a life with Guinevere Vaughn. If he could only weather these endless toasts, this drunken dinner and the wedding tomorrow, he could bundle his exotic bride back to England, where he could start transforming her into the duchess of his dreams.

Chapter Three:
So Awfully Uncivilized

The wedding went about the way Aidan expected. Flowery, country-shabby, overly emotional. Lots of tears.

His bride wept openly through their vows, wept so hard she could barely get the words out. Aidan felt some sympathy, but a greater impulse to shake her and tell her to stop. Did she think he was overjoyed to be here? He might have had a London wedding with all his friends and contemporaries in attendance. He might have wed a blueblood, a diamond of the first water, and had an elegant breakfast reception at his Berkeley Square home, rather than a drunken dinner in a dark, sooty medieval hall which still stank of the previous night's wine.

But he did not shake his bride. He was not the shaking type. He was the proper, refined type, and so he gazed at her steadily, allowing nothing in his expression to betray his disgust at her histrionics. Thank goodness none of his friends had made the journey to witness these nuptials; they would have mocked him forever. By the time the ceremony ended and they signed the marriage papers, Aidan felt in need of a very strong drink.

But he didn't partake in any strong drink. As scores of Lisburne guests grew drunker and drunker, Aidan sipped brandy and stayed close to his bride. Now that they were legally and officially wed, she had ceased crying, but she still looked miserable. Nary a smile, and very little conversation. This marriage was good for her father and her family, so they celebrated, but his bride clearly did not think it good for *her*.

And there was more to come, of course. A wedding night, and Aidan's first foray between a virgin's thighs. Another reason not to overindulge.

Finally, the ladies took his bride off to the "nuptial chamber," which was doubtless another grimy, chilly room. Aidan attempted to have words with her father, about the fine wedding and his intention to honor his daughter. The baron squinted back at him, hazy and sloppily drunk. More toasts, more wine. The men called out to each other in Welsh, bawdy sallies they were happy to translate.

Then, remarkably, all the males in the room swept him up in a mob of laughter and song and bore him toward the stairs. Aidan thought of medieval wedding night customs, beddings and shivarees. He was a duke of the realm, for God's sake. His friends would never believe this. Never. He could hardly believe it himself. *So then they carried me upstairs and crowded into the bedroom, and threw rosemary sprigs onto the bed.*

His new duchess awaited him there, shivering pitifully under the sheets as fifty or more people entered the chamber. Aidan wondered, with dark humor, whether they'd stay to witness the consummation in true medieval fashion.

When it seemed they intended just that, he reached the limits of his patience and ordered the drunken mob downstairs. Their retreat left behind a heavy silence. He rubbed his neck and muttered, "What a singular display."

"They only meant to wish us well," said his bride. "It is the local tradition, to see newlyweds to bed."

"Would you have preferred them to remain?"

She shook her head, regarding him from under her lashes. He shouldn't grouse at her, or frighten her any more than she already was. He tried to smile but imagined it came out more of a grimace. She paled. Was he so terrifying? Christ, this marriage nonsense. Best to get this unpleasant duty done.

He turned away and began to undress. Valets were not meant for wedding nights at filthy castles. His man was abed in the servants' quarters, and thank God, for he would have fainted dead away at the stampede of drunk wedding guests. Oh, to be back among civilized people. The revelries below seemed to grow louder by the moment. "Welshmen like their drink, don't they?" he said.

She pulled the covers up to her neck. "I suppose. What will you do if they come back?"

"Two of my burliest grooms are outside the door." They were not precisely grooms, being more concerned with ensuring his personal safety. Now that he was married, these "grooms" would look after his duchess too. He'd tell her about them in time, but not tonight. He laid his coat over a chair, and then his waistcoat. He took a poke at the fire, only for restlessness, but the servants had built it properly to burn all night.

There was plenty of light to see his bride. He crossed to her, ignoring the way she shrank back beneath the covers. "Take out my cravat pin, would you?" he said, sitting right beside her. "And help me undo my neckcloth."

For a moment he thought she'd refuse, but then she pursed her lips and reached to unfasten the gold and diamond pin. She was such a pretty, fluttery thing, his Welsh fairy. He recalled their moments in the meadow, the way she'd leaned against his chest as he kissed and stroked her, and traced her nipples to enjoy her soft, breathless moans. He eyed the gathered neckline of her ivory shift. "That's a pretty garment. Was it made especially for the wedding?"

She nodded and handed him his cravat pin.

"Fix it through the shirt's collar, so I don't lose it," he suggested. "Try not to stab me in the neck."

His jest went unacknowledged. Not a peep of laughter. In fact, she gave a little shiver as she loosened his neckcloth and drew it from his collar.

"Are you cold?" he asked.

She shook her head in answer, her lips clamped tight.

"Do not wag your head about like a horse," he said in exasperation. "Answer me with language."

"No, I am not cold, Your Grace."

His fingers stilled on his buttons. She had said the honorific, *Your Grace*, with considerable venom. "You're afraid then?" He stood and walked away from her. "I wouldn't have expected it, from a woman of your type."

"A woman of my type?"

He took off his shirt, shoes, and stockings, and added them to the pile. "A woman of your type. A woman who sneaks about and trysts with strange men. Are you even a virgin?"

He knew she was, but he asked it because his pride was damaged, because she didn't seem impressed by him at all. She scooted off the bed and stood beside it, a trembling figure of outrage.

"How dare you voice such an insinuation?" she said.

"How dare I? I suppose it's because you trysted with me."

"I'm perfectly pure." She backed toward the wall. "You were the one who intruded upon me in that meadow, and asked to sketch me for your own nefarious purposes."

"Nefarious," he said. "What an excellent word, although I must take offense."

"You're the one who pulled me into your lap, remember?"

"And you're the one who remained there all too willingly."

She made a huff of a sound. "You think you are above judgment, that you're so perfect as you stand about and look down your nose at me."

"Have I looked down my nose? I'm taller than you. I can't help it."

"Even worse, you have frowned and endured my father's honest hospitality as if it was some onerous burden. Do you understand all he's sacrificed? He worked for weeks to plan this celebration, and to represent our family with pride."

A crash and bellow drifted up from belowstairs. Aidan barely restrained a snort.

"Must you sneer, *Your Grace*," she said again in that derisive tone, "and behave as if you are so much better than us?"

"Those are your words, not mine, my angry little bride."

She looked angry, yes, but fearful too. He suspected this tirade was a ploy to distract him from the bedding. Unfortunately, it wasn't going to work. Aidan took off his breeches and returned to the bed. "Come here, Guinevere."

She stood where she was, regarding his stiffening cock with an expression of horror. Any lingering suspicion about her innocence fled in the face of that gaze.

"I don't want to come there," she said. "I don't like you. I don't want to be married to some toplofty English duke."

"How brutally honest you are. Remind me not to take you out among civilized people until you've had that directness beaten out of you."

She blinked at him, once. Twice. "You wouldn't beat me. You wouldn't dare."

"I've spanked you once already, if you'll remember. I can do it again, and much less playfully. You'll find I'm a kind and patient husband, but only when I'm shown respect."

"Is it respectful to deride the hospitality of your host? Is it respectful to accuse me of being a whore?"

He didn't blink at the word, but the fact that she used it told him how distraught she was. "If you don't wish to be thought common, don't behave in a common fashion," he said quietly. "Cease your dramatics, Guinevere, and come to bed."

Gwen was afraid she might faint, and she didn't want to faint. She didn't want to give this insufferable duke the opportunity to lord his lordship over her as she lay sprawled on the cold, stone floor. Especially when his lordship was so very...lordly in the masculinity department.

He'd looked so different in his plain country clothes. Handsome, friendly, non-threatening. He'd smiled so charmingly in the meadow, made her believe he was falling in love with her. How stupid she felt now.

There wasn't an ounce of love in this man. There was nothing but coldness and sneering, and insulting comments, and lofty orders as if she was his slave. How was she to go to that bed and lie beneath him, and let him have her? His muscular physique frightened her, and that daunting shaft between his legs... She was no prude, or idiot. She had lots of brothers and she knew how things worked.

And he was far too big for *anything* to work.

He had ordered her to come to him—twice—and while she didn't want to obey, she was afraid of what he would do if she dug in her heels and stayed where she was. Instead, she walked a little closer to the window. *Coward.* No, not a coward. Just someone who needed some time and space.

"I don't know you," she said, shying back against the glass. "I'm not comfortable going to bed with you."

He studied her a moment. "It's what generally happens on a wedding night."

"Even so, I don't want to do it."

He moved toward her. She tensed, fearful of his size and virility. Would he shout at her? Slap her? Drag her? She backed away as he met her at the window, and flinched when he raised his hand, but he didn't hit her. He merely tipped up her chin and peered into her eyes. His gaze wasn't angry, only very intent.

"Let's have a discussion, shall we?" he said in his polite and cultured voice. "We're married now. You're the Duchess of Arlington. My wife. Do you dispute this?"

"No, but—"

"*No, but* is not an acceptable response in this conversation. You may answer *No, Sir* or even *No, Your Grace,* provided you don't say it in that invective tone."

He wasn't shouting, but she felt as if she'd been shouted at. She moved her face to see if he'd tighten his grip. He did.

"No, Your Grace," she said with a careful lack of inflection. "I don't dispute that we're married."

"I am therefore your husband, your master, and your superior by law."

She moistened her lips, which had gone very dry. "I don't know that you're my superior, exactly."

"Then let me set you straight on the matter. I am. Now that we've married, I own your wealth, I own your property, I own the children you have yet to bear, I own this pretty little shift you're wearing." His fingers left her chin to pluck at the tie which held the neckline closed. "I don't want to be unpleasant about it, but your body is also mine now to do with as I please."

"I...I..." She stammered and hated herself for it. Why couldn't she be brave? "I...d-don't want you...to..."

His fingers parted her shift's placket and trailed warm against her skin. "Listen to me, please, darling. You're not listening, and what I'm

36

saying is very important. From this day forward, what I want will take precedence over what you want. All these years, you've concerned yourself with Guinevere's whims and Guinevere's wishes, haven't you? But that time is at an end. I'm your husband and I require your obedience and gracious cooperation. If I ask you to join me in bed, you will put aside whatever impedes you and join me in bed. Do you understand?"

She stared at him, frozen by the icy authority in his words. She was so rattled she couldn't speak. The life he described was awful, terrifying and dangerous to her soul. "I can't have whims and wishes anymore?" she finally managed to whisper. "I never knew marriage entailed such sacrifice."

"When you marry a duke, it does. Someone ought to have explained it to you."

He leaned his head closer. She had the strangest idea he was going to kiss her, but he only pressed his forehead to hers. A sob escaped as his fingers slid along her neck.

"I don't want things to be unpleasant between us," he said. "I know you don't either."

"No. But I also don't want to give up my whims and wishes."

The fingers traced from her neck into her hair, combing through it and teasing a section down over her shoulder. He was so close to her, so strong, so naked. Golden blond fur covered the sculpted muscles of his chest, and ran down toward the lower part of him she couldn't bear to think about.

"Do you know," he said, easing one side of her shift off her shoulder, "I believe our whims and wishes may correlate nicely. In one area, at least."

She reached for him as he pressed a kiss to her bared skin. She didn't want to touch him, but if she didn't brace her hands against him she feared she'd collapse. "Please," she whispered.

He drew the shift down off her other shoulder, just opened wide the neckline so the whole garment fell away. She clutched at it to preserve her modesty while he pushed it downward, so they engaged in a grasping struggle before he managed to draw it off. Now she was as naked as him. He wrapped an arm about her and drew her close, and pressed his lips to hers.

When he'd kissed her before, it had awakened all her senses. It had made her think of romance and tenderness and love, but she couldn't find that feeling now. All she could feel was his body against hers, *all* of his body, hard and rough and unfamiliar. His shaft poked against her middle, a probing threat. When she tried to push away, he caught her arms.

"Don't resist. You liked it when I kissed you in the meadow. What's different now?"

What's different now is that you're a duke. What's different now is that you frighten me and I hate you.

"We're going to go to the bed," he said in a low, soothing voice, "and I'm going to touch you and stroke you, and enter inside you as a husband does a wife. Do you know about such things, Guinevere?"

"Yes, Sir." Her voice trembled and her eyes filled with tears. She didn't know why she was so afraid, afraid to *tears*. Her sisters-in-law had explained everything that was going to happen. She didn't know why she called him "Sir" in that meek voice, and why she couldn't stop crying. It had to be someone else shaking in his arms, sniveling like a baby. Shouts rose and crested belowstairs, wedding guests deep in their cups.

"It's natural to feel nervous." He wiped her tears away, and brushed her hair back from her face. "But you should know there's nothing to fear. Just submit to me as a good wife should, and everything shall proceed smoothly. Do you think you can manage that?"

He looked at her expectantly. She knew the proper answer, as much as she hated to say it. "Yes, Sir."

She walked beside him as he led her to the bed, only because she didn't wish the humiliation of being dragged. When they got there, he pressed her back upon the covers and crawled over her, so she was trapped within the cage of his body.

"Stop crying now," he said, as if this was as easy to accomplish as opening a door or drinking a cup of tea. "I happen to remember you are a very responsive and sensual woman. I'll make you feel good if you'll let me."

"I'm not allowed to stop you, am I?" she asked, swiping angrily at her cheeks.

"It would not be advisable, no." One corner of his mouth turned up in a smile. "At least your father isn't standing at the foot of the bed to witness this, along with your brothers and all the neighbors hereabouts. That would have been more difficult, wouldn't it?"

She didn't answer, only stared at him peevishly, trying to hold onto her anger and distaste. If only he wouldn't gaze at her so intently, and bespell her with his Viking handsomeness and pleasing physique. He'd freed his hair from its queue, so it hung down and framed his face. The tousled mane granted him a wild and predatory look.

"You're trembling," he said.

She didn't respond to this observation. She was ashamed to be so afraid. She couldn't control her body's tremors now that he lay over her.

His fingers trailed up and down her arm, then traced around her shoulder. "Do you know the reason marriages are 'consummated,' as they say, on the wedding night? And why royal consummations are sometimes still witnessed to this day?"

She shook her head, even though he'd scolded her for it earlier.

"Many centuries ago, warriors and invaders used to vie for the most politically advantageous brides. You know, the ones whose fathers had the most money and the most property, and the best-situated lands. If the bride was beautiful too, well, you can imagine how men clamored for her hand."

As he said this, he stroked her breasts, light touches that sent cascades of sensation to her belly and legs. Warriors. Invaders. *Vikings*, she thought, with long blond hair, and muscular arms.

"So when one of these men married a woman, he bedded her at once, to ensure none of the other men would try to steal her away, because a marriage wasn't official until the husband had been inside the bride. Back then, marriage was a matter of staking a claim, of getting there first and planting your seed in her belly."

Gwen drew in a breath. How savage. How coarse and appalling, and yet a frisson of arousal bloomed between her legs. She prayed he didn't notice.

"Picture it," he said, his fingers circling down to her waist. "A newly married Druid princess, and the head of a neighboring clan approaching from the north. Her groom would have one thought only: to possess her well and thoroughly, in front of witnesses, before his rival arrived." He chuckled, his lips so close to hers. "You might almost be a Druid princess, with your black hair, and those jade eyes. I daresay you would have enjoyed being fought over by sweaty, growling men."

"I wouldn't," she said.

But she was imagining the entire scenario in her head, the intensity and intrigue, and her husband eager to claim her even as witnesses looked on. It made her ashamed, the excited pulse in her center. She jerked as he slid his shaft against her dampening folds.

"They were so awfully uncivilized back then." He drew back and spread his fingers where his shaft had been, touching her in unseen and unknown places. "Now we have betrothal contracts, and wedding dinners, and rosemary upon the bed."

Ohh. She pressed her legs together. He stroked her too intimately, and caused too much need and wetness down there. Only a villain would force a woman against her will. But the more he stroked her, the less resistance she felt. Desire overran her despair.

"I don't..." She couldn't complete her protest. It would have been a lie. She hated him still, but she wanted him to keep arousing her, and teasing her sensitive nipples with his tongue. Her body moved when she didn't wish it to; her hips strained against him as she sought more of his caresses. When he kissed her, it felt like a lie. But when he touched her, her body didn't care about lies or truth, or love, or honor. He slipped a finger inside her, easing it in and out.

"I got here first, didn't I?" he said with sultry satisfaction. "No marauders. No rival chieftains."

"I'm afraid," she blurted out.

But she wasn't. Sometime in the last pair of days she'd turned into a feckless liar. What she really felt was craving and anticipation. She wanted him to maraud her, like that rival from the north. Like a Viking laying waste to a captured Druid princess. *I'm afraid*, said the Druid princess.

Liar. You lie.

"Don't be afraid," he said, and she could tell by his tone that he knew her for a liar. He ran his hands up her arms, raising them over her head and holding them against the bed as if to brace her. His knees spread her thighs wide, and his hips aligned with hers. His hard length pressed against her opening. She was so hot, so wet there. He must feel how excited she was, and know precisely what sort of wanton he had wed.

40

She bit her lip and turned away from his kiss as he pushed inside her body. It hurt, a shocking, invading burn which somehow heightened her arousal to an even loftier plane. She fought against his advance, half in the moment, half in fantasy of medieval claimings, and the tales he'd murmured in her ears.

"Yes," he whispered. "That's right." He wasn't angry that she fought him. It seemed to please him. He thrust forward again, chuckling softly when she refused to kiss him. She was still too conflicted to do that, but her body welcomed the breadth of his shaft driving deep between her legs. The sensation was not to be believed. The Duke of Arlington had taken up residence *inside her*, filling her body with his body over and over, a continual ebb and flow she could not escape.

But she didn't want to escape. His chest hair scratched her nipples as he arched over her, and his breath whispered across her cheek. He let one of her arms go, and reached beneath her to grasp her bottom and angle her for his thrusts.

How she struggled then, kicking and arching, pretending she hated this invasion when she only wanted more. She *needed* more, to assuage the growing pressure in her middle. He held her down, whispering lurid suggestions she only half heard. She was more concerned with reaching the peak that had started building the moment he lay atop her. *I want. I need.*

"I need..." she cried.

She couldn't express what she needed, but he stroked her cheek and said, "I know." He buried his face in her neck and grasped a fistful of her hair. It hurt when he pulled it, but it excited her too.

This was so hot, so active. His strength no longer frightened her. No, his strength made this all the more spectacular. His power, his will, and her surrender to the way he made her feel. Each time he pushed inside her, the visceral slide triggered more waves of pleasure, until they built to a shivering peak.

"It's all right," he said. "Let go, Guinevere. Let it come."

She had never in a thousand years imagined their joining would feel like this. She wanted to let go, but what would happen then?

How easy it was to become lost in another person's body. She had done it in the meadow, to an extent, but this was so much more powerful, because he held her down and forced himself inside her again and again.

Her body clasped around him where he filled her. Her need exploded amidst his raw words and the stretching pressure, and the world fell away. Marriage, anger, love, rebellion, fear, all of it fell away, replaced by spiraling physical bliss.

Her sisters-in-law had told her nothing about this. She wondered for a moment if this was not supposed to happen, if this was some failure in her, but then she was too transported to care. She gasped because she hadn't the energy to scream, and hooked her trembling legs around his. He was still buried within her, pumping and jerking. He let out a deep groan which ended in a shudder, and then he came to rest.

Gwen lay beneath him, staring at the ceiling and hearing the occasional rumbling shout from downstairs. At last the duke raised up on his elbows and gazed at her, his blue eyes burning with a new intensity.

"That's done then," he said. "I've been inside you. You're officially mine." His voice was light, as if he jested still about marauders and consummation, but Gwen thought of his earlier words, when his voice had been resolute and deep. *I own your wealth, I own your property, I own the children you have yet to bear...*

If I ask you to join me in bed, you will put aside whatever impedes you and join me in bed. Do you understand?

Just like that, all her pleasure fled. She couldn't bear his weight upon her. "I can't breathe," she lied, pushing at his chest.

He drew back and lay down beside her. When he moved as if to stroke her cheek, she turned away and pulled up the sheets, wishing to cover herself.

"I'm cold." Lies. So many lies.

He moved again so she could hide herself beneath the ivory linens. "Are you all right?" he asked after a moment. "Is there anything you require?"

"No. Nothing. I'm very tired now."

He made a soft sound that might have been mockery. "I imagine you are."

She pressed her fingers against her eyes. After his sneering and haughty lectures, after all his hateful behavior, he had had his way with her and she hadn't said a word to stop him, nor governed her own lewd impulses. He had taken her, *all* of her, and she'd reveled in his commanding possession. It made her so ashamed.

"Are you all right?" he asked again, slipping under the sheets beside her. The bed dipped, so she rolled closer to him. His arms came around her before she could scoot away. "Are you hungry or thirsty? Would you like some wine?"

"Perhaps a bath," she said, although she felt too wrung out to rise from the bed.

"No bath," he said gently. "No washing it away."

It. His seed and her own lascivious spendings, and the humiliation that burned beneath her skin.

"You may have a bath in the morning," he said. "For now, you must sleep. We've a long journey tomorrow."

That did it. Tears rose again, and no amount of pressing on her eyelids would stop them. She held the sheets to her face and lay very still so he wouldn't notice. But the duke noticed everything.

"Are you crying?" he asked. "England will not be so bad."

England? As if she worried about England, with this fearsome man pressed against her back. He murmured soothing words and she pretended not to hear as her tears overflowed. *Liar. Wanton. Captive princess.*

"Don't cry," he said in the dim light. "It makes me want you again. And we shouldn't, tonight."

"No, not again." She bawled the words, as if he was threatening to whip her, or torture her. He gathered her to his chest and settled her head against his shoulder.

"Sleep now," he whispered. "It will get easier in time."

Next Gwen knew, it was bright morning, with banging and raised voices at the door. Her father reeled in, along with two of her brothers, the local constable, and the village vicar.

"We've come to look at the sheets then, and see that everything's in order," her father drawled. Gwen gasped as he dragged the top coverlet aside, exposing her to the cool air. She clutched her arms before her, thinking herself naked, but at some point, someone had put back on her shift. She stared down at the blood smeared on the linens. There wasn't a lot, but enough to mollify her father, who drunkenly saluted the duke and staggered back toward the door.

As for the duke, he stood fully dressed by the window. The day's light glinted in his golden hair and reflected off his tailored gray riding coat. His lips made a moue, then relaxed into something that was not quite a smile. "It's time to leave for Oxfordshire, my darling. Rise and put yourself in order, if you can manage it, and say your goodbyes."

Chapter Four: Finished

Aidan rode beside the coach until they stopped to stage the horses at midday. He didn't sit inside with her because he assumed she would want privacy to grieve. She was leaving an entire life behind with her removal to Arlington Hall. She was losing a family, a home, a secret meadow, even a much-loved horse that was too old and feeble to endure the trip. He was not the only one who'd made sacrifices for this marriage, he reminded himself. He doubted they would visit Wales very much.

But with patience and fortitude—a great deal of fortitude—he knew he could make her happy in England. She'd be impressed with the luxuries of Arlington Hall, his country manor, not to be confused with Arlington House, his Berkeley Street mansion in town.

His new duchess would socialize in kingly circles, make the acquaintance of highly regarded persons, and be invited to the *ton*'s most exclusive events. Aidan would dress her like a princess, ordering gowns so ornate and ostentatious that ladies would gossip behind their fans about the expense. He'd buy her a new horse, the best that could be had, and shower his bride with jewels until they overflowed from her trunks.

She would have a built-in social set too. His best friends would help launch Guinevere in society. Townsend and his wife Aurelia, Warren and Josephine, Barrymore and Minette. The ladies would take his new wife under their wings, and by the time the season commenced in the spring, all would be functioning smoothly. Jewels and trusted female friends to prattle with. That was all any respectable woman needed to be happy. Everything would be fine.

Then why are you avoiding her? Why is she riding in the carriage alone the day after your wedding?

After they stopped and stretched their legs, and took a bit of refreshment, he climbed into the coach with her and sat on the opposite bench. She met his eyes for a moment, then looked down at her lap. She should not be so afraid of him. He wanted her respect, yes, but not her terror. He took off his gloves and hat and placed them on the seat, thinking how quiet and still she could be, like a prey animal caught in a predator's stare. He was that predator.

"It's a few hours yet to Dryesdale," he said. "We'll take dinner there, and spend the night."

"Yes, Your Grace."

He wondered how long she would persist in calling him "Your Grace" now that they were married. "Have you stayed at an inn before?" he asked out of curiosity.

"No, I haven't traveled much."

"You ought to look at me when you speak, and not mumble."

She gave him a sharp glance, a Guinevere glance, full of conflict and loathing. It would not do.

"Come here," he said. "Come sit with me."

She hesitated a moment, as if waiting for him to slide over on the bench. Instead he pulled her into his lap. She fit perfectly there, her head beneath his chin and her back against his chest. He'd held her like this in the meadow, but she wasn't that same woman anymore. She draped her legs to the side, pressed primly together. He drew a fingertip across the bodice of her tragically sensible gown, then teased the tip of one of her nipples. Her hands came up to impede him.

"Don't," he said. "Let me touch you."

"But—"

He put his hands over hers and set them down upon her thighs. "Leave them there."

He must train his bride to trust him, using the only weapon at his command—pleasure. After a moment, he felt her capitulate. Her gloved fingers spread open over the dark beige fabric of her skirts.

"That's better," he said.

He traced over her nipple again, then searched for the other to give it the same teasing stimulation. It wasn't difficult to find it. Both of them stood out in little points against her fitted bodice. She was utterly silent, so still he couldn't even feel her breathe. Her only outward reaction to his caresses was the occasional twitch of her fingers. When he'd teased her enough, he slid a hand beneath the fabric and took one of her nipples between his fingertips. She moved her hands again as if to stop him. At his sharp sound, she returned her palms to her thighs.

"What do you think of this?" he murmured in her ear.

"It hurts when you pinch me."

"Do you like it?"

"No, Sir."

He slid his hand over to torment the other sensitive peak. He could see her biting her cheek against a cry, or a moan. With a secret smile, he withdrew his hand from her bodice and started gathering up her skirts. She wore pretty silk stockings, not as pretty as the ones he would buy her, but still very elegant upon her long, well-formed legs. "Hold your skirts here," he said, placing her hands over the bunched fabric. "Hold them up here at your waist."

"Why?"

"Open your legs for me, darling."

"What are you going to—"

"Open your legs."

His insistent tone silenced her questions. She inched her thighs apart.

"Wider." He put his hands on her knees and spread them open, and draped them over either side of his legs. "Are you holding up your skirts?"

"Y-yes," she stammered, gathering them up again where she'd let go. "But..."

He parted her curls and slid his fingers into the velvety folds of her quim. He felt her go tense again, but he had no intention of hurting her. On the contrary, he meant to enjoy her reactions, even bring her off if she could manage it in her agitated state.

"Relax," he said. "I want to make you feel good."

"Now? In the coach?"

"Why not? It's only us here." Her hips moved ever so delicately as he located her hidden pearl.

"But...you shouldn't," she said. "You can't simply molest me at your whim."

"Can't I?" He pressed his cheek closer to hers. She smelled sweet and flowery from her morning ablutions. "It's a pleasant enough way to pass the time. Besides, you like it." He could feel moisture gathering as he stroked her. He drew the slickness upward, swirling it around the swelling flower of her sex.

"This isn't proper," she said.

"I'm not concerned with propriety at the moment. Nor should you be, my wet and wanting wife."

"I'm not wanting." She could not deny the wetness, poor lady. Her body betrayed her, turning liquid beneath his fingers.

He made a gentle sound to soothe her. "It's a fine thing to enjoy your husband's caresses. This wetness is a natural reaction. Don't be ashamed."

Her hands had curled into fists around her skirts. He played with her as the coach rumbled on, exploring her pussy, discovering what made her go limp and quivery against his chest. "That's a good girl. Keep those legs open for your husband's pleasure."

She made a small, choking sound. He went back to teasing her nipples through her bodice, while simultaneously flicking, stroking, and massaging her pussy's folds. The more excited she got, the more tightly she squeezed her hands. "Take off your gloves," he said when her fingers began to tremble. "I want you to touch yourself too."

She shook her head in a very decisive way. "I can't possibly do that."

He gave her pearl a sharp pinch. "*Yes, Sir* is the correct answer. We discussed this yesterday. Now, take off your gloves. Just one, if you prefer."

With a sigh of irritation, she took off one glove and laid it aside. He collected her hand and guided it beneath his, down to her damp and heated flesh. "Touch yourself where it feels the best. Stroke yourself. See if you can make yourself come."

She didn't ask what he meant. Surely she remembered that delectable peak from last night, when she'd tossed beneath him in the throes of ecstasy. Though she resisted at first, he pressed her until she uncurled her fingers and joined him in stroking her sex. He helped her at first, until he could feel sensation take her over. Her eyes closed, her lips going soft as she leaned her head back.

"Yes, that's it. This sort of touching feels lovely, doesn't it? I'll teach you to pleasure me too, my fairy queen. There's so much for us to learn about each other."

"I'm not a fairy queen," she murmured, distracted.

"You're whatever I say you are, darling, and I'll teach you to do all sorts of things proper ladies don't do. I'll teach you to use that lovely mouth of yours on my earlobes and my neck, and my balls, and my cock." He pushed this last against her backside, so she could feel how rigid he was.

She inched forward. "I can't... You shouldn't..."

"*Yes, Sir, I am eager to learn what pleases you.*" He pulled her back against the hard evidence of his arousal. "And so I shall teach you, my dear. I'll show you how to caress me in different ways. Light, soft, rough, teasing." As he said this, he demonstrated on her pussy, and then thrust a pair of fingers inside her. "If you're a good wife, and learn all the things I like, I'll give you more pleasure than you can imagine. Does this feel good?"

"Yes," she breathed. "It does."

"Do you want to come for me?"

She tried to turn into him, to hide her face. "Oh, please. I can't."

"You can. I want you to." He eased his fingers in and out while she continued to stroke her pussy. His other hand squeezed her breasts and teased her nipples, caressing them, maintaining them in permanent, aroused points. "That's it. Make yourself feel good. Let your whole body come alive with pleasure, and when you're ready, finish it."

"How will I know—when—?"

"You'll know."

Her hips moved with her exertions, and his fingers surged into her sheath with a mounting, steady rhythm. He watched her face, saw her bite her lip hard. He wanted to kiss that poor, bitten lip. He wanted to kiss every inch of her and bury himself inside her, but this erotic show was too magical to interrupt. She gave a gasping cry, and the walls of her sex contracted around his fingers. He pressed them deep inside her, massaging, encouraging her climax to full fruition. Her feet curled around

49

his calves and her spine arched against his front. Then she fell boneless in his lap, her ecstasy spent.

"I told you that you would know," he whispered against her ear. He lifted her hand and drew her fingers into his mouth, licking them, savoring her feminine scent. She stared up at him with a combination of horror and shock.

"You're delicious," he said. "You ought to take a taste."

And like the world's most innocent courtesan, she opened her mouth and accepted the tips of his lust-slickened fingers, licking them off until his cock was far past aching, and his hand clean enough to thrust back into his glove.

Gwen sat in their private dining room at the Dryesdale Inn, sneaking glances at her husband, uncertain how she ought to feel. She wished she felt in love, but she did not feel that, not in the slightest. She felt something more akin to anxiety, and disbelief that she was actually his wife. Since they'd arrived, the staff had done nothing but scrape and bow to the duke, and hover, and bustle about bringing things and taking things away before one could even ask them to do it. *May I freshen your wine, Your Grace? Is the duck to your liking, Your Grace? Shall we bring more cranberry sauce, Your Grace?*

Gwen wanted to hate her husband, but somehow she found herself in the same sickening thrall as the servants and staff. How grand he was, how effortlessly commanding. His manners were so smooth and all his glances were the speaking type.

She wanted to defy his authority and stand up to him, but she feared she hadn't the power to do it. She was terrified to make an enemy of him. For goodness sake, she'd licked her own spendings off his fingers in the coach because he told her to. He'd said scandalous things and described scandalous acts, and she'd thought, *I know I will do them.* It seemed the whole world bowed to his will, every groom, every servant, every lady and gentleman. They all fluttered and nodded and murmured *Yes, Your Grace,* and she knew she would do it too.

"Your Grace. Your Grace?"

The endless groveling. Gwen shut her eyes, wishing she could clap her hands over her ears and disappear.

"They're talking to you, dear," came the duke's voice. "You're a 'Grace' now too."

She opened her eyes and blinked at the liveried servant. "I'm sorry. What did you ask?"

"He asked if you would like some smoked eel and black pudding."

"No," she said quickly. She'd barely touched what was already on her plate.

He waved a lazy, lace-cuffed wrist and the eel dish was whisked away. "You should eat more of your dinner," he said when the servant was gone.

"I'm not hungry."

"You'll be hungry later. I'd like you to eat."

That's precisely why I choose not to eat. Gwen knew she was being childish with these petty rebellions. Even if she could find the appetite to eat, she was sure he'd find her table manners lacking. He constantly scrutinized her—and constantly found flaws. She took a small bite of duck so he would stop staring at her.

"You must cut with your knife and eat with your fork," he said. "Not stab the flesh and gouge it from the bone. I don't see any cave fires about."

She wanted to stab him. She wanted to poke her fork right into his eye. Instead she cut another piece of duck with exaggerated gentility, then left it to congeal on her plate.

"Much more prettily done," he said. "No, don't frown at me that way. You must understand that life in London will not be like life in Wales. You'll only earn the regard of the *ton* with the finest social graces and impeccable manners." He looked her up and down, with that cool, dissecting gaze. "I suppose you'll do well enough once we get you a proper wardrobe and some finishing lessons."

"I don't need finishing lessons," she said. "I'm already finished. I'm twenty-two years old."

"Even so, you'll be obliged to improve yourself if I wish. Now that you're a duchess, you'll have to move within the highest echelons of society."

51

"Oh, must I?" Irritation gave her an unruly tongue. "Perhaps it would be more appropriate to keep me in the barn with the pigs and chickens."

His gaze didn't waver. "Why would I do that?"

"Why indeed? You behave as if I'm no more cultured than an animal, wallowing in the mud and eating from a trough."

"I mentioned a cave, not a trough."

The abominable man mocked her. "A barn. A trough. A cave," she snapped. "You might stow me anywhere out of the way, so long as I don't offend your aristocratic sensibilities. Why, it would make the most sense to set me loose in the field with the brood mares. They'd understand me perfectly."

His lips tightened. "Are you done with your tantrum? Have a bit more duck."

"I don't want any duck. I don't like duck." She put down her silverware and glared at him. A servant came bustling in to take her plate but the duke waved him off.

"She's not finished."

"I am finished," she told the servant. "You may take my plate."

The servant stared between them, goggle-eyed. The glint in her husband's eyes had frozen to hard blue ice.

"Do not think to engage in a battle of wills with me, Guinevere," he said. "Not now or ever. You'll always lose."

"Do you believe so? I'm awfully willful," she retorted. "That's why no one else would marry me."

"No one else would marry you because your father is an ambitious opportunist who was wise enough to save you for better things. I'm sorry if you were led to believe otherwise."

He said these words calmly, and studied her reaction as he studied everything else. Gwen wondered if he spoke the truth. For so many years, no man had courted her. She'd believed it was her appearance, her uncommon height, or her poor skill at conversation. But according to the duke, her father had kept her lonely and marginalized in order to fulfill his ambitions.

"Statecraft," he said as she glowered down at her plate. "It makes pawns of us all."

"I don't care."

"You do, but it's all right to deny it." He gave her a sympathetic look. "I know this is difficult, and that you are being fractious as a form of protest. No matter. I'll have cured you of such tendencies within a few days. Eat something."

Gwen gripped her silverware in rigid fingers and very properly cut the wee tiniest, most miniscule sliver of duck any person ever carved, and brought the speck of meat to her lips.

The duke watched her chew it with wee, tiny little bites, then beckoned the innkeeper, who hovered right beside the door. The portly man hurried over and sketched an obsequious bow. "How may I assist you, Your Grace?"

He turned and smiled at the man. "If you've a fresh birch rod anywhere on the premises, I'd like it delivered to Her Grace's rooms at the first opportunity."

The man nodded and bowed even lower. "I'll have one assembled, Your Grace, right now, fresh as anything. One birch to Her Grace's room without delay."

"Splendid."

Gwen found the bit of duck had lodged itself in her throat.

Her husband turned back to her as the innkeeper scuttled away. "If you're certain you're *completely* finished, darling," he said with daunting emphasis, "then let us retire upstairs."

Chapter Five: Discipline

Aidan felt rather proud to have made it one full day of marriage before spanking his wife. In this, of course, he outlasted his friend Townsend, who had spanked his wife on their wedding night, before he even bedded the woman.

Ah, well. Disorderly wives craved orderly consequences. Acting out was a plea to be taken in hand. Guinevere's stunt with the tiny piece of duck was funny, yes. He might have laughed, but there was nothing amusing about a power struggle within a marriage. By nature, he must lead and she must follow. He must rule and she must obey. He must discipline, and she must bend and take it. It wasn't anything she hadn't earned.

While the inn staff assembled the necessary birch rod, Aidan's valet freshened him up, scraping away stubble, applying cologne, and offering a somber-hued dressing gown that was perfect for the occasion. The man was excellent at reading his moods.

Aidan dismissed the servant for the night, and passed through to the adjoining chamber. He found his wife in a chair by the fire, still dressed in her traveling clothes. He regarded her a moment, then crossed to stand by the mantel.

"I brought a lady's maid on the journey specifically for your use," he said. "She would have helped you dress for bed."

"I can dress myself."

"Her name is Pascale. She's French, and came highly recommended from the Duchess of Winningham's service."

He received no thanks for procuring this most desirable of servants, the French lady's maid, who must now be stewing in the servants' chambers. He received nothing but a vitriolic stare.

"Why are you so angry?" he asked. "What have I done to you, to make you dislike me with such fervor?"

"What have you done?" She got to her feet, her hands in fists. "You questioned my virtue, repeatedly, when you were the one dallying with village girls a mere day before we were to meet."

"One village girl, who happened to be you, so I don't see how that counts."

"You've also sneered at my family and their hospitality, forced me to perform unnatural acts in your traveling coach—"

"I don't know if I forced you, darling."

"—criticized my table manners, and humiliated me before the innkeeper by asking for a birch rod to be delivered to my room."

"What else was I to do? I needed one."

As if on cue, a knock came at the door. Aidan opened it and accepted the fresh birch from a blushing maidservant. He inspected the bundle of slim, straight withes, then tapped it against his palm to test its mettle.

"Undress," he said to his wife. "Let's get this unpleasantness over with."

She stared at him. "You don't really mean you are going to... I thought you only meant to...to threaten me."

"I never threaten, Guinevere. I decide upon consequences, and then I act. Now, will you undress, or shall I do it for you?"

She answered with a bit less bravado. "I don't want to undress. I don't want you to punish me. I haven't been birched since I was a child."

"That probably explains the extent of your willfulness. As I said, I'll train it out of you."

When it became apparent she wouldn't undress on her own, he crossed to her and turned her about, and began working at her laces. One good thing about his lustful bachelorhood: he was very quick at managing ladies' clothing. He unlaced her bodice and pulled her heavy, voluminous gown over her head, disregarding her half-hearted attempts to impede him. He stripped off her petticoats next, and her underthings, her shift and stockings.

"You will tear them," she said, as he bent to tug the latter off her kicking legs.

"I'll buy you more. Better ones, befitting a duchess."

"I despise you."

He straightened and gazed at her. She glared back, her arms covering her breasts.

"All I did was ask you to eat something," he said. "It was a simple request I made for your well-being. Your peevish behavior has nothing at all to do with my actions, and everything to do with your frustration and determination to annoy me." He took her arm and led her over toward the bed. "Since I dislike being annoyed, I shall teach you not to do it again."

"You're not going to teach me anything," she cried, pulling away from him. "Except to hate you more."

"If you don't learn anything, then the lesson will be repeated until you do. Bend over, darling."

As expected, his hellion refused. With a sigh, he forced her down over the mattress, drawing her flailing hands behind her back. Pressing her to the ticking with one hand, he lifted the birch with the other and gave her a smart whack across her bottom. She made a muffled sound into the sheets, her muscles held rigidly tight. She was trying to be brave, he supposed, and remain unaffected.

But it was very difficult to pretend a birching didn't hurt.

Gwen bit the inside of her lip as the birch connected again. It hurt so much worse than she imagined. Each blow felt like a thousand pin-pricks spreading out across her backside. Before she could recover from the sting, he swatted her again. She was determined not to give him the satisfaction of hearing her beg for mercy. He was bigger than her, much bigger, so he could bend her over this bed and punish her with his godforsaken birch rod, but he couldn't make her change her attitude. He couldn't make her stop hating him. It would take much more than a birching to accomplish that.

But oh, it hurt so badly. She tried to be still, but her body jerked and squirmed instinctively. *Ow, ow, oww.* First she would hear a swish, and then a horrible whack as pain exploded in spreading heat. Then she'd wait, trembling and fearing the next.

"How many times are you going to strike me?" she asked after an especially smarting blow.

"As many times as it takes to break you, my dear."

A soft whimper escaped her, and she hated the sound of that whimper. It was her first show of weakness. Now he knew he was hurting her. *Of course he knows he's hurting you, Gwen.* Her bottom must be beet red by now, striped all over with livid birch lines. She bit her lip harder. She would not, *would not* give him the satisfaction of hearing her mewl and weep, although she wanted to mewl and weep more than anything. She went up on her toes as he whacked the underside of her buttocks.

"Not feeling it yet?" he asked.

Good God, she was feeling more pain than she'd ever felt in her life. The sting's intensity built with each stroke, or perhaps he hit her harder. The birch caught her under her bottom again and her legs kicked up in agony. How long would this go on? He would not ease his hold on her wrists, even when she began to struggle. Another whack. That one was definitely harder.

"Feeling it now?" he asked.

"No," she said stubbornly, but it came out like *noooo...*

"I suppose your punishment will continue then," he said.

Oh, how she hated him. But he would get his way eventually, she knew. She couldn't hold out much longer. Her bottom radiated heat, her buttocks clenching at each tormenting stripe of the birch. Moisture squeezed from her eyes, as much as she didn't want to cry. The tears fell anyway, dripping down until the blanket beneath her was damp. She lost the battle to be quiet. A shriek erupted from her lips, a rough, desperate squawk. Not *no*, or *stop*. She would not beg. But she cried because it hurt, and because he wasn't going to stop until she bent to his will. *Swish, whack. Swish, whack. Swish, whack.*

He owns you. He controls you. Give up and accept your fate.

She tried to steel herself, tried to keep the sobs inside, but they burst out anyway. How would she sit in the carriage tomorrow? Why was she enduring all this only for refusing to eat?

But it was not only that. She was being punished for refusing to respect his authority. Much good it had done.

"I won't— I won't—" she began.

He paused. "You won't what?"

"I won't..." She could barely talk, she was crying so hard. "I won't be peevish anymore. I'll be...respectful."

She told herself it was not capitulation. She only said it to make the punishment end. But in her heart, she knew she would guard her temper around him now, lest this sort of punishment be repeated. And so he had broken her after all, and taught her a lesson, and it made her want to scream and spit and throw things.

"Very well," he said. "Three more strokes, and then a bit of corner time so you can think about what you've just said."

She hoped the last three might be gentler, now that she had given in to him, but they were the hardest yet. She shuddered at each one, bawling into the sheets. At last he placed the birch rod on the bed and lifted her upright. Her bottom throbbed as he led her to the corner closest to the fire.

"Put your hands on the wall," he said as he positioned her. "No rubbing your backside. That sting you feel is part of your punishment."

As he said it, Gwen realized her buttocks felt almost as hot now as they had felt under the birch. Perhaps even hotter. Fresh agony bloomed every time she shifted. She put her hands on the wall and leaned her forehead against the back of them.

"While you wait there for the next few minutes, think about how you'll do better next time."

I'm going to think about how much I hate you, she said to herself.

While she endured this humiliating "corner time," she heard the duke moving about the room. He stowed the birch rod in one of the trunks, poked at the fire, and put out the candles.

I hate you, I hate you, I hate you, she thought.

And I feel so very sad.

I miss my family, and my home in Wales.

I'll never love you, and I have always dreamed of a loving marriage.

My bottom hurts almost as much as my heart right now.

After what seemed like an hour, but was probably only ten minutes, he said, "Come here."

She turned, but she didn't want to go to him. He stood by the bed, still in his rich, dark dressing gown. She felt very naked and ashamed as she crossed to his side. The worst part was the way he looked at her, as if he pitied her.

She could not bear to be his object of scorn. She wanted to go home and curl up in her childhood bed, and escape all of this. She broke down in ugly tears as his arms came around her. She didn't want him to hold her but there was no one else to do it, and she was so sad.

"It's all right," he said. "Let it out, all your misery and frustration. You've had a trying pair of days."

"I want to go home!"

He held her closer and rubbed her back. His dressing gown felt smooth beneath her cheek.

"I know it's been a difficult adjustment," he said. "Cry for a while. Let those feelings go."

So she cried, and cried, and cried until she felt too wrung out to cry anymore, and then he sat on the bed and pulled her into his lap, and she cried some more against the curve of his neck. She felt utterly demoralized. Defeated. How depressing, to yearn her entire life for love and closeness, and end up with this.

"There now," he said, when she finally ran out of tears. "I suppose that birching wasn't much fun for either of us, but we've straightened some things out. You've learned that revolt and disrespect won't be tolerated, and you've had a good cry. May I kiss you?"

Gwen sat unmoving, her face hidden in his neck.

"Very well," he said. "But I'm still going to take you to bed. You can expect to accommodate me every night. It's the best way, you know, if we wish to start a family. Heirs are important to a dukedom. Are you eager to have children?"

She blinked at his friendly, conversational tone, as if he hadn't just birched her so awfully. *Yes, I would like to have children. No, not with you.*

He slid his palms down over her shoulders and to her chest, and cupped her breasts. "Are you eager for children?" he asked again.

"I don't know."

He rolled her nipples between his fingertips with a thoughtful expression. She hated that it felt good, that he was arousing her when she did not wish to become aroused. He pressed kisses beneath her earlobe, and on her neck. He pinched her nipples again. "Spread your legs for me."

She felt too worn out to fight him, so she obeyed. He placed his palm right over the place that most liked to be touched, and teased her sensitive spot with the tip of a finger. She bit her lip again, this time to hold back sounds of pleasure. She would not make those sounds for him. She would *not*.

But it became very hard to maintain her control as he slipped his fingertip over and around that little nub of flesh. The teasing tingles set her whole body trembling. She wanted to protest and say no to him, but it would be ridiculous. She was wet as a river. Her head fell back against his shoulder as he stimulated her, urging her toward release.

"Yes, you see," he said. "These sorts of activities are very important. Not only for making children, but for encouraging intimacy between us. I like making you feel good."

"Then why did you punish me?" she moaned.

"Because you deserved it." He stood and lifted her, and laid her back on the bed. She winced as her tender bottom contacted the wool coverlet.

"Does it smart too much?" he asked. "Let's try this instead." He took her about the waist and turned her over, setting her on her hands and knees. "No, don't lie down. Stay just like this. Spread your legs wider."

Gwen swallowed hard, holding the lewd pose. Behind her, the duke removed his dressing gown and threw it across a chair. When he returned, he pressed his thick shaft at her entrance, and she realized how badly her body wanted him, even through the pain and the shame.

"There," he said as he slid inside her. "That's what you needed to feel better, isn't it? Answer me. *Yes, Sir.*"

She made a negative sound, not because she didn't agree, but because she didn't want to say it. He gave her aching backside a slap and she blurted out the words. "Yes, Sir."

"*Yes, Sir, I need it.* Answer me properly." He slid deeper inside, stretching her open. "Say it, my naughty, punished girl."

"Yes, Sir, I need it," she cried, as he smacked her bottom again. "I need it."

"And you shall have it." He drove into her with sudden forcefulness. It should have felt bad, but instead it felt marvelous and exciting. Her nipples tightened as her breasts bounced from his jolting thrusts. He pounded into her from behind, hurting her tender cheeks each time he contacted them, but her arousal grew, somehow, from the depths of this discomfort. She clenched around his driving length as he reached beneath her to stroke her quim.

"I suppose you would like to have your release," he said.

She jerked her hips against him in answer, moaning as he tugged her hair with his other hand. "Yes. Please, Sir. I would like to."

"Unfortunately, I don't think you deserve it." His delightful caresses stopped. He moved his hands to her hips and held her there, and thrust in her as before.

"I am not...allowed?" she asked.

"Not tonight. Just stay in position and let me take my pleasure. Perhaps tomorrow I'll permit you to come, if you display a more convivial demeanor."

She stared down at the bed, shocked. Why, did he think he could control her, even in this? She would show him. But as she tried to regain those heights of arousal, she found the ability had passed. Perhaps it was his command to the contrary, or his displeasure with her, or the fear of more punishment if she disobeyed him.

Whatever it was, it left her unable to continue to that needful peak. More tears dropped onto the sheets as the duke completed his business and pressed into her, spilling his seed. He was still for a moment, then withdrew and turned her about to face him. He tipped her chin up when she wouldn't meet his gaze.

"Do not pout," he said. "Show me you've learned something from that thrashing you took earlier. Be biddable, Guinevere. Kiss me now, and smile."

She offered her lips and accepted his kiss as coolly as she dared. The demanded smile was weak, very weak, but she managed.

"I'll let you in on a secret," he said, as he drew her down beside him on the bed. "Good wives get all sorts of gratifying things." He stroked her nipple. With her lingering, unsatisfied arousal, it caused a particular sort of pain. "Bad wives get bad things. Whippings and lectures. Disciplinary sodomizations."

She shivered. "What is that? Sodomization?"

"A cock up your arsehole. It's an excellent method of teaching submission to rebellious wives."

Her mouth fell open. "I've never heard of such a thing."

"Well, now you have. Lie on your front, please. Leave your birched bottom exposed to the air a while longer."

She soon realized he asked this for his own benefit, as he squeezed and toyed with her sore cheeks, and left her to fidget in helpless need. She was still wet as a well, with no hope of release. She understood now why everyone bowed and scraped to her husband. He was not to be trifled with. His cock in her arsehole? Shocking. Repulsive. She hoped he was only trying to frighten her with an empty threat.

I never threaten, Guinevere. I decide upon consequences, and then I act.

No, it was not a threat. He would do it if he thought she deserved it, and she would have no choice but to submit.

"We'll arrive at Arlington Hall tomorrow," he said, drawing her into his arms. "And I don't wish us to begin in tension and misery, so I suggest you brighten up, and resign yourself to this marriage before then."

Chapter Six:
Good Girl

Her husband didn't ride in the carriage at all the second day, which was just as well, since Gwen spent the entire journey alternately fidgeting and crying.

She had put away her traveling clothes and donned one of the finer gowns her father had ordered over the summer. It was pale green silk, with ruching and rosettes, and a matching fan and gloves. She took the gloves on and off and fussed with the fan, and avoided looking out the window lest she see him.

No matter how she sat, her bottom ached and reminded her of the punishment he'd dealt her. Her sex ached too, for he'd left her wanting. Those unassuaged echoes of desire still needled her. After tossing and turning all night, she decided she must act in self-preservation, and be the perfect and subservient wife until she developed some workable strategy to survive this marriage.

Then they arrived at Arlington Hall, and all her thoughts became this: *God save me. What am I to do?*

The duke's country estate was shockingly vast, with forests and meadows, and acres of manicured gardens, and a long meandering roadway of cobblestones that curved between a line of trees and led right up to the house. Not the house. The palace. She could not imagine the king's own residence was so fine. There was a circle-shaped courtyard at the front with a fountain in the middle, the same fountain from his sketch book. She gawked at it as the groom helped her alight from the carriage.

The duke strode across the courtyard to take her hand. "Welcome home," he said.

Lines of servants assembled in arcs beside the front doorway. Her husband approached a stern-faced man at the bottom of the stairs.

"Greetings, Dorset. The staff looks smart. Thank you for the welcome. I'm honored to introduce my wife, the Duchess of Arlington."

The butler bowed to her. "May you find great happiness at Arlington Hall, Your Grace. We are at your service."

"Mrs. Haverford," the duke said, turning to the housekeeper, "please ask the cook if she knows how to make any Welsh dishes. My wife is already homesick."

He said it lightly, but Gwen knew the housekeeper was noticing her red, swollen eyes. Gwen lowered her gaze as her husband relayed a litany of orders to the butler. *Bring the modiste at once, contact Mr. Beaumont in London, summon Lord and Lady Langton for tea, and oh, has my sister written while I was away?* Gwen hadn't even known he had a sister, but she apparently lived in Leicestershire, had four children, and didn't write often enough.

"Shall we see the house, and your new rooms?" he asked, turning to her.

"Yes, I'd like that," she mumbled. She felt utterly overwhelmed.

They proceeded up the stairs together, as each of the servants bowed or curtsied. They were all more refined than she could ever hope to be. The double front doors, which had looked so huge from the carriage, were even larger when one stood before them. The butler pushed them open and bowed again—so much bowing!—and Gwen stepped inside.

The large entry hall soared in every direction, decorated with ornate molding. A massive staircase dominated the middle, curving up and away to a second floor. The ceiling arched overhead, to a dramatic apex painted with figures of gods and angels. One hallway went to the right as far as she could see, and another to the left, and another down the center behind the stairs. The duke called these "wings" as he explained the layout of the house. The east wing, the west wing, the south wing. Her own home had been a rectangular box with battlements on top, and rough gray walls, and dirty fireplaces. There had been no wings or curved staircases. There had been no angels painted on the ceiling.

"It's very beautiful," she said. The echoing walls collected her voice and sent it back at her as if to say, *we don't want you. You don't belong here.*

He showed her some of the first floor rooms: the cavernous ballroom, the library with row after row of shelves, the first parlor, which was green, the second parlor, which was gray, the study, the card room, the third parlor, which was blue, and the conservatory, which really just looked like a smaller ballroom with more windows. Hundreds of candles helped lend each room a warm glow. He must have servants whose only job was tending all these candles. She couldn't imagine the luxury of it, the expense.

They went upstairs next, to three more hallways again, each of them lined with suites of rooms. Each and every room was aired and furnished with linens, and each had at least one large, curtained window. Today's light was fading, but on a sunny day, Gwen imagined the house was wonderfully bright. The ducal chambers—his and hers—dominated the central hall. A pair of footmen stood by the stairs, not moving a muscle as they passed. Gwen could almost imagine they were statues.

"Why are they standing there?" she whispered.

"Because they're supposed to be," he whispered back. "If you need anything, you tell them, and they'll help you."

"Oh." Her father's house had servants, but you needed to pull the bell to have them come. They weren't the sort who stood around awaiting your pleasure. What did these men do when the duke was away?

They entered a room on the right, a grand suite of chambers too huge and masculine to belong to anyone but the master of the house. The sitting room boasted deep, upholstered sofas and a writing desk the size of four of her writing desks back home. Beyond the sitting room lay his bedroom, with a wide poster bed of deep green velvet, and massive pieces of French-style furniture with carving and gold leaf. A door on the right led to a dressing room, and, as he showed her, a bathing room beyond.

She stared in wonder at the gleaming fixtures and oversized tub. "You can get hot water from below," he said. "An ingenious new system with pumps and pipes. If you wish, I'll have them outfit your bathing room too."

"I have a bathing room?" She thought of her rooms back at her father's house, her sensible bedroom with her sensible, homemade furniture, and her dressing room you could barely turn about in.

"Come, I'll show you."

He led her across the hallway to a room with the same oak doors, and doorknobs made of crystal. There was another sitting room, this one outfitted for a lady, with ivory and gilt furnishings and vases of daffodils to match the pale yellow drapes. The bedroom was an airy, feminine space dominated by a pale yellow poster bed. Two tall windows rose above cushioned window seats, and a marble mantel framed the fireplace. That mantel was taller than her, perhaps as tall as the duke. Above it hung a lifelike portrait of a man who looked very much like her husband, and a smiling woman in an elegant lavender gown.

"My parents," he said when he saw her staring at it. "You would have liked to know them. My mother died like yours, from the fever, and my father a few years later, of too much drink and an ill-thought brawl."

"I'm sorry."

"Don't be sorry. They enjoyed life while they lived it." He gazed at his parents' painting with a reverent expression. "We'll have our portrait made when we go to London. I've already engaged the artist. What else is there to do, when most everyone is rusticating in the country?"

Gwen studied the portrait, thinking what a handsome couple his parents made. She wondered if the lavender duchess had loved her drinking, brawling husband, or only pretended to with her contented smile.

"Why don't you paint our portrait?" she said, turning to the duke. "You're an artist."

He laughed. "Ah, but it's very hard to paint yourself. I'll leave the portraiture to the masters." He moved closer and placed a finger beneath her chin. "I'm not talented enough to do justice to your beauty. I want someone who'll capture the fascinating shade of your eyes, and the perfection of your lips. And those tiny freckles across your nose."

"I don't have freckles."

"You do." He brushed a finger across her cheeks. "I see them very clearly."

He guided her back into the sitting room, and led her to a pair of glass doors. They opened onto a stone patio with carved balusters, overlooking a gorgeous private garden with box hedges and flowers, and miniature sized trees.

"Would you like to go down?" he asked.

"Oh, yes. Please."

He helped her down the smooth stone stairs into the garden. How pretty it looked in twilight, how peaceful and lush.

"This was my mother's favorite place," he said. "She could make anything grow. The servants have preserved it in her honor, and they plant new flowers every year. Your rooms used to be her rooms, of course, although no one has lived in them for years now. The linens and draperies are new, because the old ones were fusty. I thought you would want to have new things."

"This is all...very..." Her voice trailed off. Such luxury, and this beautiful garden just outside her window. "May I plant things too? May I tend this garden?"

"Of course. It's yours." He smiled at her, that warm smile that sometimes made her forget she hated him. "You may muck in the dirt all you like, but not this evening. A modiste is coming to measure you for your wardrobe. No, don't frown. I didn't expect you to come to me in possession of a London trousseau. It's good that you waited. We can order things in the latest fashion and style."

She didn't have the heart to tell him that she hadn't waited, that her meager selection of gowns was the best they had been able to afford. How could he understand that anyway, here in this house with a thousand candles, and crystal doorknobs, and a patio leading down to a private garden?

"Come back inside," he said. "I've one more thing to show you."

He led her through the bedroom to the dressing room, an intimate space with mirrors and shelves and little varnished chests. He lit a lamp and began opening drawers until he found what he was looking for. He turned to her, his hands full of glittering gems, a diamond and emerald necklace with matching ear clips, and a diamond bracelet, and a gaudy diamond ring. They could not be real, these jewels, or they would have been worth an entire nation's fortune. He held the necklace up to her neck. The ornate design lay heavy against her skin and covered her entire chest.

"I didn't want to travel with these, but they are yours now. I thought you might wear them for our wedding portrait, with your silver embroidered wedding gown. Or if you'd like more color..." He turned back to the chests and brought out a ruby strand, then thought better of it and held out a pale green one. "This tourmaline bauble would look very well with your eyes. I don't know if there are earrings. Your lady's maid has recorded all the sets and organized them, so she'll know."

Gwen thought her lady's maid would be irritated that His Grace had pawed through all the jewelry she'd organized, and then she thought, *so many jewels.* A king's ransom in jewels, right here in her dressing room, and he doubtless had many more sets of his own.

"Well," he said, when she didn't respond to the proffered choices. "I'm sure Pascale will know the best way to outfit you for the portrait."

Oh. Pascale. The frowning, thin-lipped French woman she had sent away at the inn last night. Pascale would probably make her look as awful as possible in order to have her revenge. She stared at the duke as he tucked all the jewelry away, back into their wooden boxes.

"Your Grace?"

He sighed. "You might call me Arlington now that we're married, or Aidan, when we're alone together."

"Aidan." She tested the unfamiliar name on her lips. "Aidan, why didn't you marry someone more...suitable...to your social station?"

"You know why. The same reason you weren't married three or four years ago to some honest Welsh lad." He closed the last of the drawers and turned to her. "Was there someone in Cairwyn you loved? Tommy, perhaps?" he added with a note of mockery.

"There was never a Tommy," she admitted.

"I know. But was there someone else?"

The mockery dissipated, until he regarded her with a very serious look. She wished she could answer him yes, that she had loved someone. She picked at one of her fingernails, then hid it in the folds of her dress. "I left no one behind," she said. "But it would have been nice to marry for love. I always dreamed of it."

"Don't let anyone in London hear you say such things. They believe it's the worst thing, to marry for love."

"Do you believe that too?" She didn't know why she asked. She supposed she wanted to hear him admit it, that he was rich and cold and lofty, and without a heart.

"I'm not sure what love is," he answered with a shrug. "Is it intimacy, or familiarity? Is it what I felt when I saw you in that meadow? Is it what I feel now, that I would kill someone before I would let you come to harm? That I don't wish you to be..."

"To be what?" she asked when his voice trailed off.

"Ridiculed," he said. "I don't want you to be made fun of, Guinevere. That's why I correct you and annoy you, and why I will make you endure a course of finishing lessons with Lady Langton. I never thought to marry for love, but now that I'm married, my every care is for your security and happiness. Make of that what you will."

That was not what she'd expected him to say. She felt her heart ease a little as she stood blinking at him, then she said, "My close friends and family call me Gwen. It's easier to say than Guinevere."

He gazed at her in silence. She flushed red and wished she'd kept her mouth shut. She could never figure out his expressions, what was in his thoughts when he made those half-smiles.

"Gwen. I like that. Perhaps I'll call you Gwen instead of Guinevere when the situation warrants."

"Yes, if you wish." She fidgeted at her skirts and then forced herself to meet his gaze. "You have a very beautiful residence, Your Grace. I mean...Aidan. I will try...try not to bring ridicule upon it."

"Why don't you try to be comfortable in it? That would please me more." His fingers brushed her cheek, and then the fleeting touch was gone, replaced by his more familiar authoritative stare.

"We must head to London in a fortnight or so," he said, lifting the lamp and leading her back out to the bedroom. "It will be a push to have you ready by then, but the king and queen are eager to meet you."

Gwen could hardly imagine this. "Why would the king and queen be eager to meet me?"

"Because you're the new Duchess of Arlington. Ah, there is your lady's maid, right on time. We take dinner at eight o'clock in the country, if you will come down five minutes prior." With those words of dismissal, he made a slight bow and walked out the door.

Aidan thought their first day at Arlington Hall had gone rather well. It had been a risk, disciplining his wife so harshly the night before, but it had notably improved her behavior. Guinevere still spoke too quickly, and too boldly, and still exhibited rustic manners, but she didn't defy him the way she had before. She showed respect, which was exactly what he'd wanted. Now that they'd come to an understanding, he was certain things would proceed more smoothly from here on out.

He readied himself to visit her bed, thinking there was a certain coziness to married life. A convenient availability. There was no longer any need to slink out after dinner to the theater or opera, or Pearl's parlor of ill repute. Aidan had only to walk across the hallway and avail himself of his wife's charms. He might not have felt so content if she was prudish, or wilting, or horse-faced, but Guinevere was none of those things. No, she was beautiful, and more erotically sensitive than any woman he'd ever known—including his companions at Pearl's.

He was glad, for he was a man of voracious sexual appetites, and eager to tutor his wife in his tastes. Now that they were home, he wished to keep her naked all day in her rooms, so he might visit at any time and make use of her in any way he wanted, only to come back an hour later and do everything all over again.

But I would have liked to marry for love... Poor thing, when she had married into lust.

When Aidan felt he'd given her adequate time to prepare for his arrival, he tapped at her bedroom door. He waited a moment but received no answer. When he cracked open the door, he found her chambers dark, with only moonlight streaming through the windows. She lay in bed but she could not be asleep. Dinner had only ended half an hour ago.

He moved closer and gazed down at her. She was trying very hard to appear asleep. How innocent she looked in her rumpled linen shift. He would buy her silk and satin ones, scandalous, lewd garments, and tear them off her. Or perhaps he would buy her silk and satin shifts exactly like the one she wore, innocent, ruffled confections she could leave on while he did outrageous things to her body.

He reached to brush back a lock of her dark hair, then shrugged out of his dressing gown and slid into bed beside her. She lay so rigidly. Silly girl, it gave her game away. He drew her shift up to her waist, tracing lovely curves and velvet-soft skin. She was so delicious he wanted to eat her. *Mine, mine, mine.*

He kissed the base of her neck, a soft brush of his lips, and then kissed a trail down to her girlish neckline. He kissed between her breasts, sinking lower into the sheets. She still feigned sleep, although her breath came faster now. He licked her nipples right through the gauzy fabric, tracing them with his tongue until both were hard as little pebbles. Her hips jerked, a small thrust. He pressed his lips to her belly, which trembled now with the effort to stay still.

"I know you're awake," he said against her skin. "But play Sleeping Beauty if you wish."

He ducked lower and pushed her thighs apart. Funny, how a sleeping woman could struggle so firmly to keep them closed. At last she gave up and let him hold her open. In the dark beneath the covers, he bent his head and worshipped her sex, stroking, kissing, nibbling, exploring her hot slickness with his lips and tongue. She tasted like heaven, fragrant and female, and blatantly aroused. "Wake up," he murmured against her little pearl. "I have something to give you. Something you didn't get last night."

She deserved pleasure tonight, for learning her lesson. He grasped her sore bottom as he laved her, eliciting a strained gasp. A gasp of dismay, or excitement? He remembered her behavior in the meadow, her flustered reaction to being spanked. He wondered if she was sexually aroused by pain. He pinched one of her nipples, and was rewarded with another jerk of her hips. He gazed at her from between her legs. "Do you like when I hurt you?"

"No," she said. "Of course not."

Of course not. There must be some other reason she was making noises he'd never heard before.

After that exchange, he nibbled and pinched her as much as he licked her, and noted that each burst of pain made her go hotter still. His arousal grew in concert with hers. A masochistic wife? It was too wonderful to be believed.

"Yes, darling," he urged. "Show me how good it feels when I kiss your pussy."

Her thighs clamped against his face as she arched and shuddered. She was no longer feigning sleep. He explored her, discovering what excited her most, which rhythms and pressures pushed her nearer to the point of climax. His efforts were finally rewarded with a groaning gasp. He slipped a finger inside to feel her body's undulations of pleasure. Her hips twitched as she gave a few last squeezes. It must have been a powerful release.

He slid back up in the bed and gave her a long, lingering kiss. "You see," he said, "how good wives are rewarded."

She gazed back at him, her eyes glistening in the moonlight. He frowned. "Are you crying?"

"No. It only felt so... I can't explain."

"Try."

Finally she said, in a small voice, "I don't understand my feelings toward you."

He thought a moment, stroking her arm as she stared into the darkness. "I suppose that's because we've only recently met. I think marriage takes some getting used to, in just about every case. The intimacy part, especially. Speaking of which..." He gave her a reproachful look. "It would be better if you didn't feign sleep in order to shirk your marital duties."

"Are you going to punish me?" She looked very afraid that he would.

"Not punish you, no. But you're going to make it up to me."

"How?"

"By doing for me what I just did for you. Sit up please, with your back against the pillows."

"But—"

He tugged her up and arranged her as he wished, and knelt with his knees on either side of her, so his cock was on a level with her face. "You remember how I licked and caressed your quim?" he asked.

She stared at him. "I can't...possibly..."

"Of course you can." He'd gone prodigiously hard just from kneeling over her. He took her hand and placed it against his rigid length, and moved it up and down. "It feels good when you stroke me like this, but it would feel even better with the warmth and wetness of your mouth. Open for me, darling. I promise I won't hurt you."

"But..." She held him off with a questioning gaze. "I don't think you ought to put it inside my mouth."

"It's a common enough activity in love play. Didn't it feel good when I used my mouth on you?"

"I'm not..." She swallowed hard. "I'm not made like you. I don't understand...what you expect."

"I'll show you." He tried to be matter-of-fact about it. Yes, he had a big cock, and yes, even the ladies at Pearl's sometimes balked about fellating him, but he would be gentle with an innocent like her. He trailed a thumb along her chin and nudged her lips apart. "Just lick the tip of it to begin. Get it nice and wet, so your tongue can slip around the crown."

She balked, until he pressed himself to her lips and took away her choice. He held the bedframe with one hand and her face with the other, so she couldn't shrink away. She gave a tentative lick or two. Ah, God. Rapture.

"That's right," he said, pressing deeper. "It's not so hard, is it? No, be careful not to use your teeth. Wrap your lips around me as I push into your mouth."

Through some innate skill, or some miracle, she provided the perfect degree of suction as he eased between her lips. Her tongue teased along the underside of his cock. Exquisite. Heavenly. Marvelous. "You have no idea how wonderful that feels," he said.

He pressed deeper still. He shouldn't have, but she looked so tantalizing peering up at him with her lips stretched around his cock. She choked at the intrusion, and her eyes watered. He withdrew at once and stroked her cheek. "That was too much for a beginner. I apologize. Why don't you lick it some more, and cup my balls in your palm?" He showed her what he meant, placing her hand at the base of his cock. His fingers covered hers, guiding her when she was too tentative.

"Do you remember how I moved my tongue over your pussy, over your sensitive little pearl? How I sucked it and flicked it? Even though my cock is bigger, you can do those sorts of things too."

His wife complied, her technique sloppy and disorganized. It thrilled him all the same. Pleasure settled in his balls, a tensing urgency born of her submission. "Open for me again, love. You're doing so well. I'm so close to coming off."

She screwed her eyes shut and opened her mouth, and again treated him to that perfect suction. He eased his cock between her lips, being careful not to push too deep. He would not be *that* husband, even if every last nerve screamed at him to thrust into her throat to the hilt. He stroked himself as she sucked him, and sighed as her tongue teased the tip. In his rising excitement, his fingers curled into her hair and tightened against her scalp.

"Oh. God. Yes." He couldn't utter more than one word at a time. With a growl, he withdrew from her mouth and pumped his shaft, spilling his seed onto the front of her shift. He couldn't imagine what she thought of this, but it had seemed a better idea than spending without warning in her mouth.

"Good girl," he said. "You made me come."

"Oh." She sat frozen, staring up at him.

"You did that very well, especially for a beginner. Or..." He feigned suspicion. "Have you done that before?"

"No, never," she insisted primly.

He leaned to kiss her mouth, which he was certain had never sucked another cock. "I'm teasing. I know it was your first time, and you did beautifully. It felt very pleasurable."

"Oh," she said again, looking down at the sticky mess on her bodice.

"I suppose you will want another shift. Why don't we take that one off?"

She agreed that would be a good idea, although she seemed reluctant to touch it. He helped lift the now not-so-innocent garment over her head, taking care not to get any of the musky fluid in her hair. He threw it aside and wiped his hands on his thighs.

"It's better if my seed goes inside you," he said. "You can't make babies any other way. I suppose we must have relations again in a while, so I can come inside you as I ought to."

"I'm not sure we ought to indulge in so many carnal activities in one night."

"Don't you enjoy our carnal activities?"

"I... Well..." She shook her head. "No, I don't enjoy them very much, if you wish to know the truth."

He laughed and hauled her over his lap, and laid a couple good wallops over the birch marks from the night before. "A lie like that deserves a sound spanking."

"Ow!" She squirmed to look up at him. "Please, it wasn't a lie."

"Wasn't it?" He squeezed her bottom and slid his palm between her legs. His fingers came away wet. "I think it was a lie." He spanked her a few more times, playful smacks as she fidgeted across his thighs. "Lying is a very bad habit, and certainly a punishable offense. You remember what I told you." He paused to molest her again, drawing some of the moisture from her quim up between her bottom cheeks. "Bad wives earn bad consequences." He pressed a fingertip against the tight, pink bud of her arsehole to drive his point home. She tried to wiggle off his lap, but he held her fast. "Apologize for me now, very prettily. *I'm sorry I lied to you, husband.*"

"I didn't lie," she insisted. "I told you my feelings were very confused."

"Why confused? Don't you like to feel pleasure? Tell the truth, Guinevere." He nudged her off his lap and onto her back, and laid over her. The spanking and this intimate contact had him going rigid all over again. "Say it to me. *I love to be fucked.*"

"I can't say that." The poor woman was scandalized. "That is a terribly coarse word."

"Say it, or I won't let you come for the rest of the week. In fact, I won't let you have your pleasure for the next six months." That was a bluff. He enjoyed her abandoned reactions too much to deny her. He was playing with her, or trying to. He wished she would smile instead of looking on the verge of tears.

"All right then," he said. "If it's too difficult for you to admit it, give me a kiss instead. None of those reluctant ones either. Kiss me the way you kissed me in the meadow, like a wanton fairy queen."

He waited. He didn't pucker his lips or bow his head to her, or do anything but gaze at her expectantly, forcing her to take the first step.

She shifted beneath him. "If I kiss you, then what will you do?"

He pressed his thickening cock against her quim. "Surely you know the answer to that. Do you want me to make you feel good, Gwen? Very, very warm and aroused and good?" She bit her lip and turned away. "Answer me," he prompted. "Or kiss me. Either one."

He waited. After a moment, she turned back and reached to trace a tendril of his hair, a tentative gesture that seemed deeply erotic. Her fingers trailed along his neck. She kissed him, whispery-soft, at the side of his lips.

"A promising start," he murmured. "Give me more."

She blinked at him, then tilted her head to kiss him on the mouth.

Let her lead. For once. It was hard to stay still, to not to push her arms back and drive inside her the way he wished. The way *she* wished, whether she could admit it or not.

"Show me what you want," he said. "If you can't say it, show me. Arch your hips and let me come inside you. Marital intimacy is not a shameful or repulsive thing, and there is nothing wrong with you for enjoying it."

"But I don't enjoy—"

"You do. I've felt you coming, Guinevere. Don't tell lies."

He pressed into her pussy, kissing her lips and chin and neck and shoulders, all the lovely, compelling features that comprised his wife. He went gently this time. Sometimes he liked sex raw and roughshod, but sometimes he liked it sweet.

"You're so sweet," he whispered. "Let me hold you."

He gathered her close, sinking inside her warmth. She was so tight and hot, so wet. He loved the way she squeezed his cock, loved the maddeningly erotic way she moved her hips, but he also loved the way she clung to him. Beautiful, sweet girl. He didn't want her to suffer, not when they could make one another so happy.

He toyed with her, maneuvered and manipulated her until she climaxed in a trembling heat, and then chuckled when she refused to meet his gaze. "You love to be fucked," he taunted softly. "You little liar. You naughty girl."

Chapter Seven: The Letter

Gwen's hand hovered over the paper, the pen trembling in her fingers as she searched for the right words. *Mama,* she prayed silently. *Help me, please. Help me know what to say so Father will let me come home.*

She'd been at Arlington Hall nearly a week, submitting to the duke's endless scrutiny, her French maid's harassment, and finishing lessons with Lady Langton, a doddering old scold who made Gwen want to die.

No matter how hard she tried, Gwen could do nothing right. The walls of her husband's palatial estate seemed to squeeze in around her until she couldn't breathe. She snuck to her private garden whenever she could, only to be pulled back inside for lessons, or styling, or a change of clothes, or luncheon, or tea, or formal dinner, or some other pointless activity.

Then night would come and the duke would visit her bed, and stroke her and bedevil her until she lost all sense and participated in the most scandalous activities. She only realized her embarrassment afterward, when he was slumbering beside her in blissful repletion. It was an awful feeling, that lonely, shameful aftermath. It was not her fault the duke knew the precise ways to stimulate her sensual humors. And every time he lay with her, there was more chance she would fall pregnant with his child.

Gwen had never thought it possible to miss her home so much. She missed her privacy and peace of mind. She missed wearing comfortable clothes and being who she was, a simple baron's daughter. She missed having control of her own body. She missed her afternoons with Effie, feeding her apples and brushing her patchy coat. She prayed every day in her garden for fortitude, and for deliverance, but it didn't help.

It was time to take matters into her own hands, now, before it was too late.

Dear Papa, she wrote in Welsh.

I know it was important to you that I wed the Duke of Arlington. I would not write this letter if I was not in desperate circumstances.

I'm afraid our marriage is a failure. The duke regards me as little better than a savage, and treats me as such. He fears I will humiliate him before his friends, and so he is trying to remake me into a completely different person.

She wished she was a better writer, so she could explain how devastating this was. She felt like she was losing herself.

Papa, I don't know how much longer I can survive his exacting authority. He is impossible to please. Sometimes I believe he truly despises me, and when I do not behave as he wishes, he punishes me in a brutal and unfeeling manner.

Well, perhaps that was making things sound more dire than they were, but she must convince her father to come to her rescue. The duke did punish her with the birch that once, and the marks had stayed for three whole days.

Even worse than the punishments is the way my husband subjects me to his lewd whims. He commands me to do things which no gently reared woman should endure. I cannot describe them here; decency will not allow it. When I try to resist his advances, he forces me to his will.

She stopped again. *He's never forced you to do a thing,* her conscience whispered. She was the weak, wanton one who melted whenever he touched her. But he was indecent with her. That was not in question, and if her father knew it, perhaps he would find some way to extricate her from this match. They were leaving very soon to go to London, and once they were there, she knew she would never get away. They would attend an audience with the king and queen, and the duke would paint a rosy picture of their marriage and expect her to do the same.

And that would be that. A lifetime with this haughty, unfeeling aristocrat who didn't love her.

Somewhere out there, she knew there was a man who would love her, a man who would treasure her for who she was. She was not a bad person; she was only in a bad marriage. She couldn't bear to think this was her eternal lot in life.

Papa, if there is any way you can free me from this nightmare and bring me home, I beseech you to do it.

With much love (and desperation),

Your only daughter Guinevere

Perhaps it was a little over the top. There was nothing to do for it now. She must post it before her husband discovered what she was about. Even if it was written in Welsh, he would find a way to read it. She made sure it was well sealed and went to find the housekeeper with the missive secreted in her skirts.

Aidan looked down at the note in his hands, then back at his servant. "You're certain that's what it says?"

"Yes, Your Grace."

The man's tone sounded apologetic; he'd blushed red to his collar. Aidan had been blindsided by the contents of his wife's letter, and having this man witness it made it even worse.

"That will be all," he said by way of dismissal, and the footman— who had been recently hired for his knowledge of the Welsh language— bowed and left the room.

Aidan stared down at her swirling text, and then at the translation penned by his man. He could not pick out the part that disturbed him most. The entire letter devastated him, and the fact that she had attempted to send it in secret devastated him more. He'd only just returned from acquiring a gorgeous horse for his duchess, but all the pleasure and anticipation of gifting the horse had flown. He didn't want to give it to her now.

"Your Grace?"

"I do not wish to be disturbed," he told his butler. "Close the door."

"Yes, Your Grace. Shall I tell Lord Warren and Lord Barrymore to call at another time?"

Aidan lifted his head and blinked, and shoved the offending pages beneath some other papers on his desk. "No, I would like to see the gentlemen. Are they in the first parlor?"

"Yes, Your Grace."

Warren and Barrymore, thank God. He needed some friendly faces right now. By the time he reached the most sumptuous of the three parlors, his friends had already helped themselves to the brandy.

"Arlington!" they exclaimed when he crossed to shake their hands. The men waved off his handshake and gave him back-pounding hugs, congratulating him on his marriage.

"Don't spill your drinks on me," he said with feigned irritation. "It's barely three in the afternoon."

"There's the proper fellow we know and love," joked the white-blond Earl of Warren.

His other friend, the Marquess of Barrymore, was as dark-haired as Warren was light. Both men looked at him in expectation.

"Well? Tell us everything," said Barrymore. "Are you enjoying the married state? How is your wife? Is she pretty? How was Wales? How was your wedding?"

"Is she a hellion?" asked Warren. "Does she think you're grand as anything? Is she short or tall? Have you spanked her yet?"

Aidan crossed to pour his own drink. "Sorry. I've already forgotten all your questions."

Barrymore jabbed Warren. "He's forgetful. You see? I'm guessing it's due to lack of sleep."

"Let's hope so," Warren concurred in a suggestive tone.

Aidan turned back to his friends. "What are you two doing here?"

"We stayed away a week, so as not to disturb your honeymoon," said Warren. "Although the ladies begged us to come sooner."

Barrymore nodded. "We could barely hold them off. They're back at Somerton with Townsend and Aurelia, and have charged us to tell them everything about your new wife since they couldn't travel with the young ones."

"And Minette is to have her own babe soon," said Warren. "Barrymore revealed that bit of news last week."

"Goodness, Minette to be a mother. Congratulations, Barrymore." Aidan could hear the strain in his voice. His friends studied him as they took seats before the fire. "I suppose you've come to terms with it by now, eh, Warren?"

"I'm working on it," the earl replied in a grim tone. Warren had always been devilishly protective of his sister, only to lose her in marriage to his equally devilish best friend. Aidan had watched last year's dramas and agitations with smug amusement, never realizing he'd be in the midst of his own wedded drama so soon.

"Can we meet her?" asked Warren. "Where is she? Have you hidden her away? Is she ugly as sin?"

"She's not ugly, and I haven't hidden her," said Aidan. "She does a fine enough job of that herself."

"She hides from him," Barrymore said to Warren. "I can't say it sounds promising."

"We've only been married a week," Aidan said in his defense. "And my bride was not as willing as I'd hoped."

"Bother." Warren tilted his head. "I'm sorry."

"If anyone can bring her around, you can," said Barrymore.

Aidan would have thought so until an hour ago, when he'd intercepted her letter.

"If things are uncomfortable, we needn't meet her now," said Warren. "The ladies can wait for their gossip about your new duchess, like everyone else."

"No, you can meet her. She spends most afternoons in my mother's garden. We'll go look for her there."

A servant informed him that Her Grace was indeed strolling in the garden, so Aidan led his friends out to the walled sanctuary. "Guinevere?" he called. He heard a rustling, and saw her peek from a behind a row of shrubs in the corner. She'd taken off her bonnet and gloves to attack an overgrown flowerbed.

"Oh," she said as the men walked up. She brushed a bit of hair off her face, leaving behind a smudge. "I was just... Well. These plants are too close together. I was clearing some out."

"With your fingers?" Aidan asked. "You might ask the groundskeeper for the appropriate gardening tools. Or enlist his help."

"Oh," she said again, and this time she brushed her hands on the silk skirt of one of her new gowns. He set his teeth against the impulse to scold her, and considered whether he ought to dust the dirt off her face.

"I'm sorry to interrupt you," he said. "Two of my best friends in the world have come to call, and they would like to meet you. This is the Earl of Warren and the Marquess of Barrymore." He indicated each man, and Guinevere made a curtsy. "Warren, Barrymore, it's my pleasure to introduce my wife Guinevere, the Duchess of Arlington." *Not exactly my pleasure*, he thought to himself, *because I'm angry at her for her letter, and she generally hates me.* But manners were manners, so he stuck to the accepted script.

His friends stuck to the script too. Both of them exclaimed how honored they were to meet her, and took her bare, dirty hand without any indication she was soiling their fingers. Gwen ought to have spoken next, to offer tea, or inquire if they would like to stay for dinner, but instead she stood in silence, her cheeks blushing pink.

"This seems a lovely garden," said Warren. "I always wanted to come in here when I was a boy. Will you show us around?"

Aidan silently blessed his friend for easing the awkward moment. That was normally his forte, but he did not feel up to it at present. He studied his wife as she walked around the garden between his friends. She seemed nervous but polite. She gave no indication that she'd just written her father a letter of scurrilous accusations about his behavior. She did not know yet that he'd read the letter.

Oh, but he would tell her later, when he punished her for her damnable deceit.

The duke's friends stayed to tea and then dinner, telling engaging stories and drawing conversation from Gwen in such a natural way that she did not feel self-conscious. They were so easy to get along with, she could barely comprehend that they had grown up together with Arlington. Her husband occasionally gave her looks that made her think he was angry. She supposed she annoyed him with her manners and conversation, and he was unable to chastise her in front of company. In fact, his friends kept him busy the entire night, as the men stayed at drink and conversation long past the time the duke normally visited her rooms.

What a relief, not having to submit to his carnal demands. She wished his friends would stay for a week and distract him from her company, but they left the following day just after luncheon in order to return to their wives.

Gwen prayed she would be leaving soon too. She had given her sealed letter to the housekeeper, beseeching her to send it at once, and the lady had bustled off to do so. That was one benefit of being a duchess— servants listened to you and did what you asked. Now she chewed her finger and paced her sitting room. With luck, the letter would reach Cairwyn and her papa's hands by week's end, so he could come to her aid before they removed to London.

A brisk knock sounded at the door. Since she had dismissed her lady's maid, Gwen answered herself. A footman held out a silver tray with a gilded notecard. Gwen unfolded it and read the bold script.

I require your presence in my chambers at once.
Arlington

She glanced at the footman, her stomach fluttering with a frisson of unease. Was it time for the duke to berate her for all her missteps, now that his friends had left?

"I... Well... I wonder if you would tell him I am not feeling well?" It was not a lie. She didn't want to face him, not with the curt tone of that note.

The footman bowed and disappeared across the hall. Gwen closed the door and leaned back against it, and let out a long breath. She had just started toward her bed chamber when the door opened and Arlington himself appeared. He said nothing, only took her arm and pulled her from her room, yanking her across the hall to his chambers in full view of the servants.

"Do not drag me about," she complained as he forced her into his sitting room.

"When I say I require your presence at once, that means I require your presence at once. We have something to discuss." She watched in horror as he went to his desk and picked up her letter. "Do you recognize this?"

She couldn't believe he had it, and that it was not on the way to Cairwyn at all. "How did you get that?"

"Nothing goes out of this house that I don't look at."

"It was sealed. It wasn't meant for you to read."

"That seems patently obvious." His sharp voice ricocheted off the walls. "Nothing goes out of this house that I don't look at," he repeated with irate emphasis. "And thank God for that, because if your father had gotten this letter, there would have been a great deal of trouble for everyone involved. It's taken me a full day just to believe that you wrote it, that you could have been so reckless as to put these words on the page."

"Everything in that letter is true," she cried.

"None of it is true. These are the melodramatic ravings of a spoiled, self-centered child. How dare you write these things, when I have shown you nothing but kindness? When you have wanted for nothing? When I have given you my title and my husbandly care, and pleasure every night? 'Lewd whims,' Guinevere?"

She quailed at the cold strength of his fury. "You are lewd to me," she said. "I don't like it."

"That's a damnable lie. It's a lie to say I treat you like a savage. It's a lie to say that I punish you in a brutal and unfeeling manner, or force you to my will. This letter is full of false accusations and disparagement to my character."

He was not only angry, he was hurt and insulted. She couldn't bear to look at him, because she knew the letter was full of lies and exaggerations. "I don't want to be married to you," she said, the only excuse she had for her actions.

He put his hands aside his head and then threw them out in exasperation. "How many times must I explain this to you? This isn't a marriage of choice. It's a state marriage and it has nothing to do with your happiness. You're not married to me. You're married to England and Wales, and the goddamned will of the crown."

"You're not happy either," she said, shrinking away from him. "I know you don't want to be married to me any more than I want to be married to you. We don't suit one another."

"And so you write a letter full of false accusations and try to send it behind my back? Do you have any idea what would have happened if this missive had made its way into your father's hands?" He threw the letter down and advanced on her, his blue eyes glinting like tempered steel. "I'll tell you what would have happened. I would have cleared my name, darling. There are limits to what honor can take. I would have branded you a liar and shamed you and your family before the king. Your father would have been ruined for challenging me, and you would have become a despised object of scorn. Your family would have lost everything, all because you *don't want to be married to me*."

He spit out these last words as if they disgusted him. Gwen twisted her hands together.

"I'm sorry," she said, her eyes clouding with tears. "I'm sorry I did it."

"You're sorry you did it, or you're sorry you got caught?"

"I'm sorry I did it. I knew it was wrong, but I... You're right. I behaved as a spoiled child who wished to have her way."

He took her arm and leaned down so they were nose to nose. "I have servants who read Welsh, you little deceiver. In case you think to do any such thing again."

She had thought she had his scorn before, but it was nothing to the scorn he showed her now. "I'm sorry. It's only that I want so badly to go home."

He gave her a shake. "You're not going home. You're stuck in this hell of a marriage, just as I am." He turned at a tap on the door and said, "Come."

The door opened to a servant bearing a silver-lidded tray.

"Put it there," said Arlington, pointing to a side table.

The servant complied and left. The duke regarded her another moment or two, his hand still gripping her arm.

"I believe you feel remorseful. I also believe you want to go home. But you're not going home, not now, not ever. You're married to me and you are going to bear the Arlington heirs. This is your life, no matter how you struggle against it. Tell me you understand that."

"I understand it," she said, wiping her cheeks.

"And no matter how much you hate me, no matter how much you abhor my company and my 'lewd whims,' I'm going to remain your husband until one of us dies."

"That's such a grim way to put it," she said miserably.

"Grim or not, it's the truth. I will reiterate now that I require your respect in this marriage, as well as appropriate, obedient behavior, which you have not displayed." He pulled her over to the upholstered chair flanking the side table. "You're going to be punished, not 'brutally or unfeelingly,' but as befits a wife who has written a letter sorely defaming her husband's honor."

He sat in the chair and forced her down over his lap before she could gather the wherewithal to resist. His arm circled tightly about her waist as he flipped up her skirts.

"Don't, please," she begged. "I'm sorry. I know what I did was wrong."

"Then you know you deserve this spanking. Keep your legs still or I'll go for the cane."

Gwen didn't want to be caned, or even spanked, but she supposed she deserved it. She hadn't really thought about the trouble her letter might have caused. If it had come to strife between her father and the duke—or her father and the king—she knew who would have ended up on the losing side.

She braced for the spanking to begin, but instead she heard the clink of the tray. He parted her bottom cheeks, and pressed something cool and slick against her nether hole. She squirmed and tried to turn to him.

"No," he said. "Be still. You're going to have a peeled root of ginger in your bottom for this spanking."

"Why?" she cried.

"Because you've committed an especially egregious offense. The ginger will intensify your punishment by making your arsehole sting. Bad wives get bad things, if you'll remember."

It did not seem correct to do such a thing to one's wife; it seemed lewd again, and too intimate. She couldn't help but clench around the intrusion. A few moments later, she began to feel the promised sting. It felt wicked and shameful. She hid her face in her hands, trembling beneath her tossed-up skirts.

"I don't think you should do this," she said between her fingers. "It's wrong."

"Better I spank you than wring your neck," he snapped in reply. He adjusted her on his lap, over his hard, muscular thighs. The ginger hurt worse with every passing moment, and she felt so exposed and vulnerable. Then he spanked her and the burn intensified tenfold.

"Oh! *Ouch!*" She bit her lip as he spanked her again, and again.

"Don't squirm. You've earned this."

He pulled her closer to him and rearranged her until her bottom was stuck right up in the air, completely at his mercy. She kicked her legs but there was no way to get away. That's when he began to spank her in earnest.

She'd expected this spanking would feel something like the spanking he'd given her in the meadow, but it was not at all the same. The spanking in the meadow had provided a certain degree of wicked pleasure. This spanking was nothing but pain.

Firm smacks rained down on her bottom, each more heated than the last. A throbbing ache suffused her bottom, but when she reached to rub it away, he took her hand and trapped it at her waist.

"We're only getting started," he said. "By the time this spanking is over, you're going to feel like a very punished girl."

"I already feel very punished." She wailed at an especially sharp crack. Each time he spanked her, she wiggled and tensed, and the ginger in her bottom stung worse.

"Oh. *Ow, it burns.*" She kicked her legs harder but it made no difference to him. He only tightened his grip on her waist and kept spanking. Now and again his hand strayed lower, punishing the tender, sensitive skin at the backs of her thighs. Soon her entire backside felt as if it had caught fire.

How she wished she'd never written that note. She wasn't going to get out of this marriage, and there was no telling how long he'd stay angry with her, or when he would trust her again. "Oh, please," she begged. *Spank, spank, spank,* no break, no respite from his stinging palm. "Please, Sir. I'm sure I've had enough. I've learned my lesson."

"You've had enough when I say you've had enough. I don't think you know the meaning of a lesson yet." He paused and put his palm on her heated arse, then worked the ginger in and out. "Do you feel that ache, Guinevere?"

"Yes," she sobbed.

"That ache is for wives who behave badly. Do you feel ashamed? You feel hurt?"

"Yes!"

"Good. Because I felt hurt when I read your letter." The spanking resumed, mercilessly hard. Her cheeks throbbed and the ginger stung hotter than ever now that he'd repositioned it.

"Please. It smarts so much."

"I hope it does," he said without any pity whatsoever. "This isn't a game, Guinevere. You're my responsibility, my wife. When you earn a spanking, you're going to be spanked well enough that you remember it."

She whimpered and tugged at her hand but he'd caught her wrist tight, and there was no escaping his palm as it cracked against her pained cheeks. The noise of the spanks mixed with her cries and pleas until she thought the servants must come and save her. But of course, they never would.

Nothing would save her but the duke's estimation that she had had enough, and Gwen began to fear that moment would never come. She struggled over his thighs and cried silent, shuddering tears until he finally stopped.

She lay still, her bottom clenched from the pain. She hated ginger, and spankings. She hated the duke.

It's too bad, that. Because you're stuck with him forever. What had he said? *Until one of us dies...*

Gwen felt like she might die from the torturous fire of his spanking. It felt worse than the birching, or perhaps it had only gone on longer, until her skin felt raw. "Am I..." She swallowed past the miserable tension in her throat. "Am I to stand in the corner again?"

"Yes. But first..." He righted her, and set her before him with her skirts up about her waist, and the ginger still stinging in her bottom. "First, I have a few things to say."

She sniffled and wiped away tears with the back of her hand.

"You have said you are sorry," he said. "As you should be. I beg you to realize you were not my first choice of bride either. I, however, have not written any letters to anyone about your poor manners, your inconstant temper, or your abandoned behavior in my bed."

"My abandoned behavior!"

"Yes. If I wished to be cruel, I could write such things, but you notice I haven't, and I wouldn't. You're not married to a villain, as much as you wish to be. The only person behaving poorly in this marriage is the one standing before me with ginger in her sore, reddened bottom."

Gwen bit her tongue. No matter how much she disagreed, she would not reply to his lecture, or argue, or do anything that might result in him turning her over his lap again.

"I will not change who I am because of your issues and shortcomings, Guinevere," he continued. "I suggest you set yourself to your duties and stop playing a victim of fate. I have no stomach for drama unless I'm sitting in a box at the theater."

"You have no stomach for sympathy either, do you?" she said. "You don't understand my feelings. You don't even try."

"I'll show sympathy when something bad actually happens to you." He turned her about. "Go stand in the corner just as you are, with your skirts up about your waist. No rubbing your bottom, and we shall leave in the ginger. It's going to sting a while longer, which is by design."

I hate your designs. She almost said it aloud, but she knew it would not be wise. Instead she went to the corner and stood as he directed her, with her eyes to the wall and her punished bottom on display. Her buttocks ached horribly, but she dared not rub them under his watchful eye. Instead she tensed from time to time, then cursed herself as the ginger stung her. Her husband was lewd and cruel, whether or not he wished to admit it. After a quarter hour of corner time, he led her into his washroom and relieved her of the ginger, and allowed her to rearrange her appearance.

How she wished to run away and hide then. Instead the duke took her hand and tugged it. "Come with me, I've something to show you."

He marched her out into the hall and down the stairs, past servants who had undoubtedly heard her screeching and crying during her punishment. Her bottom ached with each step. Her petticoats, which were the softest, finest quality, felt like raking fingers against her freshly-spanked flesh. He took her out the side of the house, past his mother's garden and across a grassy field to the stables and paddocks.

"Look out there," he said, pointing.

A regal mare galloped about the largest paddock, a stunning specimen of strength and grace. She was pure white with a glorious mane, strong haunches and a straight, proud head. Effie had never been so glorious, even in her prime. As Gwen watched the horse cavorting in the field, she forgot for long moments that she hated the duke, and that she didn't wish to be holding his hand. Instead, she clung to it, enraptured.

"She's beautiful," said Gwen. "Will she come nearer to us?"

"I doubt it. She's young and wild yet, but when I saw her, I had to own her. If the grooms can gentle her, she'll be yours."

Gwen turned to him in shock. "Mine? My horse?"

"You had to leave your mare behind, and I felt bad about it. I planned to get you another." He turned to her, raising an eyebrow. "You see, I am not the unfeeling despot described in your letter."

He looked away, but she saw the lingering injury in his gaze. "I'm sorry for what I wrote," she said again. "I truly am sorry."

"And you have been punished. I'll destroy the letter and we'll put this episode behind us, and you can write another letter home. Just know that I shall read it, along with any letters you send, so take care that you keep them positive. Surely there are pleasant things to say about your life here. You'll have a pretty horse anyway, as soon as they manage to tame her. You must think about what to call her."

A set of grooms attempted to bridle the spirited mare. She tossed her head and fought the bit, and made whinnying sounds of protest that broke Gwen's heart.

I know, she thought. *I know what it is like to have to be tamed.*

"I wish I could go to her," said Gwen.

"You can't, not until I say." His tone was not to be argued with. "She isn't safe to ride, and I wouldn't have you hurt."

He said that so many times, that he didn't want her to be hurt. Then he'd turn around and tell her that her punishments were meant to hurt— and he certainly took care that they did. "They're tormenting her," she protested as the horse's whinnying protests rose to an equine scream.

"They're not tormenting her. They're showing her who's in charge, a necessary exercise if she's to reach her potential." His lips made a tight line as he watched the grooms. "What use is that horse, Guinevere, if she cannot be ridden?"

She didn't answer. She could see the duke was still angry, just by the way he said her name. "I'm sorry," she said once more. She thought she might say it a thousand times, and it wouldn't fix the tension between them. "And I... I thank you for buying me the mare. I'm sure I don't deserve your kindness."

He was silent a moment, then he said, "We deserve one another's kindness. Otherwise we're in for very long and miserable lives." With one last glance at the horse, he took her arm and turned her toward the house. "Go back to your room now and write another letter to your father. Lord Daniel will be here to do your dancing lesson at three."

"Oh, must I have my lesson today?" she asked. "It aches every time I move."

"Whose fault is that?"

Gwen didn't answer his pointed question, only heaved a great sigh and followed her husband back to the smothering walls of Arlington Hall.

Chapter Eight: Angry

The duke didn't visit her bedroom that night, or the night afterward. He sat silent at dinner, focusing on his plate although she sat two feet to his right. Not a single word passed his lips, except to address the servants. This went on for three days.

Gwen told herself she ought to be happy to be free of his company—especially his nightly attentions—but in truth, she felt miserable. He was teaching her another lesson, she knew. He was demonstrating all the pleasant things he'd done in their marriage by no longer doing them, and letting the empty space of his withdrawal resonate in Gwen's soul.

He had called her a spoiled, self-centered child, and then he made her feel just like a child by ignoring her and going about his ducal way, as grand and handsome as ever. Meanwhile, the mare, that living, breathing symbol of his generosity, whinnied and squealed at all hours from the paddock, until Gwen's sanity was about to snap.

Poor darling. Someday Gwen would make it up to her. She decided she'd name her Eira, the Welsh word for snow. She told the grooms so they could accustom the mare to her name, and watched impatiently as the beautiful creature refused to be tamed. *Please settle down*, she thought. *I am waiting to love you.* When Gwen was not sleeping or eating, or at lessons, or changing clothes, she was at the paddock, dreaming of the time she might climb up on the mare's back and wander with her about the duke's property. Perhaps she could find a picturesque meadow like the one she'd left behind in Wales.

The duke would take you to a picturesque meadow if you asked him.

But she did not ask him. She felt she had lost the right to ask favors. If he did not despise her before, he despised her now and it was entirely her own fault. On the fourth day, when the household was in a bustle about heading to London, he passed her in the hallway and did not so much as look at her as he continued on his way. She had become invisible. Since he did not acknowledge her, she ceased to exist.

She fled the house to see Eira, and perhaps have a little cry in private. She longed for her home, and that artist named Jack who had thought her beautiful, and kissed her. Jack hadn't cared that she wasn't a blueblood, that she wasn't well-born and elegant. Jack had been something like a friend.

Gwen found Eira prancing sideways in the paddock, her reins dangling as she tossed her head. Her saddle was somewhere farther off. Apparently she'd bucked the thing from her back. Gwen wondered if she'd bucked off a groom. There was no one about. She whickered to the horse and held out a hand.

"Come here, beauty. Come, Eira. Come see your mistress. I promise I'll be kind."

Eira turned in her direction. Gwen stood very still, meeting the horse's gaze with all the placid calm she could muster. She made another soft sound, a sweet, welcoming cluck that held the horse's attention a few more moments than before. "Please come," she whispered. "Let me stroke your mane. I won't ever hurt you."

Eira's ears flicked up and back, and she started toward Gwen. Oh, she wished she had brought some treat, a carrot or apple, but the mare didn't seem disappointed when she arrived and found her palms empty. Gwen reached slowly, so slowly to pat her sleek neck and tangled mane.

"What a pretty girl," she said in her most soothing voice. "You aren't bad at all, are you? You're only misunderstood. You want to gallop about and be free, and they want to truss you up in harnesses. They are awful here about things like that."

Eira nodded her head up and down as if she understood, and pushed her muzzle under Gwen's hands. Gwen laughed and stroked her some more, gazing into her liquid eyes.

"I can't wait until we can ride together every day," she said. "You know, I'm from Wales, where the ladies can ride as well as the men, or better. I've ridden horses much wilder than you, naughty girl. When you learn to bear your saddle and bridle, we'll have so many adventures, and be best friends."

Now that Eira was calm, Gwen ducked under the fence and stood beside her, petting her withers. The horse neighed in approval and tossed her head again, and twitched her shoulders until Gwen giggled.

"Yes, I understand you've got personality. You'll make a fun pet, and you're so lovely and strong. Look at those muscles! I wish I could climb up on your back and ride you now, the way I did with Effie when she was younger. Will you let me on your back, if you won't tolerate that tiresome saddle? We can take a stroll around the paddock if you promise you won't toss me off."

"Guinevere!"

Gwen heard the duke's voice from far away, somewhere near the house. Somewhere too far away to stop her, at any rate. She climbed up on the fence, which she'd done many times as a child, and hopped onto Eira's back. She'd always preferred bareback to saddles, because she loved to feel the strength and movement of her mount.

"Beautiful girl," she crooned, patting Eira's neck. "How kind you are, to let me climb atop you. How still and polite you're being."

"Guinevere, get down. Get down at once," the duke shouted. "Palmer! Gandiston! See to the duchess!"

Her husband's voice was closer now. In fact, he was running full speed to the paddock, his coattails flying out behind him. A groom stuck his head out of the stable and came running too. Gwen could feel Eira go tense. Gwen didn't want to attempt to get down, not while the horse was agitated. She said her name softly and stroked her mane as she gathered the horse's dangling reins.

"Guinevere!"

Eira sidled away as the duke arrived at the fence. Gwen met Arlington's gaze, surprised by the depth of his alarm.

"Please stop shouting," she chided. "You're frightening her."

"Frightening her?" The duke was still yelling. "You're frightening me. Get down from that untamed beast before it snaps your neck."

"I promised her a ride around the paddock."

"She's not yet fit to ride. She isn't even saddled."

One of the grooms approached from the other side of the paddock. Eira danced around to watch him, spinning between the duke and the groom. Gwen imagined it must be terrifying to the mare, to be surrounded and yelled at in such a confrontational fashion. Gwen leaned down and whispered in her ear. "Go, Eira. Let's go."

The duke snatched at the reins but couldn't reach them. "Don't dare."

"A short jaunt only," she told him.

"Don't dare!"

But Gwen did dare. She nudged a heel into Eira's side and urged her forward. The mare needed little encouragement. Within a pair of strides the horse had gained speed and accelerated to a gallop.

Poor thing, to be restrained all the time when she only wanted a good run. Eira's legs pounded, carrying them on a collision course with the paddock fence. Gwen heard shouting behind them but she didn't turn around. "Fly for me, girl," she whispered instead, and the horse went up and over, smooth as silk, strong as the sun. Gwen laughed with the joy of motion as her hair came loose from its pins and tumbled back over her shoulders.

"Go, go, go," she urged as they streaked toward the woodlands. "The duke will be angry, but there's nothing for it. Fly while you can, my darling, as far as you can go."

Aidan was struggling in this marriage, and he didn't know how to fix all the things that were wrong. He had always been good at everything. He had always been well-liked, the sort of chap people were pleased to count as a friend. Even in his rakish exploits, he had always been fondly regarded by the ladies.

Now he was failing. Two weeks into this mess, he was failing at marriage, failing as a husband, failing at protecting his wife. Despite his orders to the contrary, she'd swung onto her wild horse's back and galloped away. They were gone, run off into the woodlands toward the thickest area of trees. His wife would be killed, he was sure of it. What would he tell Guinevere's family? What would he tell the king and queen, who were expecting them at audience in London?

He never should have bought the horse. The mare was beautiful, yes, but she was too wild. He never should have shown her to Gwen in the first place. And damn him, he shouldn't have ignored Gwen in the hallway. He should have swept her up and taken her to bed instead, and put an end to the freeze between them. He might be putting a child in her right now, instead of galloping out with the grooms in pursuit of a satanic horse which may or may not have trampled his wife by the time they caught it.

He should have locked her in her room. If she survived this, he would lock her in her room for the rest of her life.

"There she is," said one of the grooms, pointing into the distance.

Gwen was still on the mare's back, thank God. Aidan gestured toward the tree line. "We'll go around. They're headed for the lake."

"It's a young horse, Your Grace. If the duchess can keep her seat, the beast'll get tired soon enough."

Aidan's eyes stayed riveted to his wife as they sped in faster pursuit. Through his panic, through his anger, he realized Gwen was a magnificent horsewoman. He'd never seen an Englishwoman ride like that, bareback, neck or nothing, hunched over her mount with the reins loose in her hands. The wind caught Gwen's black hair and whipped it behind her like streaks of dark lightning against the horse's white coat. She was a fairy queen on her enchanted steed. *Please, please, please, don't stumble. Don't lose control.*

"The horse is slowing, Your Grace."

Aidan nodded, looking over at the white-faced grooms. Now that the race was over, now that Gwen had apparently survived, Aidan could not seem to collect his emotions. He rode into the clearing by the pond, where the mare drank and his wife stood beside it, stroking its neck.

He slid down off his horse, so weak with relief he was not certain his legs would hold him. Gwen glanced at him, saying nothing. They had said nothing to each other all week.

"Walk the mare back," he said to the grooms. "I would speak privately with my wife."

His men took the reins, and the now-tired horse followed them without resistance. Gwen stood with her chin high and her hands clasped before her, and Aidan thought for the hundredth time that he would never understand her. Why was she not afraid of him, especially now? Why was she not in awe of him like everyone else? Why was she always doing things that made him want to shout at her?

"Well," she said. "You have that look about you. Are you going to spank me again?"

"If I had control of my temper, I would. That horse might have killed you, you know. If you ever pull such a stunt again, rest assured I'll whip you to within an inch of your life."

"I don't understand why you're angry. You said she was mine."

He wanted to murder her. He did. "Do not be obtuse. You heard me yelling at you. You heard me say the horse was not fit to ride."

"But she was fit to ride. She carried me beautifully."

"Beautifully?" He stalked toward her. "She ran from the paddock like the devil was at her heels."

"Because you shouted at her and startled her," his wife retorted, backing away.

"You're lucky she didn't break your head open and snap your bones under her feet. I thought you'd be dead. I thought I'd come upon your broken, lifeless body, God damn you."

He had no more words, only emotion choking him inside. He'd grasped her arms without even realizing it. She infuriated him beyond reason but he didn't want her to die. He pulled her down to the ground and trapped her hands over her head, and yanked up her skirts. She didn't resist him, and he didn't look at her face. He only knew he had to be inside her, because she was alive and whole, and not in a thousand bloody pieces.

"Oh," she said as he yanked at his breeches and released himself. He pushed into her hard. He might have hurt her if she hadn't arched to him, if she wasn't already wet. But of course she was wet. He'd learned in their marriage bed that she liked force. She liked sexual wildness and abandon. It was one of the only things they had in common. Perhaps that's why he ravished her now, because it was the only way to reconnect with her, and they needed to reconnect. *You scared me. I care about you.*

He would not say he loved her. She wasn't lovable in the least, the way she constantly challenged him, but he should have been going to her bed all this time. Five days lost, when he might have been between her legs, giving her the only thing she seemed to want from him: a hard, rough fuck.

He dug his knees into the grass, surging inside her, lifting her, taking her in an animalistic temper. He'd never fucked a woman angry before, never. Not until now.

Their clothes would be ruined by dirt and grass. Everything would be ruined, but he didn't care. He couldn't think of anything beyond taking her as he ought to have taken her earlier. He'd never pass by her again without dragging her into some room and possessing her. Perhaps he'd fuck her on sight, then and there, pull her beneath him in the corridors, in the parlors, or push her up against a marble column in the main hall.

At some point he'd let go of her hands. He wrapped himself around her so she couldn't get away, but she wasn't trying to get away. She gripped and pulled his hair as she strained against his front. He wasn't taking the first care for her pleasure, but she was ardently aroused. It made him angrier, and the anger spilled over into passion for this hellion who was not the wife he expected to have. *I hate you*, he thought, but he meant, *I love you, and I don't know why.*

She cried out and bucked beneath him. He fucked her harder, cursing, biting off oaths as she climaxed. Her sheath tightened around him in rhythmic, ecstatic ripples that signaled her release. He sought his own, driving into her so firmly she panted for breath. No, it was not civil, not well done of him. As soon as he emptied himself inside her, he became aware of how barbarous he'd been. He'd never fucked a whore so violently. He should not have done so to his wife, not for any reason. He made himself look at her, and endure her righteous outrage.

But there was no outrage. She closed her eyes a moment, then blinked them open again. She unwound her fingers from his hair, and let her arm drop back about her head. It was a sensual pose, lazy and content. He didn't understand her. He would never understand her.

"Aren't you angry?" he ground out.

He felt her squeeze around his cock.

"You were the angry one," she said. "Do you feel better now?"

Did he feel better? He couldn't tell, and it didn't matter. "I shouldn't have taken you in anger. That was not respectful of me."

"I suppose it turned out all right."

He realized then why he could not be pleased. It was because a proper lady would not gaze up at him and say *I suppose it turned out all right.* A proper lady would not gain pleasure from being ravished beside a lake. But his lady did.

So what was he to do? He could not be angry and rough again, that was certain. And he couldn't ignore her, because it only made things worse. He couldn't change her, not without a great deal of angst and willful disobedience. He didn't have the answer, and he always had the answer.

He sighed and rose on his elbows, and pulled away. When he glanced down to fasten his breeches, he saw crimson on his cock, and her thighs, and experienced a sickening jolt of horror. "I've injured you," he said. "There's blood."

"You didn't injure me. I believe my courses are upon me. They were due." She pushed down her skirts to hide the stains. "I'm sorry."

"Sorry? Why are you sorry?"

"Because I haven't yet conceived your heir. I know that's all you need me for."

He pursed his lips as he did up his breeches. "You know nothing of what I need. Nor do you care." He stood and held out a hand. "Get up."

She ignored him and stood on her own, and arranged her appearance, brushing away leaves and dirt. "I wish you would stop being angry all the time," she said.

"Then I wish you would stop angering me." Aidan turned away. "They took your horse, so you'll have to ride back on mine."

"Her name is Eira."

He stopped on his way across the clearing. "What?"

"The mare. I've named her Eira. It's the Welsh word for snow."

He started again toward his horse. "Don't get attached to that mare. I'm going to get rid of her."

"What?" The word rang out among the lake and trees. She ran to his side. "You can't get rid of her. You can't!"

"Why not? She won't be broken to the saddle, and you can't ride bareback in London. You can't streak through Hyde Park clinging to her damned mane."

"I won't then," Gwen cried. "I'll wait to ride her, as long as it takes you to be satisfied she is tame. The grooms will train her, I know." She grasped his arm, tears brimming in her eyes. "Please, Aidan, you were so wise to choose her. She's smart and lively, with so much potential. She only needs a little more time."

"I was wise to choose her, you say, but not wise enough to know when she's ready to be ridden?"

"I'm sorry. I'm so sorry I didn't listen to you. Please! Please don't take Eira away from me."

She threw her arms around him, sobbing against his chest. He wanted to stay angry, and he meant to get rid of the mare at the first opportunity, but Gwen's grief was so raw, so deep, he couldn't steel himself against it.

"That beast might have killed you," he said, running a hand over her hair.

"No, she wouldn't. It wasn't her fault. She didn't do anything to endanger me. It was my fault for galloping off when you didn't want me to. I won't do things like that anymore, I promise."

"I understand that you're upset, but she's not working out. We'll find a better tempered one, just as beautiful."

"No, I love her. Please." She gripped the front of his coat and gazed at him through tears. "Eira and I talked together. I know that sounds silly, but I looked into her eyes and I saw that she belongs to me. She knows she belongs to me too. I can't explain it, but she's special. I know she'll get better and...and so will I. I'll be a perfect, obedient duchess from now on. I promise. I swear."

He loosened her fingers before she started popping off his buttons. "That's a pretty promise, but I don't believe you."

"Please! I'll say whatever you want, and do whatever you want. Please, please, don't take my Eira away."

He'd seen her upset, and he'd seen her cry, but he'd never seen her like this. *My Eira.* How could she care so much about a dumb, wild creature and yet think so poorly of him? He brushed away her tears before she could wipe them again on his coat.

"All right," he finally said in exasperation. "I won't send her away yet. But you are not to go anywhere near the paddock unless I allow it, and if the grooms aren't able to improve her, we'll have to let her go. Do you understand? You're too valuable to me, more valuable than any horse."

She gripped his sleeves and sniffled. "Do you swear? You aren't just saying it so I'll stop crying?"

"I swear. I'm a man of my word." He frowned as he stared down at her. "And I wait with great anticipation for this perfect, obedient duchess you've promised to be."

She took a step back and sank into a low curtsy, bowing her head before him. It was certainly the most graceful reverence she'd ever shown. "Very pretty," he said. "I hope you'll be as biddable in London."

He doubted her sudden reformation would last more than an hour or two, but with her love for the mare, he had a threat to hold over her head, a surefire way to bring her to heel. She might even make it through their audience with the king without setting Welsh-English relations back a century or two.

"Come along then," he said, guiding her over to his stallion. He mounted first and hauled her up before him. She settled in his lap, her body still shuddering with the occasional sniffle. He slid an arm about her waist to hold her in the saddle.

Perhaps later, when he had calmed down completely, he would spank her for shearing a full ten years off his life. But he knew he probably wouldn't.

He was still too stricken by the idea that she might have been lost.

Chapter Nine:
In London

A few days later, Gwen bid farewell to Eira and her private garden in Oxfordshire, and set out with the duke on her very first journey to London. Being a perfect, obedient duchess wasn't easy when one was trapped in a carriage with one's demanding husband. But no innkeepers were asked to assemble any fresh birch rods, so in that way, this journey went better than the last.

Arlington House, her husband's London home, turned out to be even grander than his manor in Oxfordshire, comprising twenty-two windows across the front and eight windows across the side. By this particular form of measurement, Gwen perceived that his town house was one of the grandest in the city proper, with an elevated portico and staircases and a long balustrade along the front with shining iron gates.

There was not as much land around the house as he had in the country, but still more than any of the other homes about. Behind the house stretched a landscaped garden with walking paths and follies, including a great Greek temple carved and detailed to look like the real thing. When she asked him the purpose of this temple in the midst of his gardens, he winked at her and said, "For fun."

A house that was twenty-two windows wide and eight windows deep was not very fun for Gwen, because she was constantly lost in its corridors. While she flailed about trying to find her place in this new London home, Arlington came and went, riding out on his prized black stallion. She did not ask his business, although she supposed he had any number of ducal interests to see to now that he'd returned to town. He still visited her each night, exposing her to more perversions. As much as she wished to resist him, he made her crave ever more wanton things.

Sometimes she wondered if he did it as an exercise in power, for he dealt skillfully in power. She watched him now in the looking glass, as he scrutinized her diamonds and the silver gown she wore. It was the same gown she'd worn at their wedding, the gown the duke had chosen for their formal portrait. London's best artist waited downstairs in the grand hall. Pascale had done her hair to the duke's specifications, some of it curling down over her bare shoulders, and the rest of it braided and piled upon her head, rather as it had been the first day she met him. Well, officially met him. He came over and smoothed one of the coils, and adjusted the pin that secured it.

"Your lady's maid does well," he said. "Are you pleased with her?"

"I suppose." In truth, Pascale was nearly as lofty as the duke.

He smoothed a hand down the bodice of her gown, to the fitted waist. "I like this color with your eyes. The diamonds too. Anything else would be too showy, and you are already showy enough." He stood back and met her gaze in the glass. "How do I look? Our grandchildren and great-grandchildren will study this portrait one day, and remember us as we appear."

"But you've had other portraits made." She had seen them, expert renderings of him as a child, and as a willowy, slightly sneering young man. There was a more recent likeness of him in the gallery that perfectly captured his powerful masculinity. She stood from the bench and turned to assess him. "I think you look very fine."

"Fine" was always an understatement when it came to her husband. He wore a deep blue coat and breeches embroidered with silver to match her dress, a lace-cuffed shirt, and a sumptuous fur-lined cape that buttoned at the neck with a garish jewel. He flipped one side of the cape back over his coat, revealing decorations and medals, shining ducal things. In truth, he awed her, clad in such finery. He seemed at home in it, while she felt stiff and overdressed. "I have never seen you wear a sword," she said.

"It's ceremonial. It was my father's, and my grandfather's before him. Would you like to see it?"

He drew the gleaming thing from its scabbard and Gwen jumped back.

He chuckled. "If I haven't stabbed you yet, I won't do it now." He stepped to the side and adopted a ready stance, his sword arm extended before him. "Like any well-reared man, I took lessons in fencing and swordplay. I've never cut anyone to pieces, but I could if I wanted to."

"A useful talent."

He shot her a piratical look. His hair was pulled back, shining gold even in the dim dressing room. She felt a pang of arousal, a craving for his touch. His force. She wanted him to threaten and subdue her, and run her through. Not with the sword, of course, but something else. Then she remembered that he disdained her, and only valued her as another exercise in power. *My elegant duchess. My obedient wife. My cooperative lover.* She was here to please the king and give the duke children.

And to look pretty in his portrait.

"I suppose we ought to go down," he said, sheathing the sword. He still retained the dangerous aura that attracted and repelled her at once. "Are you ready to sit motionless for an hour or more? Have you sat for a portrait before?"

"Once." Her voice sounded more wistful than she meant it to.

"Ah, yes." He looked at her with a ghost of a smile. "I remember you did very well that day, sitting still for me."

You approved of me more that day, she thought, *than you have ever approved of me since.* "Do you still have that sketch?" she asked aloud.

"Of course I do." His eyes raked over her, from her face to her breasts, to her waist and hips and skirts. "And I have something better, too. A fairy queen for a wife." He took her about the waist and pulled her close against his hard, tall body, then tilted his head down and pressed a kiss to the curve of her neck. Her stomach fluttered. He pulled away and touched her diamond necklace where it rested against her chest.

"The portrait," he said, as if reminding himself. "We must sit for the portrait now. It may take a few days."

"Yes, Your Grace." She whispered it, because he didn't like when she called him by his title. But sometimes, when she looked at him in his rich capes and finery, she couldn't think of him by any other name. Not Arlington, and certainly not Aidan. He was the duke at his essence, *Your Grace* through and through.

"I've received good news from Arlington Hall," said her husband the following week over dinner. "Your horse is responding at last to her handlers. Perhaps your wild ride across the fields exorcised some of her demons."

Gwen knew why Eira was responding now. It was because someone had finally shown her some sympathy and understanding. "I'm happy to hear she's doing better."

"If she continues to improve, I'll have her brought to London. We can take the air in Hyde Park when the weather permits. You'll look quite striking atop your pretty mare, as Mrs. Gerrard is putting together several riding habits for these colder months. Everyone will note your horsemanship."

"I hope so."

"If you are ladylike, that is."

And there it came, the eternal insult, the constant reminder that she was not good enough, not "finished" to his standards, which were impossibly high and impossibly shallow. All he cared about was her appearance, her presentation, her manners, and how much she might increase his esteem among the denizens of his social set.

She wished there was more to him. She wished she could know him better, even love him, instead of being held at arms' length and used mainly to satisfy his sexual needs. His *excessive* sexual needs.

She wondered when he would begin to stray in their marriage. Most men did, as a matter of course, and they'd been wed for a month now. The duke was frequently gone for hours, "making calls," he said, or "going to the club." She imagined him going instead to tryst with other women, fine, genteel women he might have married if he'd been allowed to. She didn't know why that should bother her, since she didn't like him anyway, but it did.

"In other news," he said, "we've a time and date for our royal audience. One week hence, at four o'clock in the afternoon." He glanced up at her briefly. "I pray you will not become anxious."

Become anxious? She'd been anxious about it since before she married him. "What if they don't like me?" she asked.

"You must make them like you. Otherwise things shall go poorly for you in society, and for me. Not to burden you with undue pressure," he added as an afterthought.

She rubbed her eyes, and jabbed her finger rather inelegantly into the corner of one.

"Stop that, please. You must refrain from showing disquiet in public. It's impolite to frown and poke your fingers into your eyes."

"I can't help it." She forced her hands back to her lap. "Why did you marry me, when I can't do anything right?"

He looked to the heavens. "Not this again. Come here, Guinevere."

His expression was sharper than his voice, but he had a way of speaking softly even when he was angry. She never trusted his tone, only his eyes, and of course his hands. When she went to him, he turned her about and tugged at her laces, loosening her bodice. When he had it as he liked it, he retied it and turned her back around, and reached within her clothing to cup her breasts. She tried hard not to react as he rolled her tightening nipples between his fingertips.

"You shouldn't," she pleaded. "Not at dinner. The servants will see you."

He gazed into her eyes, that wily, hungry gaze that always made her squirm. He went to the servants' door and shut it, then returned and sat before her again, his gaze now fixed upon her chest.

"Take your breasts out," he said. "Fold down your bodice so they're plainly in view."

"Must I?"

"You know what happens when you defy my commands, darling."

It was bad enough for him to fondle and expose her. It was infinitely worse to be made to expose herself for his sordid amusement. She reached within her bodice and lifted her breasts so they crested the taut neckline of her gown. The bodice pushed them up and out. Her pink nipples hardened to stiff points. She flushed and stared at the opposite wall, avoiding his gaze.

"You're not still shy?" he asked. "After all we've done together?"

"I believe the word is modest."

He burst into laughter. "You're as modest as a peahen in season. If I lifted your skirts right now, you'd be wet as Noah's flood. It's one of the things I like most about you."

She braced for him to do it, to lift her skirts and discover the damp heat that blossomed alongside her humiliation. "I only get wet because something is wrong with me," she said. "I feel things I don't want to."

"No." He gave a slight shake of his head. "You feel things I want you to, like a perfect, obedient duchess. What a good girl you are to keep your promises, if only for love of a horse." He tugged one of her nipples as his lips curved in a wry sort of smile. "Kneel down, Guinevere."

She glanced toward the closed door. It was not locked. She knew it wasn't locked. He could not ask this of her, not now. He demanded it in the bedroom all the time, but it surely wasn't proper to do it at dinner. He spread his legs to make a place for her, and leaned back in his chair. She could see the thick outline of his cock behind the falls of his breeches.

"I do not like to wait," he said quietly.

She went to her knees because she had no choice in the matter. If she didn't obey him, he'd force her, or punish her, or both. He toyed with her breasts as she undid his breeches and drew out his manhood. She closed her eyes and took him into her mouth, and attended to him as he'd taught her.

"Oh, yes," he said in that same quiet voice. "This is why I married you. You certainly do some things right." He pinched her nipples again, hard enough to make her whine against his skin. Then he shoved his cock deep in her mouth, so she gagged and choked. When he withdrew, she gasped for air, licking his balls and the base of his cock to compose herself. He laid back and let her do it, emitting the occasional ragged growl. The untamed sound resonated between her legs. She wished she could touch herself at the same time she served him. She wished he would touch her too and make her come.

He fisted his cock and guided it back to her mouth, and thrust between her lips, even deeper this time. He was so wide, so thick, she couldn't breathe. She drew air through her nose and nearly cried in relief when he thrust in her more shallowly. She used her tongue to tease and entice him, and one of her hands to stroke up and down his length. Her other hand delved within her skirts, sneaking under her petticoat to find the part of her that ached for stimulation.

"What's the matter, love?" he asked in lazy amusement. "Is your pussy wet and empty? Do you want to be fucked?"

He would make her admit it if she did not admit it herself. She gazed up and said the words to him, rather than be ordered to do so. "Yes, Sir. I want to be fucked."

"Perhaps I would rather spend in your mouth." He gripped her head and surged into her throat again. "Perhaps I'll avail myself of your arsehole."

She coughed as he withdrew. "You said—only when I was bad."

He chuckled and released her. "So I did. And you've been very good." He hauled her up and bent her over the table, between asparagus and potatoes and cream sauce. He gathered up her skirts until she felt cool air on her bottom, and then he delivered a brisk spank. "I want to take your arsehole, you know. Right now, I want to be inside you there. It makes me cross that you don't deserve it. Not yet," he said in a portentous voice.

He drove into her pussy instead, a careless, pumping possession. The china rattled and the silverware jumped. She feared a goblet would overturn and stain the tablecloth with wine, but the heavy crystal stayed standing.

"It will take you all of a minute or two to come off," he said, squeezing her shoulders. "The food won't even be cold. All you need is a cock inside you. Isn't that true, darling?"

It was true, because of his rough voice and his large hands, and the demanding way he forced her to his will. It aroused her beyond bearing. He slapped her arse again and she shuddered from the thrill of it, and the shame. The tablecloth chafed her exposed nipples, but he wouldn't let her up. He pounded into her until her walls clenched around him, seeking that last bit of stimulation she needed to find release.

"Not yet," he said. "Wait for me."

She laid her forehead against the tablecloth with a moan of supplication, only to be spanked again, and fucked harder. "Don't be a spoiled duchess," he chided. "You will wait for your pleasure, or not have it at all."

She scratched her fingertips against the tablecloth, trying to hold off so he wouldn't punish her. She wanted to knock off all the plates in her frustration, but instead she panted, and waited, trying to hover just at that tipping point until he allowed her to come. The need increased to the point she could barely stand it. "Please, please," she begged as he surged into her, hitting her perfect spot.

He grabbed her hips and drove in her to the hilt. "Now," he gasped. "Now you may come." He held her shoulders down against the table and that pressure and force was as thrilling to her as anything else. Her legs gave way as her climax overtook her. The goblet finally tipped, shattering and splashing wine upon the table.

The duke pulled her up and away from the jagged pieces, supporting her from behind. He squeezed her breasts, which spilled wantonly from her bodice. One more thrust and groan, and he went still, dropping his head to her shoulder. After a moment, he pressed a kiss against the curve of her neck.

"A minute and a half," he whispered in her ear. "That's how long it would have taken you if I hadn't made you wait."

"It's not my fault," she said. "It's your fault."

"Don't place blame. Kneel down and clean me off so I can pull up my breeches."

She gave him a pleading look, but he remained firm.

"Do it," he said. "You promised to be a perfect and obedient duchess."

She sighed and sank to her knees for the second time, and applied herself to tidying his cock. He might have let her use a napkin or something to do it, but no. Nothing would satisfy him except that she perform the task with her mouth. And she had learned to be quick, lest he become aroused and begin things all over again.

"Now," he said when she was finished, "stand up and let me fix your gown. I'd be pleased to let you finish dinner that way, but the servants would be dropping dishes left and right."

Her eyes went to the spilled wine and broken goblet. When they were situated, and she was seated primly at her place, he opened the door and the servants streamed in as if they had been waiting in a line outside the entire time. They whisked away the crystal fragments and covered the soiled part of the tablecloth with extra napkins. The dinner plates were cleared away to make room for dessert.

She stared down at the fruit tarts and assortment of cheeses and then looked back at him. He'd just bent her over the table and ravished her, and now he wanted her to take dessert?

He waved a fork at her. "Eat, Guinevere. And don't frown so."

"The thing is…" she said, cutting into the tart, "I don't think it's fair."

"What's not fair?"

"I must be a proper duchess at all times, but you do not behave like a proper duke."

"I made no promises to be a proper duke, did I? Not like you."

"You're not a very nice person." She narrowed her eyes as she said this, even though he might punish her for it later. "I think you play with me, and treat me like a toy, like something to bat about for your amusement."

"I do not bat you about."

She glanced at the napkins piled atop the stain. "Yes, you do."

He ate for a moment, the fine Arlington silverware sparkling in his long fingers. "If you do not wish to be played with, Guinevere, then I suppose I will take my pleasure tonight without bothering to arouse you as I normally do." He gave her a positively satanic smile.

She sucked in a breath. "You know that's not what I mean."

"Then what do you mean? That you *do* enjoy when I play with you?"

This was a perfect example of being toyed with, not that the duke cared. "You love to twist my words and make me uneasy," she said.

"And you love to paint me as your lewd and heartless assailant. I can't remember now what we ultimately decided. Would you prefer to have pleasure tonight, or not?"

There was only one way to answer. "I would prefer to have pleasure, Sir."

"For your own amusement? Not only mine?"

She sighed. "Yes, Sir."

"Please do not accuse me of being a villain in order to assuage your own disordered feelings. We've spoken of this before."

His voice was light, cold, casual in its evisceration. How hateful he could be. She made no response, only took another bite of her tart so he would not see how he provoked her, and swallowed hard when the delicious morsel stuck in her throat.

Chapter Ten:
Perfectly Matched

The duke's friends visited a couple days later, since they had all arrived in town to spend the holidays: the two marquesses, Lord Townsend and Lord Barrymore, and the Earl of Warren, that ceaselessly cheerful man. This time they brought their wives, who seemed eager to meet Gwen. She endured the introductions with a sense of gloom. She was certain they would find her wanting in some way.

Lord Townsend's wife was named Aurelia, and was the daughter of a duke. Gwen's first thought was that Aurelia would have made Arlington a better wife, except that she was enamored of her towering, dark-haired husband. Lord Townsend seemed enamored of her too, hovering around her with loving glances. The Townsends' daughter Felicity was back home napping, along with the Warrens' infant son George.

The other dark-haired man, Barrymore, was married to Minette, who was apparently Warren's sister, and Warren was married to Josephine, a countess with lavish auburn hair and the occasional spark of mischief in her eyes. The three ladies seemed to know one another quite well, and kept up a steady stream of conversation as they sat at tea on the terrace. Below them, the gentlemen romped in the chill air, playing a loosely organized game of cricket.

"Look at them," said Aurelia, pulling her cloak closer around her. "The older they get, the more they behave like boys."

The other ladies laughed. "I think they're only happy to be together again," said Minette. "My husband always worried that marriage and children would put a strain on their friendship, or end it altogether."

"Your marriage to Barrymore nearly *did* end it altogether," Josephine said with an unladylike snort. "Warren spent more than one night pacing and cursing August's name."

Gwen listened to all this in confusion. "I'm sorry, but who is August?"

"Barrymore was Lord Augustine before his father died," Josephine explained. "We called him August, and Warren was bound and determined that he would not marry his sister, even though Minette had adored him for years. But now they're Lord and Lady Barrymore, and they're going to have their first baby in the spring, so everything worked out for the best."

"Congratulations," Gwen said to Minette. "You must be very excited."

"You're finally starting to show, dear," said Aurelia, "even beneath all those skirts and petticoats, and winter capes and cloaks." The honey-haired lady smiled, and again pulled her cloak closer about her.

Minette studied her friend. "Do you have something to share with us, Aurelia? Townsend's barely left you alone all day, and you keep wrapping that cloak around you as if you're hiding something. Not only that, but you look a little green."

"Are you not well?" Gwen asked. "Can I get you something? A tonic?"

"She's well enough," said Minette with a grin. "Except that she's expecting again."

"Oh, are you?" Josephine clapped her hands.

"It's very early," said Aurelia, blushing. "But I might be. Townsend thinks so."

The lady practically glowed with happiness. She was living the life Gwen longed for. She was in love, and obviously loved by her husband. She was pretty and refined, and would doubtless give birth to a steady stream of pretty, refined babies as her husband doted upon how perfect she was. Gwen hated Aurelia a little bit.

The men gave a shout, so the ladies turned to watch them tumble in the grass. Arlington came up with the ball, and the others chased after him, trying to tackle him.

"What game are they playing now?" Josephine asked.

"Some variation of beating each other up. The same game they've played for as long as I can remember," said Minette. "Arlington usually wins."

"He was always best at everything," Aurelia agreed. "I don't think it ever bothered my husband. They all conceded his greatness from a very young age. I imagine he makes a fine sort of husband."

The three ladies turned to Gwen expectantly. She felt a blush steal over her cheeks. He made a fine sort of husband, if one enjoyed being tormented on a daily basis. She could not think of a word to say.

"Do you like being married?" Josephine pressed.

Gwen thought a moment. "I'm still getting used to it. I miss Wales. I miss my family, and the life I used to know." Her eyes misted. She tightened her jaw and willed the tears away. She would not cry in front of these women. They might seem warm and friendly, but they were Arlington's friends, not hers.

Minette reached to pat her hand. "Don't worry, my dear. Things will get better. I was newly married this time last year, and oh, I thought I'd never survive the first few months."

"Yes," Aurelia agreed. "Husbands take some getting used to, especially when you meet them just before you wed. It must have been difficult for him to show up at your father's house in Wales and take you right to the altar."

Gwen grimaced. "There was something awfully businesslike about the whole thing. It still feels businesslike sometimes. I thought marriage would be different. I thought there would be more...love." Her voice wobbled on the last word. She ducked her head, feeling terribly embarrassed that she had even said such a thing.

"Oh, Guinevere," said Josephine softly. "There will be love. Don't give up yet. It's hardly been a couple of months."

"I haven't given up," Gwen said, which was an utter lie. She had given up that first night, when he had declared himself her master, and her superior by law. He'd never love her because she wasn't his equal, and she would never love him because it hurt to be found wanting all the time.

The men were running about now, throwing the ball and converging on whoever had it. Warren shouted in protest as Barrymore tackled him. She couldn't hear Warren's muttered remark, but Arlington gave a great laugh and clapped him on the back as Townsend swooped in to steal the ball. How happy Arlington could be around those he esteemed. It hurt her to see that easy, joyful happiness when she could not so much as make him smile.

"Do you think it's getting colder?" Gwen asked. "Perhaps we ought to go inside and leave the gentlemen to their sport."

She pretended not to notice the concerned look the ladies exchanged before they all agreed to finish tea inside.

Aidan flopped on the ground with his friends, lying back and studying the sky as they traded a few last insults and brushed the grass from their clothing. They'd discarded their coats when they first started horsing about. Now that they rested, the chilly December air settled over him. The ladies had disappeared indoors a few minutes earlier. He hoped the four of them would become friends. Gwen seemed homesick still, and he thought she would benefit from some female companionship.

Female companionship. That term used to mean something different to him. He used to seek it out on a regular basis, and consort with wickedly talented whores. Strange, that he hadn't been tempted to visit Pearl's since he married. Or not so strange. For all Gwen's prickly moods and homesickness, his fairy queen suited him wonderfully in bed. He'd expected to grow tired of his wife by now, but instead he felt more interested than ever to explore her sensual depths.

"Well, he'll come back to us one day," said Warren with gentle mockery.

"What?" asked Aidan.

Townsend and Barrymore laughed. "We were just talking about the mare you got from Halliday in Oxfordshire," Townsend explained.

"Oh, the mare." Aidan sat up straighter and rubbed his neck. "I was ready to give her back a fortnight ago." He didn't tell them the story about Gwen tearing off on the horse, or his panicked pursuit. The memory still disquieted his mind. "She's been a challenge to train, but my grooms tell me she's making progress. She's meant for Guinevere, if she can be tamed."

"Your duchess rides?" asked Barrymore.

"She rides like a dream," he said in a hollow voice. "She's a Welsh hellion, perfectly capable of handling a spirited mount."

"That's good to know," said Warren, with just enough lascivious insinuation to make Aidan scowl over at him. "Hellions aren't all bad."

Aidan didn't know if they were talking about the mare still, or his wife, or Warren's wife, who'd been something of a hellion too when they wed.

"How are things with your duchess?" Townsend asked, definitively changing the subject. "Barrymore and Warren told me there was tension between you two when they visited in Oxfordshire. Forgive me, but I sense it's still there."

"I told you you'd have the hardest time of all," said Warren. He looked around at the others. "Didn't I tell him?"

"Shut up," said Barrymore, throwing a handful of dried grass at his brother-in-law. "Arlington's having problems."

"I'm not having problems." Aidan pursed his lips. "And I'll thank all of you to stay out of my marriage. When I need your assistance, I'll ask."

The men exchanged looks but let the subject drop. Soon after, his friends and their wives departed for home, for warmth and children. They made marital happiness look so easy. He caught Gwen before she could disappear upstairs, and drew her cloak back around her. "Will you walk with me a while?" he asked.

He didn't know why he asked, or why she agreed to do it, except that he felt vaguely ashamed that they were not in accord as the other couples were. He had no plan. He did not know what to say. *How do we connect? What can I do?*

She took his arm readily enough as they set out through the back, to the winter-silent gardens. He led her onto a lesser-used path, setting a leisurely pace.

"Do you know," she said, looking about, "the gardens here are even more beautiful than the ones at your country house. Not that the ones at your country house aren't lovely as can be."

"Why do you call it *my* country house? You live there too, now that we're married."

She made no answer to that. A few moments later, he asked, "How did you enjoy the ladies' company? They were anxious to meet you."

"They were very nice."

Her short, stiff answers pricked him. "You know, out of all the ladies in London, they are the ones you may trust to have your best interests at heart."

"Will there be ladies in London who don't have my best interests at heart?"

"Yes," he said bluntly. "There will be ladies in London who will scrutinize you for every flaw. The queen is one of them. There are ladies in society who delight in others' social failures. I am not trying to frighten you, only giving you a warning."

"You've given me plenty of warnings," she said in that tone that always made him want to turn her over his lap.

"I suppose I'm saying that Aurelia, Minette, and Josephine wish you only the best. You may believe in their friendship. Goodness knows they've put their necks on the line for each other these past few years, and gotten into all kinds of scrapes together."

"They do not seem the sort to get into 'scrapes.'"

"Well, they are, so however shy you feel around them, they are quite similar to you. Imperfect and emotional, and given to mischief when it suits them."

"They're not like me."

He could feel his wife's mood darkening, sense it in the tension of her hand on his arm.

"They're nothing like me," she said. "They are happy and poised, and bubbly, and content. I understand now why you're not well pleased to have me as your wife. I know that something is amiss with me."

"The only thing amiss with you is that you choose not to be happy in this marriage."

"It's not a choice. You should never have agreed to wed me. I'm not like them. I'm...horrid."

He stopped walking and turned to face her, lifting her chin when she avoided his gaze. "In what way are you horrid?"

Her pale green eyes filled with tears. "You know."

"I assure you I don't know."

"I'm not…good. I'm not a proper lady, like them."

"You most certainly are. You're a duchess. You outrank them all."

She shook her head. "That doesn't matter. They are more cultured than me, more polished. If they knew the things you do to me…"

"The things you enjoy?" he said in a sharp voice. "Those things?"

"But I should not enjoy them!"

His poor, conflicted duchess. He held her chin harder when she would have pulled away. "Who told you you shouldn't enjoy them? Not me. Never me." He released her and took her hand. "Come along. I want to show you something."

He took her down another path, the one that led to his mock Greek temple. He'd built it in his younger, wilder years, and outfitted it inside for all kinds of sensual mayhem. Today he hoped to use it to teach his wife some important lessons about herself.

He unlocked the door and ushered her inside. It was a cold, still space, not least because it was entirely made of marble, save the benches and chests of equipment, and the tall wooden pole in the center. It was also dark, having no windows.

"Take off your clothes," he said as he lit the sconces affixed to the walls. "Remove everything."

"What is this place?" she asked, eying her surroundings.

"A temple dedicated to lascivious games. Don't worry. No one will come." His voice had taken on the stentorian tenor of some ancient Greek nobleman or judge. Perhaps that was why his wife obliged him without further comment. She took off her cloak, and bent to remove her shoes and stockings. He helped her unlace her gown and pull her shift over her head. Then he leaned to retrieve one of her stockings, and twisted the fine silk length of it about his palm. "I'm going to tie you to that pole," he said.

"Why?" Her nervousness had transformed to full-blown fear. "What will you do to me?"

"Give me your hands."

"Please. I'm cold."

"Give me your hands."

With a shudder, she held them out, and he wasted no time binding her wrists before she changed her mind about cooperating.

"You know," he said, "there's a certain type of person who gains pleasure from feeling pain. It's not uncommon."

She turned her face away. Her hands twitched as he lifted them and hooked the silk binding over one of the wooden pole's hooks. "Turn," he said, when she tried to pull away. "Turn and face the pole. It's called a whipping pole, this thing. I'm sure you can figure out why."

"Why do you have one here? Why are you tying me to it?"

"That should be obvious."

"But I haven't done anything," she said, straining at the bonds. Luckily, the hooks were too strong for someone her size to escape.

He rubbed her shoulders to soothe her. "As I said, there is a certain type of person who enjoys being overpowered, even abused for someone's pleasure. I'm not that type of person, but I think you are." He slid a hand over her bottom and up her trembling spine. "Are you still cold?" He pressed himself against her back and embraced her shivering body.

"I wish you would let me go."

"You don't. You're so excited right now you can barely breathe."

"It's because I'm cold."

"It's because you're aroused." He reached beneath her and drove two fingers into her quim. She was wet as anything, as hot as the temple was cold. "Let's do an experiment, shall we? I'm going to whip you, not because you've misbehaved, but so we can find out if you're one of those people who is aroused by pain and bondage. Because I strongly suspect you are."

"You can't do this. You shouldn't," she said desperately.

"On the contrary, I think it's time we settled this question once and for all." He went to the chest in the corner for a true whip, a short, flicky devil of an implement that imparted a great deal more sting than a spanking, or even the birching he'd given her. Her eyes went wide as he turned.

"You'll kill me with that!"

"Only in the most lovely sense, my little pervert."

"I'm not a pervert."

He sent the tip of the whip cracking at the back of one thigh. She sucked in a breath, making fists of her hands. It was all he could do not to fall on her right then...

The pain was a shock; it radiated out from the strike on her thigh to her breasts and belly, and yes, the throbbing center between her legs. She let out the breath she was holding, and thought she would die if he struck her again.

And he did.

And she didn't die. No. She gripped her bindings and processed the thrill of it, and arched for more. It was exciting somehow, even though it hurt. Oh, she didn't understand it. It was so troubling.

"There exists a perfect counterpart for those who enjoy pain," said her husband, "and that is a person who enjoys dealing pain for someone else's pleasure, as well as their own." She shrieked as the whip caught her across her bottom. "As you may have guessed, I'm that sort of person."

"It hurts," she said, panting through the aftermath of pleasure.

"I know."

He flicked her again and she danced on her toes, pulling at the stocking that held her fast, ruining it, probably. In that pulling and that struggle, she felt a lengthening of her body, an opening. A release of resistance, and a craving for worse pain if he would want it, as mad as it seemed. She always felt that way when he hurt her, that she ought not to take pleasure from it, and yet she did. He had called her a pervert in jest, but that was exactly what she was.

"I don't want to be this way," she said. Tears squeezed from beneath her lids as the whip's bite stung her bottom, and sometimes her thighs. "I want to be like them. I want to be proper, the way you want."

"You can be both." She heard him toss the whip back onto the chest. "This is not about your struggle with me, Guinevere. This is about your struggle to accept yourself."

She had felt cold before, but now she felt hot, feverish. Sore and endangered, and needful as ever. "No, it's you who won't accept me," she cried.

"Is it?" When she turned, he was half undressed. His coat and waistcoat were thrown down next to the whip, and his shirt soon followed. He rummaged in a drawer. "I think I've been very accepting, considering what a complicated wife you've turned out to be."

He returned with a small porcelain jar, and held it in one hand while he took down his breeches with the other.

"Are you going to release me?" she asked.

"Not yet. I've another experiment to do first."

"I don't want to be experimented on anymore."

"And yet you shall be," he said, stilling her straining hands. She could feel his cock against her bottom. She heard him take the cap off the porcelain vessel, but he was too close behind her to see. He parted her sore, whipped cheeks and caressed her intimately, smearing slickness against her arsehole. His broad chest trapped her so she couldn't squirm away. He pressed his shaft against her, not where he normally did but...back there.

"No," she cried, trying to escape him. "No, please. Don't do that."

His arm encircled her, forcing her to be still as his other hand poked the tip of his thick member into her clenching orifice.

"Shh. Let me try," he said. "You might like it."

The pain was not exciting or arousing like the other pain. It was dull and achy, and frightening. "Please, you'll hurt me."

"I won't." He tightened his embrace and pressed his cheek against hers. "Wait. Take the pain for now, just for a moment." His voice rumbled as his long hair brushed her cheek. "Wait and see what happens."

Gwen didn't want to wait and see, because this was not the sort of hurting she liked. He worked his way inside her there easily enough—the aromatic oil accomplished that task—but it ached and stretched her awfully.

"Feel me inside you," he said. "Feel me forcing you open, using you however I wish."

She made a sound, a moan or cry. "It hurts."

"Yes, but you like to be hurt. Let me have you this way. I'll make it feel so good."

His rough-edged words settled in her pussy, along with the force of his embrace, and the way he pinched and flicked her nipple as he held her tight. He eased his shaft all the way inside her, so his hips pressed against her aching bottom cheeks. "Does it still hurt?" he asked.

"Yes," she sobbed, but it didn't really, not as much as it had. She felt very full, and very scared, but it didn't hurt in any unbearable way. He withdrew a little and pressed back in, and her quim pulsed in reaction. No, this couldn't feel good. It *shouldn't* feel good.

"I like hurting you," he said, his cheek still pressed to hers. "I like the way you gasp and whine when I hurt you. I like the way you shudder. I like the way you get so very, very wet." He stroked a hand across her center, then grasped her in a rough, squeezing way. She tensed around the thick intrusion in her bottom and moved her hips forward against his palm. She shuddered as he teased her and bit her earlobe.

"Yes, you like that," he said. "I know. Desire and pain get all mixed up for you in a wonderful sort of way. Don't fight it. Don't try to hide these things you feel."

She wasn't hiding anything now. She was grinding her hips back against him, then thrusting forward against his hand, trying to make him touch her in just the right place. Sometimes he did, murmuring encouragement, and sometimes he just held her hips and drove in and out of her arse. There was nothing for her to do but submit.

"I thought you said this was for bad wives," she said after an especially deep thrust.

"Sometimes it's for bad wives. Sometimes it's for confused, conflicted wives who need to be shown that it's all right."

"That what's all right?"

"To like it when things hurt. Do you like being sodomized? Do you like being forced to take my cock in your arse?"

"No," she said, because she didn't want to like it.

"Tell the truth," he said against her ear. "Now, of all times, tell me the truth. How does it feel to be tied up and whipped, and used in this appalling fashion?"

She couldn't answer. Her arsehole clenched around him. He invaded her, stretched her, filled her so she couldn't get away.

"I... I like it," she admitted miserably. "I do like it. It feels frightening, and exciting."

"It feels that way for me too." He held her hips and took his pleasure with long strokes of possession. Her hands strained at her bonds, but now it was a different sort of straining. She was reaching for completion, about to lose her mind.

"I wish I could whip and bugger you at once," he said, wrapping a hand about her neck. "You'd like that most of all."

That hand at her neck, the firm squeeze made all the rising, molten need within her overflow. "Ohh," she cried, alarmed by the sheer force of her climax. He was deep inside her, his body a cage around her as she constricted on him in ecstasy.

"Yes, that's right." His hand gripped her throat tighter. "I've got you. Let everything come."

She shook in his implacable embrace, impaled, wrung out, and still the aftershocks lingered. He groaned and uttered an oath, and surged deep inside her once more as he found his own release. She didn't want him to let her go. She couldn't bear it if he did. She couldn't bear to turn around and face him, and admit he was right about everything he said. Yes, she liked when he did cruel and shameful things to her.

They were indeed perfectly matched.

"Rest a moment," he said once he'd pulled away. "Does it still hurt?"

"Yes. A little." It wasn't her poor, buggered arsehole that hurt, it was her sensibilities and her pride. "Will you unbind me now?"

"I'd like to leave you here forever," he said. "But yes, I suppose you must be released."

He took her hands down and unwound them, and chafed them to be sure they still circulated blood. He kissed each wrist, studying her face. "All right?" he asked softly.

She didn't know if she was all right, so she didn't answer. Instead she said, "I'm cold."

He did up his breeches and then he helped her dress, touching her more, perhaps, than he really needed to. She felt warmer now, but still cold. The stocking that had held her was impossibly stretched and flopped down over the garter. She felt dirty and embarrassed. She wanted to wash.

He watched her as he pulled on his shirt and his fine afternoon waistcoat, and did up the gold buttons, and tidied up the echoing temple until it looked the way he'd found it. He extinguished the candles and shrugged on his coat, and guided her to the door.

"Say goodbye for now," he said. "Although I'm sure we'll be back."

She wasn't sure she wanted to come back. Well, yes. She did. "How often will you bring me here?" she asked.

"As often as I think you need to come. There is nothing 'amiss' with you, my dear, except that you have deviant sexual tastes. It's not as if this is shocking to either of us. I've known you were like that all along. I knew when I spanked you in that meadow, and so did you."

Yes, she had known then, but it didn't make the conflicting emotions any easier to bear.

"You say you don't like the things I do to you in private," he said, "but I think what you really don't like are your abandoned reactions. Which is silly, because they're perfectly normal, and magnificently exciting to me."

"What I don't like is that...that you don't like me."

He gave her a puzzled look. "Of course I like you. You're my wife. I feed you and clothe you like a princess, and shelter you in my house. And also occasionally tie you to a whipping post and sodomize you, but I'll reiterate: you like that sort of thing."

He jested. He refused to understand. He would never understand that she wanted more than to be used by him, and dressed like his doll, and perverted at his whim—even if she enjoyed said perversion. "I don't want to like it," she said peevishly.

He pulled her closer as they neared the house. "You don't want to like anything," he said. "But you will continue to behave as I wish, and be a proper duchess. The rest of it is nonsense."

"Nonsense?" she repeated in irritation.

"Yes, nonsense." He waved a lace-edged hand. "All your struggles and tantrums. Totally unnecessary. At some point you will realize that I know what's best for you. If we've learned anything this afternoon, it's that I know you better than you know yourself."

He raked her with his gaze, a knowing, lurid assessment that made her want to slap him. Then he smiled and placed a lingering kiss on her forehead, and she thought, *you don't know everything you think you know, you pompous man.*

Chapter Eleven:
Audience

"Remember to curtsy to the king and queen," Aidan said, pulling on his best pair of gloves. "And don't speak unless you're asked a question."

"Yes, Sir. Lady Langton told me."

His lips tightened. Why did his wife persist in addressing him as if he were a bloody stranger? He was her husband, for God's sake. The least she could do was smile at him.

You are not smiling at her either.

He forced a smile to his face, but by that time Gwen had turned to look out the carriage window at the people milling about the palace.

"Are all of them here to see the king and queen?" she asked.

"No. Most of them are only here to gawk. Not everyone is admitted to the palace. Audiences are only granted to the proper sort."

"The proper sort?" His wife rolled her eyes.

"Yes, the proper sort," he said a bit heatedly. "And there is a proper sort, whether or not your wild Welsh heart believes it should be so."

He sat across from her, since her ornate court gown took up her entire bench. It had been specially made of heavy gold satin, to match the trimmings on his black formal coat and breeches. The skirt was at least four feet wide, and twice as long behind with the attached train. The entire ensemble—bodice, skirt, petticoat, train—was encrusted with ruffles, embroidery, and French lace. He didn't envy her the challenge of walking in it, and the cost... When she asked the cost, he didn't tell her. She would have considered it a fortune. Enough to keep her father's household in wine and servants for a year or more.

But the expense didn't matter, or the fact that she would probably never wear this gown again, since it would be gauche to appear in the same outfit twice to a royal audience. The priceless jewels she wore didn't matter, or the gold and diamond tiara nestled in her dark hair. What mattered was that they had made this marriage at the crown's behest, and the crown wished to look upon them and believe it well done.

She sighed and clasped her gloved hands in her lap.

"Why the sigh?" he asked. "You ought to be happy. I'll be glad to have this over with."

"I will too." His wife studied him from beneath her lashes. "Must we act like we're in love today?"

"What?"

"Will the king and queen expect us to be in love? They're rumored to be in love."

Aidan stared at the rose and ivy embroidered along the hem of her dress. "They know ours is an arranged marriage. You needn't feign love or affection for their benefit. It's only been a few weeks. But you should express thanks for their hand in bringing us together."

"If they ask, you mean. You said I should not speak unless I'm asked a question."

"Why don't you let me do the talking? I'm accustomed to these audiences."

Gwen looked back out the window. "How long do you think it took them to fall in love?"

"I don't know. I'm not privy to their private life." Had he sounded too sharp? His wife had a great fascination with romantic love. It made him wonder if she'd carried a flame for someone back in Wales. Tommy, he thought bitterly. Sometimes it seemed she would prefer the fictional Tommy to his own status and wealth.

Aidan was not sure how he felt about love. He knew his friends were in love with their wives, and yes, King George adored his Charlotte. Did Aidan love Gwen? He tried to. He tried to be patient with her, and understanding. He was generous in bed, and catered to her need for rougher pleasures, needs that aligned beautifully with his. All of that ought to add up to love, but somehow, with them, it didn't.

Even so, he felt protective of his wife. He could feel her trembling as they made their way through St. James Palace, past bewigged servants and haughty courtiers to the royal chambers. He couldn't even draw her close to comfort her, due to the exaggerated proportions of her gown. At last they stood in the presence of Their Majesties, and Gwen made a creditable curtsy, for all her trembling.

"Arlington," the king said warmly. "You have brought us your new bride as we bade you."

Aidan bowed. "I am honored to introduce my wife, by your wisdom and grace. Guinevere, the Duchess of Arlington."

Lady Langton had taught Gwen well. His dark-haired wife sank into another obeisant curtsy. The queen's face lit up in an approving smile.

"You have our congratulations," said the king. "And what did you think of our heroic Lord Lisburne? Was he pleased with the match?"

"Exceedingly pleased. I found him in excellent health," Aidan replied. "He showed admirable hospitality, and I enjoyed my time in Wales."

"And here is his daughter. Come forward, duchess. Let us look at you."

Gwen curtsied again. Well, she certainly had the curtsying thing down. The king would appreciate her gentle modesty, even if it was all an act. Aidan could see the man was charmed.

"And how do you enjoy being married to our Duke of Arlington? He is a much-admired man."

"Our marriage has been well enough," she said.

"Well enough!" exclaimed the king, grinning at her husband. "Not the most resounding vote of confidence."

Aidan played off this misstep with a smile. "The duchess and I are still coming to know one another, Your Majesty. We have not been married long."

"One of the greatest joys of marriage is coming to understand and feel affection for the other person," said the queen, smiling at Gwen. "Do you spend time together with your new husband, pleasant time at leisure?"

Gwen flicked a glance at him. "We do spend time together."

Well, she might have smiled when she said that. The king and queen regarded Gwen curiously, as did some of the other courtiers in the room. *Smile, damn you*, he thought. *We are supposed to seem grateful for this match.*

"I imagine it has been an adjustment, coming to England from your homeland," said Queen Charlotte. "It was an adjustment for me."

These were very kind words on the part of the queen, a gracious likening of their situations. Gwen accepted them in silence, so Aidan was forced to speak instead.

"It has been somewhat of an adjustment for my wife, Your Majesty."

"But her English is good," said the king. "Barely an accent, and her manners are fine."

Aidan could feel Gwen tense beside him. Whenever they discussed her manners at home, she became agitated in the extreme. He gave her a look that said, *Do not dare*. He could cope with her tantrums at home, her sharp words and peevishness. He could not deal with them here.

"She is excited for the upcoming season," said Aidan, to change the subject. "She will be pleased to make the acquaintance of your loyal subjects and settle into English life."

"Yes, indeed," said the king.

And then Gwen spoke. "If you want to know the truth of it, I would have rather stayed in Wales."

One sentence. One miserable sentence she might have kept inside. But no, she hadn't. The room fell silent. Someone tittered, almost inaudibly. The king and queen looked shocked.

"What my wife means," said Aidan quickly, "is that she is homesick for Wales. She might have said it a better way." He bowed in apology, and shot his wife a scathing look.

For long moments, the king and queen only looked at them. Aidan felt heat rising beneath his collar.

"I remember what it was to be homesick," said Charlotte after a moment.

The king turned to his wife and squeezed her hand. Yes, that was love, that glance between them. Perhaps, in this case, it would save them. Charlotte seemed to like Gwen, even if the king thought her terribly rude.

"The best thing for homesickness," Charlotte continued, "is patience and prayer. And subservience to your husband. You must focus on your duties as a wife."

"Do you mean bearing his heirs?"

By God, he wished he could clap his hand over her mouth. What had he told her, in no uncertain terms? *Don't say anything at all unless you're asked a question.* He would make her write it out a thousand times as punishment for this debacle. But this debacle was his fault. She was his wife. She was not adequately under his control.

"Well, yes. Heirs are important," agreed the queen, as more titters sounded from a corner of the room.

Aidan hoped his expression communicated the remorse he felt for his wife's uncouth behavior. One did not speak of "bearing heirs" in a royal audience. He prayed the king would end this meeting before she made any more mistakes.

"We hope that you shall feel more at home here soon," said the king with a sharp hint of remonstrance, and with that, they were dismissed.

Aidan wasn't sure how he made it through the press of courtiers to the carriage without unleashing his temper on his wife. She had utterly humiliated him in front of his contemporaries, not to mention the highest sovereigns of the land. She blinked at him as he collapsed on the seat across from her.

"What is the matter?" she asked.

"What's the matter? Did you think that went well, that audience?"

He saw a shadow of guilt on her face. "I did my best."

"Was that your best? The part where you insulted the king—not to mention your husband—by suggesting you would rather have stayed in Wales? What about the part where you said our marriage was 'well enough'? That was lovely. Oh, and taking up the discussion of bearing my heirs with Queen Charlotte, that was absolutely stunning in its couth. My goodness, Guinevere. You've outdone yourself today."

She shrank at his vicious tone. "You never specified what I could or could not say."

"Because one would assume you would only say polite things to the crown of England."

"It seemed that everyone was speaking plainly. I was being honest."

He held up a hand to silence her. "I'm too angry to speak with you right now."

"But—"

"No."

No, he didn't dare look at her, or say another word. He didn't want to attempt to spank her in her court dress, in this carriage, but if she riled him any further, that was what he would do. How was he to proceed from here? He'd have to beg pardon of the king, and he would have to fix his wife and his marriage before the season began. He did not like to be a laughingstock. He would not be made a laughingstock by a slip of a Welsh girl, at any rate.

They were nearly back at home when she asked in a troubled voice, "Will you still let me see my horse?"

"Your goddamned horse." He wanted to throttle her. All the turmoil and irritation she'd brought to his life, and all she cared for was the blasted horse. "I ought to take her away from you," he said as the coach rattled to a stop. "It would be an appropriate punishment, since you have taken away my pride, my reputation. You knew exactly what you were up to during that audience, and believe me, you shall be brought to account for it, as soon as I have regained my temper."

"What does that mean?"

"It means you won't sit comfortably on that horse, even if I decide to let you keep her."

With those words, he disembarked from the carriage and stalked into the house, leaving the grooms to extricate his lavishly skirted wife.

After her lady's maid divested her of her court clothes, Gwen waited to be called to the duke's room—for she knew she'd be called to his room. She deserved to be. She had acted foolishly, because she was nervous and reluctant, and irritated by the outfit she had to wear. She understood about royalty, but she didn't see why she had to participate in all the pomp and circumstance.

Well, she knew why.

A somber-faced footman escorted her to Arlington's private sitting room an hour or so after they'd arrived home. He still looked angry, but his color wasn't as high as it had been in the carriage.

"I'm very sorry," she began. "I've spent this last hour reflecting—"

"Take off your clothes."

"Please, Sir—"

"Do not infuriate me further by refusing to comply. Remove your clothes."

His gaze darkened as his words snapped across the distance between them. Gwen swallowed hard and removed her slippers, and her stockings and garters. She reached behind to unlace her gown but could not manage it. Arlington crossed to her and unlaced her himself, with rough, impatient tugs. The dread that had fluttered in her stomach the past hour rose and settled in her chest.

"I'm sorry," she said. "I'm so very sorry I embarrassed you."

He ignored her, yanking her gown over her head as she tried in vain to impede him. She fumbled at her petticoat's ties to have something to do besides panic. Once they dropped to the floor, she was bared to his gaze.

She searched his face for any softness, any comfort. Nothing. He took her elbow and drew her toward his bedroom.

"What are you going to do?" she asked.

"Punish you."

"But you are still so angry. You're frightening me."

He stopped beside his great, raised bed and forced her to face him. "I think you deserve to be frightened. And I think I deserve to be angry. There is nothing more humiliating to a man than a wife who is not within his control. I'm tired of battling with you, Guinevere. One of us is going to break in this marriage, and it shall not be me."

"It won't be me, either," she said with false bravado. "You're not allowed to hurt me."

"I'm allowed to discipline you, and you are due a correction for your insouciance today. Lie on your stomach on the bed. You are going to be caned. Ten strokes."

"Ten strokes!" she cried. "I said I was sorry."

"And I said to lie on the bed."

Gwen had never been caned before, but she knew it was a vicious form of punishment. "Please don't do this," she begged him.

"Would you like me to help you lie down?" he asked, fetching the whippy looking cane from the bedtable. "If I must help you, I'll add five additional strokes."

If she was not so naked and frightened, she might have resisted him, but what good would it do? He was determined to make her hurt because she had offended his lofty English pride. She climbed onto his bed where he indicated, and lay on her front with her legs pressed together.

"I think this English tradition of husbands punishing wives is very uncivilized and cruel," she said.

"And yet you live in England now, whether you like it or not."

Goosebumps rose on her arms as the duke positioned himself beside the bed. He tapped her bottom with the cane, once, twice, as if perfecting his aim. She gazed up at him in entreaty.

"Must you? Please, Sir!"

"Keep your hands out of the way. I expect you to remain still for the entirety of your punishment."

She barely had time to prepare herself before she heard a swish and a thwack, and the most painful stripe of agony she'd ever felt in her life. She hissed as her backside caught fire, and reached back to rub the throbbing weal.

"That was only the first stroke," he said. "Move your hands."

"I can't!"

"I've explained before that you are not permitted to rub away the sting. Remove your hands and lie still the way you're supposed to."

Gwen gave a little sob and returned to the commanded position. The second stroke landed just above the first, and then a third stroke beneath it. She reached back and covered her bottom again. "Oh, it hurts."

"If I don't make it hurt, you'll only enjoy it. Remove your hands or we'll begin again."

She pressed a fist to her mouth. How was she to bear this? She still had seven strokes to go. "Please," she said. "I can't."

When she saw him raise the cane for the next stroke, she reached back so he was forced to arrest the movement in midair.

"I suppose I ought to have done this at the start," he said, yanking off his neckcloth. He took her wrists and wrapped them in the fabric, and knotted them tightly before she knew what he was about. Then he stretched her arms over her head and threaded the tail of the linen through the headboard, and tied it off.

"You must not do this," she said. "It's reprehensible, to bind my hands in order to punish me."

"I'm binding your hands so you don't lose a finger. Shall I begin again, or will you be content with seven more strokes?"

"I don't want any more strokes."

"You don't sound very remorseful for your behavior today. I suppose I had better begin again with ten."

"No," she said, trembling at the very idea of it. "I'm remorseful."

"I don't believe you are. If you don't wish to begin at the start, I suggest you remain still."

She went still, as still as she could be with a cane whistling through the air. The implement connected, the pain making her yank wildly at her bonds. A burning line of heat bloomed upon her flesh.

As she panted through the agony of it, she berated herself for a fool. Why did she cross him? She had been impertinent during the audience to prick him, because she was unhappy, but she only made herself unhappier. He was too great an enemy, and too powerful. She would never defeat him. "I can't bear any more," she wailed. "Isn't there some other way to punish me?"

"What? A spanking?" He put the cane down, leaned over the bed and gave her a couple smart cracks. "I don't think a spanking will hurt enough. I don't think you'll learn your lesson."

"I've already learned my lesson." She sobbed as he spanked her again. Her already-heated bottom felt ready to burst into flames.

"There is another way you might be punished." His fingers delved between her clenching cheeks. "Another way I might put you in your place."

Oh, God, no. Gwen tried to squirm away. "You can't," she said. "Not that."

"Or I can resume your caning. Six more strokes to go."

Her bottom still throbbed and burned from the four strokes she'd endured. When he stood to retrieve the cane again, she cried, "No! I would rather... I would rather...the other..." She looked over at him with narrowed eyes. "You're so horrible."

"And you're so stubborn. Bad wives get bad things. Didn't I tell you that?"

He began to take off his clothes, as Gwen pulled at the neckcloth and questioned whether she'd made a wise choice.

"Please don't do this. Let me go," she said. "I'm sorry."

"Who is the master in this marriage, Guinevere?"

She closed her eyes at his dire tone. "You are."

"I warned you the day after our marriage not to get into a battle of wills with me. Why do you persist?"

She heard him drop his breeches, and turned at the rattle of a jar. The aromatic oil...

Gwen bit down on her lip as he climbed onto the bed and turned her on her back. His cock jutted between them, rigid and daunting. She'd survived this once before, but she'd been more relaxed then, and he had been patient and gentle.

He seemed a lot less patient and gentle now. He pulled her legs apart and held them open, and probed between her bottom cheeks, depositing the slick stuff around her hole. Was this allowed by law, this sort of punishment? She didn't think so.

She blinked up at him, her emotions in a turmoil of confusion. "I'm afraid. Please..."

"Hush." His voice was low and rough. He held her gaze as he pressed his cock against her arsehole. *Disciplinary sodomization...an excellent method of teaching submission to rebellious wives.*

She could do nothing to impede him, since her hands were still fixed to the headboard. It hurt as he pushed in, and she moaned as if it were unbearable. The truth was, while it was painful, it also excited her in some shamefully base way. The bondage, her vulnerability, and his stern admonishments...

"Please, you mustn't," she cried in some vain attempt to push away those feelings.

"On the contrary, I must. You need this, Guinevere." He started to move, to take her tender bottom with steady thrusts. "You're my wife, my possession. You will obey and respect me. You will be made to understand."

She whimpered, gazing up at his hard eyes, his broad chest. "I understand, I just—"

"You just choose not to behave properly." His pace quickened as his fingers dug into her hips. "If you will not obey and respect me, you will be put in your place by any means necessary. Spankings, canings, sexual ordeals and sodomizations. I'll take great care to make sure none of it feels good."

What he was doing to her now didn't feel very good. She knew he could make it feel good if he wished to...he had made it feel good the first time, in his Greek temple. But he would not let her feel good today, because this was a punishment. The pain of his initial entrance had dulled to an uncomfortable ache as he used her—punished her—in this debasing way.

"How does this feel?" he asked.

"Bad."

"Do you like feeling bad like this?"

"No, Sir."

The sheets, soft as they were, hurt her caned arse cheeks. She never would have survived the entire caning, but this... He loomed over her, tightening his grip on her legs whenever she tried to draw away from him. His lips were parted, his expression intently focused. *What would your king think of this?* she wanted to ask. *What if I told him these things about you?*

But she would never dare say such things to the king. She couldn't tell anyone about this, or explain the conflicted way it made her feel.

After long, excruciating minutes of surrender, her husband's breath came faster and he pressed deep inside her bottom. Gwen closed her eyes and wished she could disappear. He grunted, pumping a few more times, and finished with a drawn-out, satisfied sigh. How unfair, that he should be allowed release when this was a punishment. But nothing between them ever seemed fair.

For a long time afterward she didn't move, didn't say a word. His shaft still impaled her, an intrusive reminder of his mastery. His hands still grasped her legs. She wanted to pull away, but she was afraid to do anything that might irritate him further. At last he withdrew, leaving her empty and cold.

"Open your eyes," he said. "Look at me."

She obeyed, even though she would rather not. What if he made her admit that she took some sick pleasure in being used this way? She couldn't have owned up to it in that moment, not even under torture. Not even if it was true.

"I'm sorry," she blurted out. "I won't embarrass you again."

"I'm sure you'll find a way," he said with sharp impatience. "But you've been punished for this episode, so we'll move past it."

He reached up to the headboard to release her bonds, and Gwen thought, *I don't know how to move past it.* She hated him, with his orders and his threats and his lecherous forms of punishment, but when he released her and took her in his arms, she clung to him as if she loved him. Maybe it was only that she had no one else to comfort her and hold her.

"I'm sorry," she said again. "I'm sorry, please forgive me."

She began to cry, silent tears that leaked from beneath her eyelids. He wiped them away and murmured that her punishment was over. As if that mattered, as if that could calm the storm in her heart! How pleased he must feel, that she begged his forgiveness. He would believe that she had learned a lesson, but the real lesson was that she was a harlot who could not control her yearnings.

No wonder he demeaned her.

No wonder he punished her.

She didn't know if she was relieved or devastated when he finally dismissed her to her room.

Chapter Twelve:
Folly

His duchess did not come down that night to dinner, and he didn't order her to attend him. Instead he sat alone at the head of the table, the silent ruler of his broken, miserable estate.

Her horse had arrived that afternoon—lamentable timing. He went to the stable after he'd punished his wife, and watched the grooms put the mare through her paces until he was satisfied she had been tamed to bridle and saddle. He would not get rid of the creature now, as much as he wished to. He could only hurt his duchess to a certain degree before he crossed a line.

Perhaps he'd already crossed that line.

Aidan tried to convince himself he'd only been trying to teach her a lesson. The caning, perhaps. The buggering, no. He might pretend it was a punishment, but it had been his own lustful vice, his perverse reaction to the way she struggled after he bound her to the bed. Gwen knew it too, but she let him have his way, and then reviled herself for it afterward. Horrible.

Their relationship was bleak and dishonest, and broken at the core. He had reduced his wife to tears in some misguided attempt to soothe his ego, and then sent her away for the remainder of the afternoon because he couldn't deal with the guilt. He'd never imagined he'd be so awful a husband, that he'd be such an abject failure at nurturing his wife.

But he could give her the horse.

After dinner, he climbed the wide marble staircase and walked down the echoing corridor to her chambers. She was curled in a chair in her sitting room. A tray of food sat beside her, mostly untouched. He crossed to her and stopped a few feet away.

"How are you?" he asked.

She sat up straighter and clasped her hands in her lap. "I'm fine."

She was not fine; nor was he. *I'm sorry, Gwen. I'm sorry...* He almost wished she would berate him for a monster and a pervert. Even now, he wanted her. He wanted to be inside her, inside this beautiful, wild duchess who made his life such a hell.

"Aren't you hungry?" he asked, nodding to the tray.

"No, Sir. I'm not."

She thought he was here to take her to bed. He could see it in her resigned expression. It pricked him, that resignation and dread.

"I know it's late, but there's a full moon and plenty of light," he said. "Are you too tired to ride?"

She blinked at him. "Ride...now?"

"Eira arrived today. She's developed fine manners, but she's in need of a mistress, if you are up for the job."

Gwen stood at once, no longer woebegone but breathlessly ecstatic. "She's here now, in the stables?"

"She is. Go put on something for riding. Be quick."

She started toward her dressing room, but then she hurried back and threw her arms around his waist. "Thank you," she said. "Oh, Sir. Thank you."

The exuberant hug shocked him. He raised a hand to stroke her hair, but then she was off again, calling for her lady's maid.

Aidan sat at her desk to wait, and noticed a half-finished page of Welsh scribblings. Letters had begun to trickle in from Wales, though she had not done a lot of writing in return. The letters she did write were carefully lacking in detail. She didn't say anything negative, but he could glean her loneliness and homesickness from the translations his servant provided. The spidery lines of her writing made him feel very glum.

When he took her down to the stables, Gwen squealed and stroked and caressed her Eira, and whispered Welsh words in her ears as they pricked to the sound. What was she saying? *Thank God you're here. I'm trapped in this mansion with this horrid man who ties me to his bed and beats me, and sodomizes me for his pleasure.*

He told the stable hand to saddle Gwen's horse, and his stallion. "We can ride on one condition," he said.

"Yes?"

"You're not to kick your heels into her side and run away into the night. Your mare has been tamed to city manners. You must stay abreast with me and hold her with a firm hand."

"Yes, Sir," she agreed, and then she turned to the horse with a sympathetic gaze. "Is it true? Have they tamed all the life out of you? All your spirit? I still love you, pretty lass." She patted her mane and spoke again in Welsh. He wanted to ask what she said, what she and the horse were plotting. Was she promising her a wild ride as soon as his back was turned?

"I mean what I say about sedate horsemanship," he repeated. "If I learn you've been riding her neck-or-nothing, I'll leather you *and* your horse."

But none of his dire warnings could dampen her joy. She climbed on her mount and took up the reins like a proper lady, even correcting the horse in Welsh when she danced a step sideways.

"You ought to speak English to her," he said irritably. "She's an English horse."

Gwen turned to him as they headed out of the paddock. "Does it bother you that you can't understand?"

"It bothers me that you talk more to the horse than you talk to me."

"What would you like to talk about?"

Aidan didn't know. He didn't know what he wanted to talk about. Any topic seemed fraught with peril. Her homeland, her life, their marriage.

"How did you learn to ride so well?" he asked.

"I've ridden since before I could remember. I grew up a lonely child, with gruff older brothers who found me very tiresome. Horses were my favorite friends."

Perhaps that explained her manners. If only London's court were made up of horses rather than people. He allowed himself to picture King George and Queen Charlotte as rough Welsh mounts with glittering crowns.

"Did you have a pleasant childhood?" she asked. "A happy family life?"

Had he? Perhaps. "It was just me and my sister, but we got on well enough. I rarely saw her most days. I was raised very strictly, and spent a lot of time at lessons."

"Because you were to be a duke?"

"Yes. I was my parents' only son. I was a boy when I inherited the dukedom."

"I suppose you were sad when your parents died."

In truth, he had barely known his parents, only the grand and glittering aristocrats. His childhood had been consumed by statecraft and manners, and the occasional paternal audience, during which he was stringently measured and judged.

The same way you judge your wife now...

They fell into an uncomfortable silence as they rode deeper into the woods. Gwen was sitting high on her saddle. Poor, sore bottom. He had done that to her. "Are you cold?" he asked. "Do you wish to go back?"

"No, Sir. Unless you wish it."

"How do you like your horse? She is not completely docile, is she? Her good manners are only for show."

He spoke about the horse, but he realized he might as well be talking about his wife. No matter how much he bullied her into proper behavior, and *yes, Sirs* and *no, Sirs*, underneath she would always be that wild, lonely girl from Cairwyn who'd grown up in a dark castle, and seduced him in that meadow.

Gwen patted the mare's neck and smiled at him, and he remembered her abrupt hug up in the room. It seemed she was always flitting to him, and then flitting away again before he could capture her in any lasting way. She was not a duchess, not by nature and especially not by will. Like her horse, she would always be pretending, waiting for the opportunity to rebel. Perhaps that was why he plagued her every night with his caresses. That was the only time she stopped pretending, and rebelling.

The horses had taken them into the garden clearing, by the temple folly. He stared at the marble edifice and stone columns, and remembered their encounter there, when he had made her admit she liked perverse and common pleasures.

"Let's stop here a while," he said.

She looked wary. Well, he had given her the opportunity to return to the house, and she hadn't taken it. He would not let her go now. They tethered the horses to a nearby tree, and then he put a hand at the small of her back and led her toward the temple. When he took her inside and shut the door on the moonlight, the space went pitch black. She clutched at his coat.

"I can't see," she said.

"You don't need to see."

He found her lips in the darkness and kissed her, the sort of violent, grasping kiss one only gave in the absence of light. As he did so, he hiked up her skirts so her arse was bared. She whimpered as he ran his palms across her cheeks.

With a muttered curse, he yanked off one of his gloves so he could trace the lingering cane tracks. He would not say he was sorry for putting them there—she had earned them. But he was sorry that it aroused him to feel them now. She shuddered as he pinched one of the welts.

"Please, that hurts," she whispered, pressing closer.

He was sorry that her shivery little plea inflamed him beyond bearing. She clung to his coat, his lovely wife who was aroused by pain. He circled her waist and drew her against the hard, thick line of his erection. He wished he could explain to her how she excited him, but he could only kiss her madly, assaulting her lips and reveling in her eager response. He caught her lower lip between his teeth as he worked loose the flap of his breeches. He was rigidly hard, bursting to be inside her.

There was no light, but he could see the outline of a trunk in the dark. He turned her around and pushed her toward it, and bent her over it, hauling up her skirts from the back. He held them out of the way and nudged open her legs with his knees. She gripped the edge of the trunk for balance; he could see the pale outline of her gloves against the wood as he positioned himself behind her.

Like Jack in the meadow, he was taking what he wanted, whether offered or not. He could not seem to stop taking from her. He pushed her legs wider and stroked her quim, and found her copiously wet. He slid two fingers inside her, pumping them in and out. "Naughty little duchess. How hot you are. Stop squirming about, and let me have you."

"It's so dark," she said. "I'm afraid."

"You're not afraid. You want this."

"Please don't hurt me."

She meant *Please hurt me.* He heard it in her tone, and felt it in her arching spine as she wriggled back against him. He shoved inside her, driving through her tight, hot slickness all the way to the hilt. "Oh," she gasped. "Oh!"

Oh, indeed. He thrust into her again, not caring for the dark or the hard floor beneath his knees. He set up a steady rhythm, capturing her arms and pinning them behind her. She struggled with a low moan. By God, she stripped his control with her responsive reactions. He couldn't resist her, and he couldn't restrain his animalistic urge to possess her.

He reached beneath her to yank down her bodice and expose her breasts. He grasped one of them, worrying the nipple between his fingers before treating her to a hard pinch. She gasped and threw her head back.

"Does it hurt, darling? Yes?" He chuckled at her distracted nodding. "It hurts in the best way, doesn't it?"

He released her arms and squeezed her breasts until she wailed and shuddered. Her pussy's clenching sent waves of need through his cock and balls, an intense building of energy. He pumped inside her, losing his mind, losing control.

"You should always be like this," he growled, twisting his fingers in her hair. "You should always be beneath me, moaning like this, taking my cock."

"No," she cried.

"Yes. You're mine."

Her hips moved wildly to meet his pounding thrusts. She was so beautiful, so powerful, even in her surrender. He pulled her hair harder, yanked her head back so he could kiss and suck the smooth column of her neck. Her pussy pulsed and her breath hissed through her teeth.

"Please," she begged. "Please."

"Please what?"

"Please don't stop. Don't stop. I'm so close…"

"Come for me," he ordered. "Come for me now."

She obeyed with a ragged cry, arching back as he grasped her breasts. He climaxed deep within her, his own pleasure heightened by the intensity of her release. For long moments they remained still, gasping for air.

"Are you all right?" he asked when he could manage it. He tried to turn her in his arms, but she resisted. He realized she was in tears.

"What's the matter?" he asked. "Did I hurt you?"

She pulled away, readjusting her clothing and wiping at her cheeks. "You always hurt me," she said. "You make me ashamed of myself."

He squinted to see her in the dark room. She wouldn't let him hold her. She got to her feet and moved toward the door, searching for the handle in the dark.

"You've done nothing to be ashamed of," he said, following after her. "There's no need to cry." He did up his breeches as she stumbled into the moonlight. He could see her well now, her tears and her agonized expression. He caught her before she reached the horses.

"Do not," he said, taking her face between his fingers. "Do not be ashamed of what just happened. Do not dare."

"You can't control me in everything. You can't tell me how to feel!"

She tried to turn away, but he forced her face back and looked into her eyes. "I can tell you how *I* feel. I don't want you to cry when we've just shared such pleasure." He frowned at her tears. "You ought to be happy. In this, you please me."

"In this." She gave a bitter laugh. "What a laudable duchess I am, to be able to meet your basest carnal desires."

"Your carnal desires too. You enjoyed yourself well enough, for all your tears."

She pulled away from him when he would have comforted her. Why were they back to anger, after the closeness they'd just shared? He took her arms and made her look at him. "If this is the only thing that works for us as husband and wife, so be it. It's the only necessary thing to perpetuate my family line."

"Of course your family line is the only matter of importance in this marriage."

"It's the most important thing, yes."

"What about love? What about caring?"

He scowled at her. "Why are you harping at me in that shrill tone? You're never angrier than after you've just been fucked. If I could contrive a way to keep my cock in you all the time, you'd be a lot more biddable, I think."

"You are crass."

"And you are peevish. Again. No matter." He lifted her and put her on her horse. "I'll be ready to take you again by the time we return to the house."

"I don't want you again."

"Is that so?" He put on his gloves and mounted his own horse. "In the end, one has little to do with the other. Especially when I am so much more powerful than you will ever be."

Gwen rose the next day feeling mentally and physically exhausted. Arlington had seen fit to lay with her twice more after they returned from the temple. He had proved his point—that she enjoyed his caresses—but it had come at a cost to her peace of mind, and her pride.

The last thing she wanted was to spend more time with her husband, but the portrait artist was there for the final sitting, so she put on her silver dress and her jewels and reported to the grand hall to pose primly with her hands in her lap. She wondered if the painter could see the strain on her face, or intuit somehow the stresses of the previous night. Arlington stood proud and pompous behind her, having shown yet again that he ruled supreme.

Only fitting, that he should stand tall in their painting, while she sat below him, his dog at heel. She didn't smile. She refused to smile in this portrait so that generations to come might imagine she had been happy as his wife.

At last the artist declared himself finished, with the preliminaries at least. To Gwen, the painting looked half done, with white spaces and shaded areas, but the artist would finish the rest from his sketches, and promised delivery within a couple of weeks. The duke, at least, seemed handsomely outlined. The artist had captured his attitude perfectly, his regal aura and bearing. Gwen seemed an afterthought. Her face was only partially sketched in. That was how she felt these days, only partially sketched in.

Once the artist was gone, Arlington told her to dress for riding. His commanding tone reminded her of the night before, of firm touches and carnal manipulations. She didn't want to be aroused by the memories, but she was.

"I would rather not go out today," she said.

"You'd rather not go out? Or you'd rather not go out with me?"

When she clamped her lips shut and refused to answer, he took her arm and led her into the breakfast room.

"Do you know that we are famous this morning?" he asked.

"I don't know what you mean."

"I'll show you what I mean." He snatched up a paper from the sideboard, the newspaper he scanned every morning at breakfast, and read from the third page with great dramatic flair.

"*It appears the Duke of A---- is not as lion-hearted as he is lion-haired. The admirable duke took his wife, recently acquired from W----, to meet with the Crown, whereby the Duchess of A---- alluded to a less than satisfying marriage.* Look, darling, there's even a likeness of me frowning at you."

She swallowed hard, and forced herself to glance at the drawing when he shoved the paper under her nose. "Horrid gossip," she whispered.

"I don't know if one can call it gossip," he said, taking it back to scowl at the picture. "The paper's only saying exactly what you did."

"That drawing is ridiculous," she said to placate him. "You don't have lion hair. And I don't know why they bother to use initials when everyone knows who they mean."

"It doesn't matter if I have lion hair or not," he said, throwing the paper back down on the table. "What matters is that, thanks to you, everyone in London is talking about our failed union and laughing behind their hands. We're going out riding, Guinevere, like the happiest married couple ever. Go get dressed."

Gwen hurried upstairs to change, to obey him, yes, but also to get away from him. He was in a very prickly mood.

"You must make me look happy," she told Pascale. "The duke commands it."

"Are you going to ride in Hyde Park?"

"I think so."

"You need bright colors then," said the French maid. "The cerise riding habit, or the orange."

They ultimately decided on the deep yellow-gold, since it looked so well with her hair, and because yellow-gold was one of Arlington's favorite colors. Anything to quell that quiet fury in his gaze.

"If you want to look happy, Madam, you must smile," said Pascale in her strident way. She adjusted Gwen's hat again, seeking that perfect angle. "People go to the park to see and be seen. Make sure that they see what you want them to see."

What did Gwen want them to see? That she loved her husband? It was hard to capture that feeling in the confusion of her muddled thoughts. He was waiting when she came out of her dressing room, and inspected her with a critical gaze.

"Will I do?" she asked tightly, as his perusal strung out.

"You'll do fine if you keep your temper," he replied with a warning note.

At least Gwen would be able to ride Eira again. She'd been overjoyed to see the mare yesterday, even if she was a different animal now. Tamed and subdued. Gwen would still love her forever, and Eira seemed to understand that love. She nickered softly when Gwen appeared, nosing her hand for a treat. Gwen tsked and petted her muzzle. "I see. Is that how they trained you so prettily?"

She went to the stable master and secured a bit of apple to feed her pet, as Arlington looked on impatiently. At last they set off to the park. Eira did very well among the sounds and sights of the busy London streets, so Gwen could relax and look about. London was still new to her. In fact, she doubted she would ever get used to all the people. Everyone gawked at the duke, and Gwen had to admit he looked very fine in his deep hunter green coat, atop his oversized stallion.

When they arrived at Hyde Park, it was even more crowded, and people still stared, although they stared with a great deal more judgment. She was glad now that Pascale had taken so much time with her hair and clothes, and so carefully adjusted the tilt of her riding hat.

Arlington stayed beside her, his black crop tucked beneath his arm. "Smile, would you?" he said between his teeth. "Or there'll be another *on-dit* in the paper tomorrow."

She tried to smile but there were people everywhere, staring and shouting back and forth to one another. A few gentlemen addressed the duke, and he introduced her as the Duchess of Arlington. She would never remember all the names. Lord this and Lord that, and Lady something-or-other who giggled behind her hand.

"Was that woman laughing at me?" asked Gwen when the last group moved along.

"I told you how things would be in London," he said. "Didn't you believe me? People are vicious. That's the way the *ton* works. You've stopped smiling again."

"I don't feel like smiling."

"You'll do better to smile and pretend, than keep frowning that way."

She looked down under the pretense of smoothing her gloves. She tried to curve her lips into a smile before she looked up again. They were garnering a great deal of attention, and yes, furtive mockery. One bold gentleman pointed before lowering his hand. This was why Arlington had punished her so angrily, she supposed. She had not only embarrassed him before the king and queen, but before his entire social set.

"I'm sorry," she said quietly.

"There's nothing for it now. Hold your head up another moment, and we'll go."

Thank God. Her face hurt from forcing a smile and pretending to be happy. She wanted nothing more on earth than to be away from these crowds, but then...

Then he'd take her home. She glanced at the square set of his jaw, framed by his queued hair. She noted his strong legs and broad shoulders, and thought about the things he did to her in private. She didn't know if she dreaded them or wanted them again. Perhaps both. At least in his arms—or his Greek temple—she passed muster.

They rode back to Arlington House in silence. She could not divine his thoughts, although she guessed them quite unpleasant. How long would they be laughingstocks? How long would those crowds in the park judge her, and judge their marriage? Forever, she feared.

As they neared the house, there was a great clatter of carriages out front. She recognized the duke's Oxfordshire friends and their wives, and wondered why they had come to call. Arlington went to speak to Lord Warren, and then Lord Barrymore appeared. It was a relief to see them, in a way. It meant he wouldn't be taking her to bed again, for a few hours at least. She did not enjoy his perverse and sadistic tastes.

Or perhaps she didn't enjoy the fact that she enjoyed them, when she really didn't want to.

Oh, it was all such a terrible coil.

Chapter Thirteen: Frank Talks

Aidan watched helplessly from the foyer as the servants bustled back and forth with trunks and baggage, and the Warrens' baby crib. The ladies had gone upstairs to consult on sleeping arrangements. Aidan went into his parlor, where his gentlemen friends had gathered before the fire.

"So you've come to stay," he said. "All of you?"

"We've come to bide a fortnight or so, if you'll have us," said Warren. "The ladies decided you had the grandest house, and the best place to throw a Christmas party."

"A party?" Aidan echoed.

"We're not just here to throw a party," Townsend said, nudging Warren's shoulder. "Tell him the truth." He turned to Aidan. "We've come to save your marriage, which is reportedly in a shambles."

"You read it in the papers?" he asked acerbically.

"And heard it at the club, and in the park, and in the ladies' circles," said Barrymore. "Sorry to give you the news, but it's on everyone's tongue."

"Is it as bad as they say?" asked Warren. "Did your duchess really appeal to Queen Charlotte for an annulment?"

"Dear God. Is that the gossip?"

His three friends gazed at him in sympathy.

"Well, of course that isn't true," he said, pacing across the room. "I mean, she didn't specifically say that. She said something more along the lines of wishing she'd never left Wales."

"Blast," said Townsend. "That's not much better."

"She also conversed with Queen Charlotte about 'bearing my heirs.' Neither she nor the king was charmed."

"Goodness, Arlington," said Warren. "What an uncomfortable audience that must have been."

"Uncomfortable does not begin to describe it." He poured a drink for himself, and for all his friends. "As for saving my marriage, I doubt it can be done. Once she gives me a handful of children, I suppose I'll let her go back to Wales the way she wants."

"What? Really?" said Barrymore. "Things are that bad?"

Aidan tossed back his drink, feeling cross and humiliated. "I know you three bunglers managed to make a go of your marriages, but Guinevere and I are poorly suited. We don't get along. I would go so far as to say she despises me."

"Why?" they all asked in varying degrees of outrage.

"Perhaps you shouldn't stick your cock so deep in her mouth," said Warren under his breath.

Barrymore smacked him on the side of the head. "This isn't a time for laughs, Warren."

Townsend glowered at him. "I agree. Show some respect to our old friend, and more importantly, his wife."

"Forgive me," said Warren, throwing up his hands. "I only feel rather helpless. Out of all of us, you've always been the finest, most stand-up chap, and the ladies adore Guinevere. There must be a way for the pair of you to come to terms."

"The marriage is young yet," said Townsend. "There's still hope."

There were times Aidan had hope, but those times were always followed by some wretched scene of emotional destruction. He wondered what his friends would say if he described his last twenty-four hours with his wife. *I caned her for embarrassing me before the crown, then sodomized her as a form of punishment while she was tied to my bed. Later, I took her to the temple, bent her over a wooden trunk, and fucked her...*

"You're welcome to stay, of course," Aidan said. "But I'm not sure if you can help."

"It's not as if we didn't all have our own problems," said Barrymore. "I broke my wife's heart to pieces before I managed to get my head on straight."

"And I made Josephine run away from me twice," Warren said. "Once all the way into the country."

"Shouldn't have stuck your cock so deep in her mouth," Aidan said.

"I couldn't help it," Warren retorted.

Aidan refilled their drinks, and the three of them looked at Townsend. He glanced over his shoulder and back at them. "What, my turn now?"

"C'mon, Towns," said Barrymore. "Confess."

He lifted his arms with a woebegone expression. "I don't know where to begin. Before we even married, I tried to duck out of my engagement by trysting with another woman, who, thanks to you all, ended up being her." Townsend continued enumerating his missteps on his fingers. "I also spanked her on our wedding night, forced her to learn bedroom techniques more suited to a courtesan, then bought her an insect to try to win her affections."

"An insect?" Warren snorted. "You've always been a hopeless romantic."

"I've never been a romantic." Townsend glared at them. "Must I go on?"

"I wish you would," said Aidan. "I'm actually starting to feel better."

"Let's see... I took her to an orgy at Wroxham's country estate to cure her of a *tendre* for a certain gentleman who shall remain unnamed, who happened to be embroiled in a scandalous assignation."

They all looked at Warren as a blush spread about his ears.

"I had my cock out and everything," said Warren. "It was not well done of you, Towns. Our friendship barely survived."

"My marriage barely survived. Aurelia and I had a screaming fight in the carriage on the way home, and..." He fell silent. "Well, I had a lot of apologizing to do afterward, to you and everyone. Love makes people do stupid things."

Aidan gave a mirthless laugh. "I wouldn't know about that. There's no love between us."

"That doesn't mean you aren't being stupid," said Barrymore in his typically forthright way.

Aidan leveled his friend with a glare. "What are you saying?"

"I'm saying that when I was hurting Minette, I didn't even know I was doing it. I thought I was being a caring, honorable chap. I was incredibly stupid. Maybe you're being stupid too."

"In what way?"

Warren jumped in to smooth rising tempers. "We don't know in what way, Arlington, or what's going on between the two of you, but maybe we can offer advice after we've watched you muck about for a while."

"So you're going to make a study of my marriage?" Aidan leaned back in his chair. "Is this absolutely necessary?"

"Yes," they all said in unison.

He let out a sigh. "I'm only warning you, our problems run deep. We're not at all similar. Unlike your wives, Guinevere is hardly part of our class."

"Our class?" Barrymore tilted his head.

"Well, there's your problem," said Townsend. "If you're lording it over her with your riches and title—"

"It's not that," Aidan interrupted. "She scorns my riches and title. We don't have the same world view. We are not the same."

"And yet she's your wife," said Warren. "You must find some way to connect with her. You must have something in common."

Aidan pursed his lips. *After I fucked her in the temple, I molested her all through the night, kissing her and stroking her and hurting her. Oh, did I mention she likes erotic pain?* "We have things in common," he bit out. "Just...not enough. Not enough to build a workable marriage."

"Not yet," said Townsend. "But we'll help you figure things out. The ladies will help too. You know how the three of them get when they put their heads together toward a common goal."

The other gentlemen groaned. "Yes, we know," said Warren. "All too well."

"In this case, their scheming can be put to good use," insisted Townsend. "This is important. Our friend's happiness is at stake."

The other men nodded and agreed that the women could be capital schemers when the situation called for it.

Good Christ. Aidan needed another drink.

"Dearest Gwen," said Minette, crossing the sitting room to put an arm about her shoulders. "We have all become the most smashing of friends over the past week. Don't you think?"

Gwen regarded Barrymore's wife warily. *What now?* she thought.

It was true they'd become closer friends. She called all of them by their first names, and knew a great deal more about their marriages than she had ever really thought to. She had learned that Minette was the chatterbox of the group, while Aurelia put great stock in propriety and manners. She'd learned that Josephine grew up in India and even communed with tigers. Her friends were interesting and kind, and well-loved by their husbands.

"I'm so grateful for your friendship," said Gwen politely. "Shall I call for more cakes?"

"Forget the cakes," said Josephine, who tended to abruptness. "The time has come for a frank talk. A talk about you and Arlington."

Gwen took another sip of tea. Bless them, they were so interested in her marriage, even though Gwen resisted talking about it. The three of them were in such affectionate accord with their husbands, it made Gwen feel hopeless. Even if Arlington could find something to love in her, he would never love her that much.

"A frank talk?" she echoed, forcing a smile. "That sounds serious."

"You and Arlington have been married for what, six weeks now?" said Minette. "And, well, to be perfectly honest, people are still gossiping that the two of you don't get along very splendidly. Which seems a shame, for you are both friendly and wonderful."

"Oh," said Gwen. "Well, ours was an arranged marriage."

"So was ours." Aurelia regarded her with sympathy. "And it is so awkward at first."

"Yes, it is," said Gwen, pouncing on this truth. "It was especially awkward for us, because he didn't want to marry me. And honestly, I didn't want to marry him either."

"But you're married now," said Josephine. "Don't you think he's a fine fellow? He seems a caring enough husband."

Gwen couldn't say anything to disparage him when they all admired him so much. She couldn't explain how he made her feel common and ugly in manners. She couldn't explain how he brought out her wanton side, then pointed to it as evidence of her Welsh "wildness." She couldn't explain how she both adored and hated him.

"He is very admirable," admitted Gwen. "I guess that's part of why it's...difficult."

The ladies all watched her, waiting for her to elaborate.

"Why would it be difficult, if you find him admirable?" prompted Minette.

Gwen took a deep breath. "I suppose it's because he's so much finer than me. So much more confident and polished. I think he finds me wanting. No. I know he does."

This confession brought tears to her eyes. She'd thought it to herself a thousand times, but to confess it out loud was embarrassing. It made it feel so awfully real.

"I'm afraid he's not content in me. That I am not good enough. We cannot seem to...connect."

Josephine, Minette, and Aurelia exchanged more glances. Aurelia rose from her chair. "I'll be right back."

After she left, Minette took her hand. "You are certainly not the only woman in history who's had difficulty connecting to her husband. We all struggle with it, especially when you are wed to a particular sort of man, who is very strong in temperament, and titled and rich, and used to having his way. And when it comes to our husbands, well, you know, the lot of them had a rather infamous past."

"A 'rather infamous past'?" Josephine laughed. "You might as well say it plainly. They were rogues through and through."

Gwen looked at them in surprise. "Your husbands? Rogues?"

"Yours too," said Josephine. "They were known for it, I'm afraid."

"But they are such family men now."

"So is Arlington," said Minette. "He's different now that he's married. He's never been one to dote on women, so it's novel and charming, the way he looks at you in that longing way."

Gwen stared at her friend. If Arlington looked at her with longing, it was for carnal reasons only. "I think he mainly married me to have children," she said. "And to have a portrait to hang over the fireplace. He sent for an artist right away."

"Oh, how fun," said Josephine. "I hope it turns out beautifully. Arlington looks so smart when he's done up in his cape and sword and medallions. He wore them for the painting, didn't he?"

"Yes," said Gwen. "And I wore a lot of jewels. If nothing else, he'll have something impressive to hang on the wall."

"I'm sure you mean more to him than a painting," said Minette.

Aurelia returned with a pile of books and papers clutched to her chest, and carried them to the table where they were taking tea. "I've brought some things to show you, Gwen," she said. "Books that have to do with...marital connection. In a sense."

Josephine gave the other two ladies an exasperated look. "Are we really going to do this again?"

"Why wouldn't we?" said Minette. "She deserves to be educated, considering whom she married. We all had to be educated too."

"Yes, but I seem to remember all of us getting spanked last time we 'educated' ourselves with these materials," Josephine pointed out.

Gwen gawked at them. "Your husbands spank you?"

The three of them stared back at her.

"Your husband hasn't spanked you yet?" asked Aurelia. "I mean, that's wonderful." She looked at her friends. "Only a bit difficult to believe."

"He has," said Gwen, a blush rising in her cheeks. "I didn't realize it happened to other women. Your marriages seem so happy."

Minette laughed. "Oh, that has nothing to do with it. In fact, our marriages are probably happier because our husbands turn us over their knees once in a while. It dissipates emotional tension."

Josephine giggled along with her. "Along with other kinds of tension."

"There will be no spankings this time around," said Aurelia. "Hunter encouraged me to bring these along, since..." She gave Gwen another apologetic look. "Well, you see, we came to Arlington House to try to help your marriage. And a great part of being married... Well, our husbands in particular have a fondness and reputation for..."

155

"Just say it," said Josephine. "All of them are perverts of the highest degree."

"They are all perverts," agreed Aurelia with a sigh. "Josie has the right of it."

"But perverts in the nicest way," said Minette. "And once you learn about the sorts of things that arouse gentlemen, it becomes easier to maintain marital harmony. Because men can be very harmonious when they are having a good time in bed."

"Prettily put, Minette," said Josephine. "Aurelia, let's dive into the naughty books."

Gwen blinked as the ladies spread the books and drawings out on the tabletop. They were of fine paper and craftsmanship, at odds with the lurid subject matter. Naked, cavorting ladies and gentlemen engaged in all manner of shocking pursuits, and each drawing was accompanied by an equally sordid description. *The Milk Maid shows her Master an extra "Measure" of Service. The Horned Gentleman makes Merrie with Lady Diddle's Quim.*

Aside from the sexual drawings, there were a great many drawings depicting corporal punishment: maids getting spanked, housekeepers getting spanked, wives getting spanked, even gentlemen getting caned like schoolboys. There were drawings of Far Eastern harems and parlor-room orgies, and abandoned masquerade balls. Gwen had never seen such materials in her life, never even imagined they existed. If she had, she might have been more prepared for the things Arlington did to her.

"Oh, this one is my favorite," said Josephine, pointing to a pair of lords standing over a wide-eyed servant girl, brandishing birch rods and outrageous erections.

Aurelia smothered a giggle. "Josie, you trollop."

"There is something about the look in that one's eyes," said Minette with a theatrical shiver. "When Barrymore looks at me like that, I run away."

"But not fast enough to avoid being caught," said Josephine. "I know how that running-away thing works."

"Nothing like a chase to get the blood flowing," agreed Aurelia. "It's another form of teasing. Like this." She slid a page across the table to Gwen.

Gwen flushed as she regarded it. The woman in the drawing was tied to a bed while her partner caressed her curves with a garishly colored rose.

"How…interesting," she offered, too ashamed to admit that she'd been tied to a bed in that same way. She turned it over, only to be confronted with another drawing that reminded her of Arlington. It was the expression, the intent authority on the man's face as he fondled his lover's nipples. She realized, on further inspection, that the woman had whip marks on her breasts.

"Oh, my," Minette said, studying another drawing. "Does Townsend do such things to you, Aurelia?" She turned it sideways with a goggle-eyed expression. The pictured couple did have a lot going on, with bondage, avid sex, and a line of waiting footmen with cocks jutting from their breeches.

Aurelia took it from her and nodded. "Of course. We do this every week."

All of them erupted in laughter. Even Gwen couldn't help but smile. For sex to be funny… But in a way it *was* funny. It was funny and confusing, and enjoyable, and terrifying. Gwen's gaze fell on a drawing of a naked woman tied to a pole, being whipped by her stern-faced captor. She sucked in a breath.

"These materials are quite explicit, aren't they?" she said, to cover her distress.

Aurelia gave her an apologetic look. "My husband amassed this collection in his younger days. It *is* a bit shocking, isn't it? But you needn't do the things in these pictures. You need only browse over them to feel inspired, and gain new ideas. One of the most lovely things about marriage is the pleasure you can give one another in private moments. Perhaps you'd like us to help you think of things to do with Arlington to increase your marital happiness. Improve your 'connection,' as you say. If you have any questions, the lot of us have been married awhile."

"Yes, to utter perverts," said Josephine.

"And we would be happy to be very open about anything to do with marital intimacy," Minette assured her. "You needn't be embarrassed at all."

"Goodness," said Gwen. "How very kind of you. But…" She leafed through a few more of the pages, only to be polite. "But this is not our problem. Our intimate life is…in good order."

Josephine looked at the other two and shrugged. "Well, it *is* Arlington. One imagines he would ask for what he wanted." She turned to Gwen with an expression of concern. "Does he ask you for all sorts of troubling things?"

"Josie," Aurelia chided. "That's private."

"Don't pretend you're not curious," Josephine said back to her. "Tell the truth, Gwen, he's awfully commanding, isn't he? I always imagined he'd be a very demon in bed."

Minette giggled behind her hand. Aurelia tried to look outraged, but ended up looking curious too. "Is that the problem, Gwen?" she asked. "Is Arlington...too much?"

Gwen rubbed her temple and took another sip of tea. "Sometimes he seems too much," she admitted. "But I..."

She looked at the three of them. They had been so forthcoming, even bringing Lord Townsend's naughty books for her to look over. She decided to be forthcoming also. "He can be a demon, yes," she said, using Josephine's word. "But I like it. I enjoy it. That part of our marriage is all right. Maybe too good."

"How can it be too good?" asked Minette. "If you enjoy one another, it's nothing to be ashamed of. Goodness, when Barrymore gets going sometimes, he rather shocks me, but I'm the first to admit I enjoy it all the same."

The other ladies nodded in unison. "If you and Arlington are well matched in that way," said Josephine, "it bodes well for your marriage all around."

"I don't know," said Gwen. "I'm afraid it just reinforces his feelings that I am not a proper lady. That I'm not some duke or earl's daughter, with courtly manners and an impressive pedigree. I came to him a plain miss, reared in the country. My father isn't a wealthy man. He only earned his barony from being in the war. I'm afraid that—" Tears welled in her eyes again. "Oh, the duke disdains me so. I'm not even sure he means to do it, but he does. I'm tired of feeling that I don't make him a worthy partner."

Aurelia reached to squeeze her hand. "Oh, Gwen, you mustn't think that."

"Everyone thinks it. Not just him. There has been much gossip about our uneven match."

"This for gossip," said Josephine, snapping her fingers. "And Arlington has never seemed a man to stand on circumstance and titles. I'm a baron's daughter too, you know, and he's never thought the lesser of me."

Because you are not married to him, Gwen thought. *Nor are you Welsh, or common-born.* "It's not even a matter of social inequality, or gossip," she said aloud. "It's that I always dreamed of marrying a man who loved me. I know that sounds silly."

"It doesn't sound silly," said Minette. "We all dream of a loving marriage. I don't know a woman in the world who doesn't. But it doesn't always happen right away, especially when it comes to arranged marriages. Sometimes love takes time. Please, Gwen, don't give up on Arlington yet. He's a wonderful, caring person. I pray for your happiness every day. We all do. We've all become something like family, and families help one another."

"Yes," said Aurelia. "You must give your marriage more time, and as for the gossip, our holiday gathering will put those wagging tongues to rest. You and Arlington can welcome everyone to your home, and they'll see how perfect you are together."

"I don't know about having a big party," said Gwen. "If I cock it up, like I did the royal audience—"

"You won't cock anything up, not with us to help you," said Josephine. "Minette can do the guest list and Aurelia will do the planning, and I'll handle the music and decorations. All you have to do is spend time with Arlington, and let love develop. He cares for you, Gwen. Minette was right when she said he's changed. I think marriage shall suit him nicely, once the two of you have got things in hand."

"And then there shall be babies," said Aurelia, "and laughter and love, and all the things you've always wished for."

Oh, how Gwen wished for happiness. If only it didn't seem such a great distance away.

Aidan walked through the rain to the stables, cursing under his breath at the weather. Their dinner party was to take place tomorrow, and the heavens had seen fit to send down a mixture of ice and rain.

You cannot control everything.

He was coming to understand that. He could not control sunny skies or callous gossip, or his friends' good-natured meddling. He could not control his feelings toward his wife. He could not tame his emotions into neatness or reason, and the more his friends goaded him, the less self-assured he felt.

He opened the door and walked within the dim interior, down the row of stalls to the one at the back. Eira lifted her head at his approach. "Hello, pretty girl," he whispered, stroking her forehead. "Have you seen my wife? I thought she might be here."

Had he been reduced to conversing with horses, then? Things were no better than before his friends appeared. There was only more pressure, and an ever-present shame that they did not rub along so comfortably as the other couples. When he tried to behave comfortably toward her, it always went wrong, or felt awkward. He'd grow embarrassed, which in turn made him angry, and he didn't want to be angry with her. None of this was her fault. It wasn't her fault that her father had petitioned the king, who had then requested them to marry. It wasn't her fault she wasn't at home here.

He heard a sound above, in the hayloft. Was she hiding from the chattering ladies, or from him? He climbed the ladder and found her curled against the back wall, under the window.

"You're going to get wet," he said. "You'll take a chill, and you won't be able to go to the party tomorrow."

She looked almost hopeful at that. "It's not wet here," she said. "Your stable doesn't leak, or your windows."

"I thought you'd be down with your horse." He walked over, brushed away a bit of straw, and sat on the boards beside her.

"I visited Eira for a while, then I came up here to listen to the rain." She tilted her head. "You can't hear it in the house when it rains. I miss the sound of it. I always heard it when it rained at home."

His lips tightened. *Not her fault.* "Still miss home, do you?"

"I miss some things about it. I miss the hayloft." A smile flitted across her lips. "I used to play with my cousin there. Tilda and I would make dolls out of straw, and sew clothes for them. We played the most imaginative games." She shrugged and turned to him. "Are the ladies looking for me again? I'm sorry. It's only that I need a break from them now and again."

"I know what you mean," he said ruefully. "It's the same with my fellows. They mean well, as overbearing as they are."

"I know. I don't wish to hurt their feelings when they've been so kind to us."

"I don't think they are hurt. I think they are concerned." He picked up a bit of straw and split it into pieces. "They wish us to be happy. They want this party to be a success."

"They say everyone will want to come see me. Am I such an exotic creature?"

He looked over at her in the loft's dim light. "Yes, you are." How beautiful she was, and how unknowable, and sad. He reached to trace a lock of her hair, as blue-black as Eira was snowy.

"Why haven't you come back to my bed?" she asked.

He let the bit of hair go. "I don't want to trouble you while the ladies are here," he lied. The truth was, he didn't trust himself. The more frustrated he got, the more he feared hurting her again, holding her down, taunting her, using her in ways no man ought to use his wife.

He wanted to have a good relationship with her, like his friends had with their wives. If only it was as easy as doing some particular thing, or saying some particular right words, but he didn't know what those words were. "Sometimes I think about that afternoon in the meadow," he said quietly. "I wish we could always be those people, Jack and Rose, flirting together without a care in the world."

"I had a care in that meadow," she said. "I was to marry a duke the day after the morrow. A man I'd never met."

He frowned at her grim tone. "So you were."

"And you were to marry me. You didn't even care."

"I hadn't met you yet," he said in his defense.

She looked away from him, at the rain pelting the glass. "You speak of that time in the meadow as if it was a pleasant thing, but you took advantage of me. You thought me someone of no consequence, and so you toyed with me, and manipulated me into doing inappropriate things."

He did not remember it that way at all. He remembered bright sun, charming kisses, and her dark hair blowing in the breeze. "I wouldn't say I toyed with you."

"I felt toyed with, afterward. You lied to me in that meadow, and played me for a fool."

"You lied to me too. You said your name was Rose, that you had a beau named Tommy. You made up any number of falsehoods."

"Between the two of us, you were more false."

The depth of her hurt surprised him. "I made you feel good that day," he said. "There was nothing I did to you that you didn't heartily enjoy."

"You believed you had a right to flirt with me, and kiss me, even spank me on my bare bottom. Because you are a duke, you believe you can do anything that suits your fancy, no matter who's harmed."

"I didn't harm you." He let out a sharp breath and threw up his hands. "No matter how I come to you, we end up in an argument. No matter how pleasant I intend to be, you make me want to snap off your head. I loved our time in that meadow," he said with injured passion. "I'm sorry you don't agree."

"You will not understand," she said, curling her body away from his. "You'll never understand. You don't even hear me when I say things. You only hear what you believe is true."

"What do you want? An apology?" He rolled his eyes. "I'm sorry I flirted with you that day, and kissed you. I'm sorry I spanked you, no matter if it made you excited."

"I wish you would not talk about that time in the meadow ever again," she said. "I wish we could forget it."

"Why would I want to forget it? It's the only damned time in our godforsaken history that we ever got along." He stood with a grunt of irritation. "Very well. I will leave you to your solitude. Perhaps, with the way things go, it would be better if we never tried to talk."

"Perhaps it would be."

He went to the ladder and climbed down, trying to convince himself the tears in her eyes hadn't mattered. She cried all the time, about everything, him most of all. He was damned tired of being painted as her tormentor, the evil duke, when all he ever wished in life was a happy and respectable marriage. He wouldn't talk to her *or* go to her bed, if that's what she wanted. There were plenty of other women who would be ecstatic to accommodate him. Once his friends left, he'd send Gwen to the country for the rest of the winter, and go on about his life however he intended.

As long as she had her damned horse for company, he doubted she'd even care.

Chapter Fourteen: Christmas Dinner

Gwen went downstairs at the appointed hour, in the festive red gown and matching jewels the ladies and Pascale had advised her to wear. She stood at her husband's side with the appropriate smile and greeted the guests for the dinner party, two dozen or more persons, not counting his friends and their wives.

Arlington had no kind words for her, but he was all smiles for the guests, and she understood that she was to be all smiles too. This world was their stage, and she had to play her part, or he might punish her again in some horribly painful and sexually depraved way.

Minette, Aurelia, and Josephine had certainly done a laudable job with the planning. The ballroom and dining hall were festooned in greenery, ribbons, and hundreds of candles, and holly decorated each place setting. The company was jovial and the musicians were splendid, playing carol after carol in honor of the season. Even the cold and ice outside couldn't dampen the celebratory atmosphere.

Christmas was but a week away. If she was home in Wales, she would be relaxing before the fire with her family, enjoying merriment and conversation. She'd be chattering with Tilda and playing with her young nieces and nephews, and looking forward to the cook's special Christmas

164

pudding. She would not be in this stiff velvet gown pretending to be a happy duchess. She felt so alone.

The duke, on the other hand, was surrounded by friends and admirers. He looked striking as ever, and was so good at his role. Why couldn't she be shining and confident like him? What if all the discord between them was her failing? *If you were prettier, wealthier, with better breeding...* It was the same thing she had said to herself in Wales, when no one would offer her marriage. Now she was married and wished nothing more than to go back to Wales.

"Come, Gwen," said Minette, as Josephine and Aurelia flanked her on either side. "You cannot hide here in the corner. You must walk about and speak to your guests."

"But I've already forgotten their names," she said, pushing down panic.

"Stick with us," said Aurelia. "We know all their names. And half of them are active gossips, so once you impress upon them that things are lovely in the Arlington household, it will put all the whispers to rest."

"You look beautiful tonight," Josephine murmured, "so lift up your chin and smile."

Gwen tried to smile, she really did, but she felt so scrutinized. Ladies and gentlemen nodded to her and asked her questions, all of which were a variation on "Aren't you so very lucky to have married the duke?" She wondered if those couples had love in their marriages. The duke told her that society disdained love, that it was a common pursuit reserved for the lower classes. She watched Arlington, tall and strong and handsome, as he conversed with some of the guests.

I love you, she thought, looking hard at him. *I love you, I love you.* She wanted to love him, even if it was common or coarse. If she could go back to the meadow and pray again to the vague heavens, that was what she would beg for. Accord. Understanding.

Love.

They went in to dinner and Gwen tried to be merry. She sat near Minette, who was cheerful all hours of the day. She and Aurelia were both going to have babies in the new year. Gwen wondered if she would too. Her appetite fled at the thought of bearing the duke's child. Then he wouldn't only criticize her as a wife, but as a mother. She wouldn't be able to bear it. She glanced up to the head of the table and caught his eye.

He stared back at her with an inscrutable gaze. He was not thinking that he loved her, that was for sure.

"Gwen," said Minette, leaning close to her. "What's the matter? Aren't you having fun?"

"Oh, yes, I am," Gwen replied, forcing a smile. But she wasn't. She was thinking how horribly lonely it was, to be looked at in that distant, detached way. Maybe love didn't matter to the upper crust, but it mattered to her. Arlington's physical attentions weren't enough. His title and his protection weren't enough either. Her heart cried out for something deeper. *Please love me.*

Stupid girl. He would love you by now if you were good enough.

Lonely, so lonely, while all around her, animated couples smiled and chattered about the holidays. Their easy voices rose and fell, but she didn't know what to say. She hated the woman seated beside Arlington, because she spoke so easily to him and made him laugh.

Gwen tried to eat, but she couldn't swallow past the tension in her throat, and the food on her plate began to blur. Oh, no. She could not cry, not after all their work to plan this party and show how happily married they were. Minette watched her, so sincere, so troubled that Gwen might be troubled.

"What is it, dear?" asked Minette, taking her hand.

"I wonder if I'm not feeling quite well. My head's begun to hurt."

The first tears fell. She wiped them away as quickly and furtively as she was able, but more rose in their place. The loud-mouthed gentleman across the table stopped talking and stared at her. She heard two ladies whispering as she swiped at her cheeks.

"I think I..."

Minette gazed at her with such tenderness. "Perhaps the music is too loud."

"Perhaps."

"Let's go and find you a quiet place to rest." Minette hustled her up and out of the room, assuring the others it was only a bit of headache. Arlington followed after, his expression one of dark concern.

Aidan had reached the limits of his patience. Who cried at a holiday party in one's own house? In front of thirty-odd dinner guests? He burst into her chambers. Minette was comforting his weeping wife, murmuring to her and patting her arm.

"Minette, please," he said. "Don't make a fuss. Go downstairs and rejoin the guests, and assure them everything is all right. We'll be down in a moment."

She looked sideways at his wife. "Gwen is very upset."

"My wife and I are going to talk about things," he said in as steady a voice as he could muster. "If you would allow us some privacy."

"Of course," said Minette. "I'll tell everyone you'll be back shortly."

"Thank you."

She cast one last concerned glance at her friend and let herself out, shutting the door.

Aidan crossed to sit beside Gwen. "Whatever's the matter?" he asked gruffly as she sniffled into her handkerchief. "You realize you're making a muck of this party. If you want to cry, you can do it later, for as long as you want."

"Don't you even care why I'm sad?"

"I know why you're sad," he snapped. "Because you're unhappy, because you don't like it here, because you can't hear the rain on the roof or some such nonsense. There are children starving in London, you know. Men and women dying in the streets of violence and disease. There are families freezing in this unseasonable weather. What a spoiled, sniveling piece of work you are."

This only made her cry harder. She ought to cry. She had stolen his peace of mind this past few weeks, made him a miserable man in his own house.

"That's enough," he said. "You will dry your tears, go back downstairs among our guests, and do your goddamned duty."

"I can't," she said, covering her face with the handkerchief.

He took it from her and mopped the tears from her cheeks. "You will. You're the Duchess of Arlington and you owe it to me. You're wearing the gown I bought you, the shoes, the damned rubies around your neck. You have responsibilities which I will not allow you to shirk. You will go downstairs and pretend that you are eminently happy."

She pushed away from him and took to her feet. "No, I will not! I am not happy. I am miserable here. You can give me a thousand gowns and a million jewels and I'd still be miserable because you have no heart."

She was shouting at him. He knew how to shout too. "I have no heart? What about you? You antagonize me in every way possible, and delight in making me look like a villain. You delight in humiliating me."

"I most certainly do not."

"You've embarrassed me repeatedly before my friends, before the king, before those guests downstairs. I can't guess why, except that you hate me."

"No." She shook her head, pacing to the window. "You are the one who humiliates me. You have no care for me unless I'm in a bed, or your perverse Greek temple."

"That is not true."

"You do what you must to keep up the appearance of a happy marriage. But you have never thought me proper, or worthy of your vaunted hand."

"You don't act worthy," he retorted. "You act like a petty brat the majority of the time. You say I keep up appearances...what did you think marriage was about?"

"Love!" She burst into tears again. "Marriage is supposed to be about love."

"Oh, now we're going to go on about love again. I suppose you wish you had married some bloody farmhand back in Cairwyn."

"I do wish it, if he would have loved me," she cried.

"And you could have cooked and cleaned all day, and dropped his brats, and swept the hearth in his shambling cottage, wearing threadbare rags. Of course, all women dream of such a life."

"They do, if they are loved."

He crossed to her and took her arms. "You say you want love, but you offer me no respect. You have crossed me from the beginning, from the inn the night after we wed. *Oh, he wants me to eat this duck. But I won't, because that's what he wants.* Never mind that it's just a piece of fucking duck that any normal person would eat without thinking. Everything has to be a fight with you." He gave her a little shake. "If you want me to love you, Guinevere, stop being so hateful. Our marriage was not my fault."

"But you blame me," she said. "You blame me for not being up to snuff. That night at the inn, you looked at me as if I were something you'd found on the bottom of your boot."

"I looked at you like a wife whom I did not know, and did not understand. I still don't understand you. I don't know how to make you happy. I don't know how to make you smiling and content. I don't know how to convince you that I mean you no harm."

"Meaning no harm is not the same as loving someone. And I know you'll never love me."

"So you'll live a whole life unfulfilled, is that it?"

"Yes." She swiped a hand across her damp cheeks. "It makes me desperately sad."

"Your nonsense makes me sad," he said, walking away from her. "Please collect your wits so we can return to the party and salvage what we can of this debacle."

She stood where she was, her hands clasped in front of her skirts. "I'm not going back to that party with you."

He glared at her, feeling helpless frustration and rage. "What if I say I love you? What if I really, really pretend I mean it?"

"Kind of the way you want me to go to that party and pretend I'm your happy wife?"

"Yes. Why don't we do that? I'll pretend I love you, and you pretend you're happy. Will that do well enough?"

Her bottom lip trembled, her expression set to crumble again. "I want to go home. I want to go back to Wales."

Perhaps it was that trembling lip that set him off, or perhaps it was the way she stood there in her grand velvet gown, with her black locks tumbling over her shoulders. His fairy queen had never been his queen. She didn't want to be. He felt like a toad, him, the Duke of Arlington, whom everyone had always admired. He was not good enough for her, no matter what he did, no matter his commendable attributes. It infuriated him.

"You know what? Go then," he shouted. "Pack your bags and go to Wales. If it will fucking make you happy, then go. Leave tonight if you want, in the rain and the ice. Get out of my damned house, if you hate it here so much."

"I can't wait to get out of your house," she shouted back.

He went to the door, yanked it open, then spun to face her with a skewering gaze. "Only use the back door, would you? The door for the servants and common people."

That was too cruel, wasn't it? But he didn't stop to apologize, or take her in his arms. He went down to the dinner party and sat at his place, and told everyone his wife had unfortunately exhausted herself planning the event. He avoided Minette's gaze, and those of his friends.

Gwen had made him exactly what she accused him of being: a cold and haughty tyrant without any heart.

Chapter Fifteen:
So Cold

Pascale had made herself scarce while she and the duke were arguing, so Gwen undressed herself, taking off the ruby necklace and earrings and placing them in their specific drawers. All must be in good order for the duke, excepting his own wife, whom he seemed to believe a lost cause. He had told her to get out. She knew he hadn't meant it, that he had only been ranting and waving his arms in anger.

She was still leaving. Tonight.

She squirmed out of her gown by pure determination. She heard a seam rip at some point, but she didn't care. She laid the dress over a chair and went to one of her trunks from home, and pulled a drab gray traveling gown from the bottom. A bonnet, gloves, even a coarse wool cloak that was perfectly nondescript for her purpose.

She would indeed take the back door. In fact, it was the easiest way to slip out without being noted. The servants were busy with the party, and the kitchen was in an uproar of pots and trays. Gwen pulled her hood about her face and snuck out as the cook was calling for more wine to be served. The stables were equally busy, managing the horses and carriages of the guests. She went to Eira's stall and saddled her for riding. She'd always saddled her own horses at her father's manor. Eira snorted with pleasure to see her, and regarded her with great shining eyes.

"We are not really going to Wales," Gwen assured her as she led her out the back way, beneath the shadow of night. "But you must take me away from here, as far as you can go."

The London streets were quiet because of the holiday, or perhaps because of the miserable weather. Everyone seemed to be at home, inside, out of the icy cold elements. The air hurt Gwen's throat, but she trusted her cloak would keep her warm enough on this journey, wherever it took her.

She did not have a specific plan. She only knew she would ride west as far as Eira could go before her legs tired, and then Gwen would find a respectable lodging and use some of her money to hire a room. While she was there, she would write an explanatory letter to her father and ask his advice, and this time the duke would not be able to stop her from sending it. She would tell her father she was too homesick to stay here. Perhaps he would come and meet with Arlington, and realize the duke didn't really want her. Perhaps they could create some arrangement where she only spent part of the year with her husband, enough time to fall pregnant, and mollify the king.

Even as she thought it, she knew Arlington would never agree to any such arrangement. How many times had the man named himself her owner and master?

Perhaps she could hide at an inn long enough for him to give up on her, or consider her dead. Perhaps she could ride all the way to Wales, if he was not able to find her. Perhaps she would meet a farmhand there who loved her, and live in his shambling cottage and sweep his hearth and bear his babies. She would not mind to do it.

Perhaps she was an utter fool.

It was so cold. She hadn't imagined England could be so cold. Her anger's heat warmed her at the outset, but now, a mere half hour into her journey, she couldn't stop shivering and she couldn't get warm. She had not gone far enough to take a room. The duke would find her before sunrise if she stopped hereabouts. She grasped the reins with stiff fingers and urged Eira to a canter.

"We might go to Wales," she whispered, patting her mane. "I ought to. I might meet a handsome stranger there."

But she had already met a handsome stranger. She lived in his house, ate his food, entertained his friends, wore his priceless rubies.

"I want a different handsome stranger," she said to Eira. "One who loves me for who I am."

Are you sure he doesn't love you?

Who had spoken those words? The horse? Gwen was so cold now, she was hearing things. And what a ridiculous question to ask. If he loved her, he wouldn't scold her, and punish her with birchings and spankings and canings, and make her feel something less than what she was. He wouldn't use her body the way he did, holding her down and hurting her, and...

You love the kind of hurt he gives. You crave it. Even now, you crave his touch.

"I don't," she whispered. "I know I don't."

It had started sleeting again, the moisture chilling her face and seeping into her cloak. She couldn't control her shivering. She'd long since ceased to feel her feet, and now her hands felt frozen about the reins. She tried to shake them, to waken them and reassert her grip, but Eira took it for a signal and lurched into a gallop. The mare lost her footing and Gwen slid from her back. It barely hurt. In fact, it all happened rather like a dream, as she tumbled into an overgrown hedgerow. It felt almost like falling into a bed.

She was so tired and cold, she could not pull herself out of the enveloping branches. She tugged her cloak around her and put her hands over her face, and looked around for Eira, but the sleet had turned to great flakes of snow. She wanted to cry but her tears felt frozen, so she prayed instead, the way her mother had taught her. *Ask the heavens for what your heart wants...*

"Please," she whispered. "Please help me, Mama. I don't know what to do."

They only found her because of the horse. The shivering beast had stayed beside her mistress in the frigid cold, so that the snow-dusted hedge revealed itself to be more than a hedge. It was a lost, fallen duchess, half-frozen, wrapped in a common wool cloak.

Fifty men had spanned out, and they had found her in time to save her. Townsend had opened his own shirt and held her hands and face against his skin, and carried her back while the others went to fetch Aidan.

Now Townsend was suffering from the cold too, and the house was in an uproar. Most of the guests were still there. Ladies were crying, servants were scurrying to and fro with water and towels and more wood for the fires. Aidan carried his wife's limp figure toward the stairs. "Are you the physician?" he barked at the nearest stranger.

"No, Your Grace. I've a delivery, promised today. The painting you commissioned from Master Oglesby."

"Damn your painting. Get out of the way."

He carried Gwen upstairs as fast as he could without risking a tumble from his iced-over boots. They said she was alive, but she was so still. She ought to at least shiver, as Townsend had shivered when he brought her inside.

"Where is the physician?" he roared as he took her to his chambers. "Where are the blankets? Who is building up the fire?"

The housekeeper and butler hovered about him, but he didn't hear any of what they said. He kicked off his boots and threw off his cloak, and stripped his wife of her sodden clothes. The housekeeper came behind to wrap her in a blanket. Pascale wept in the background, praying in French. He stripped down to his breeches and got into bed beside her, and pulled her against him so he could warm her. Servants brought hot bricks and more blankets, but she was still too cold.

Get out of my damned house. He had shouted that at her earlier, mere hours ago. He deserved the torture of her cold flesh against his. He deserved more, much more. At last she moved, and trembled, and began to shiver. Around that time the physician arrived, and checked Gwen over, listening to her heart and rubbing her hands and feet. Now and again he murmured "hah" and "hmm," and Aidan had to bite his tongue against shouting at the man.

"She's lucky, Your Grace," he said when he finished. "She'll survive unscathed, although she may be weak and feverish for a spell." He poked at her wool cloak on the floor. "If she'd ridden out in a fine silk cape, I fear she might not be with us, but this servants' garb is hardier stuff."

Aidan recognized her traveling clothes, and her cloak from home. "It's not servants' garb," he said tautly.

174

The doctor pulled the blankets closer about her. "Well, Sir, you must keep your wife warm, and feed her hot tea and broth until she regains her strength. Don't overheat her, lest you give her body a shock."

"Why won't she wake?" Aidan asked.

"I warrant she is exhausted. She must conserve her energy." The silver-haired doctor packed up his instruments.

"She has to get better," Aidan said. "You have to make her better."

"She has to rest," said the physician firmly.

"Is there no medicine? Nothing you can give her?" He rose from his sleeping wife's side and pulled on his shirt. "The fire is not warm enough. Are the guests still downstairs? They must go home."

The housekeeper curtsied as Aidan threw logs onto the fire.

"The guests have gone, Your Grace, except for your friends," she said. "They are belowstairs. The ladies have asked if you will move the duchess into her rooms, so they can help attend her."

"She's not moving anywhere. She's warm where she is." He didn't want her out of his reach, not when she was so wan and lifeless. He'd come so close to losing her, and it was all his fault. If not for that bloody horse, they would be planning a funeral. They would never have found her in that blasted hedgerow, not until daylight had melted the layer of snow.

He went back to the bed and helped the housekeeper clothe Gwen in her warmest flannel gown, a red, beribboned nightmare that made her look even paler than she already was. Gwen stirred as they laid her back down, the first sign of life she'd shown since he brought her inside. He lay beside her and caressed her cheek, and fought back terror.

"As soon as you are better," he whispered, "I'm going to kill you."

"It's c-cold," she said in a hoarse stammer. "So cold."

A fever afflicted Gwen in the middle of the night, raging hot and relentless. She suffered paroxysms that terrified him, and then fell into a torpor-like sleep. The physician came again and checked her heart and listened to her lungs, and told Aidan he must control the fever and make her drink. So Aidan spooned liquid into her mouth, bit by bit, weak, cool tea and broth which she would not keep down. He sponged her and soothed her, the ladies taking over for him when he thought he would lose his sanity.

It went on like that the entire next day. Her long, slender limbs trembled and her cheeks burned. He lay beside her on the bed and whispered that she had to recover, that he couldn't live with himself otherwise. He watched her chest rise and fall and imagined her breath extinguished. When the fever let her sleep, he held her hand and prayed in a mindless panic, *Give me another chance. I'll try harder this time. I'll never stop trying, if you'll only let her live.*

But his prayers seemed to do nothing. He ate and drank only to sustain himself enough to tend her. She suffered into the night, until the ladies had to rest, and the housekeeper took over with her trusted staff.

"When will you sleep, dear man?" asked Aurelia before she left with the others.

"When she is better."

"When she is better, she will need you to be strong and rested."

"No. She needs me to be strong now," he said. "Now, when she is in danger."

"She is in good hands with Mrs. Fleming. At least go down and speak with Townsend and the others. They're worried too."

He'd forgotten his friends were even here, but of course they would remain until the end of the crisis. He still hadn't thanked Townsend for finding his wife. He took a last look at Gwen and headed downstairs to the parlor. Exhaustion dogged him but he couldn't sleep, not until her fever let up. The men looked up at his appearance.

"How is she?" Warren asked.

"Struggling. She won't drink. She can't keep anything down, and the fever won't break."

"She's a strong woman," said Townsend. "She'll pull through this."

Aidan started to pace. "Damned little fool, setting off in the cold of night like that." He turned back to Townsend. "Thank you for warming her the way you did. The doctor said she might have lost her fingers to frostbite otherwise. Thank you for…bringing her back to me." His voice went ragged on the final words.

"You ought to thank her horse," said Townsend. "But you are welcome. Eira is fine, by the way. We went to check on her after luncheon. She's being spoiled rotten with currying and treats."

"I almost got rid of that horse. She was so difficult to train."

"Why don't you sit down?" said Barrymore, when Aidan resumed pacing. "Rest for a moment."

Instead, Aidan walked over to the large, rectangular parcel propped near the doorway, leaning against a pair of chairs.

"What is this?"

"Oglesby's painting of you and Gwen. It came a couple days ago, the night..." Townsend didn't finish the sentence.

Aidan turned to them. "You haven't looked at it?"

The men exchanged glances. "It didn't seem the thing to do," said Warren. "With her struggling so terribly upstairs."

"She's not going to die." That was what they meant, that they hadn't looked at it because they might be looking at a ghost. He hated Warren in that moment, hated them all for having healthy, happy, well-adjusted wives. "Gwen's going to recover. We're going to hang this damned thing over the fireplace."

"Of course you will," said Barrymore. "We just didn't want to look at it without you."

Aidan tore the wrappings back. Barrymore came over to help him, collecting the paper, and holding the painting while he studied it.

Master Oglesby had a gifted hand. He had captured Aidan's likeness exactly, and Gwen's too, down to the otherworldly luminescence of her gaze. He stepped back to study the two of them, taking in every detail. His medals, her curls, the drape of his cape, and the tension of her gloved fingers upon her lap. Her expression, which was not quite a smile but not quite a frown.

"It's handsome," said Warren. Townsend and Barrymore agreed.

Aidan said nothing. He did not find it handsome. He found it far too representative of the chasm between them. She sat directly beside him, beneath him, and yet she might have been a thousand miles away. His expression was one of haughty disconnectedness. Lord of his manor, master of his wife. He shuddered and shut his eyes, and opened them again. It looked the same, only worse. The painter had captured everything that was wrong between them.

Without thought, on pure impulse, he attacked the horrid thing. He tore at it, shredding the image and ripping it from the frame. The canvas rent in great swaths, across his chest, down to her lovely sad face. Bits of paint peeled off, smearing on his fingers. He realized he was shouting at it, *no, no, no. Damn you.*

His friends pulled him away, hauled him back by his flailing arms and pinned him to the floor.

"Easy, man," said Warren as he kicked to be let free. "Rest a minute. You're beside yourself."

He saw Barrymore's white face beyond him, and the butler's. Townsend brought a drink but he wasn't thirsty. "Let me up," he yelled.

"In a minute," said Warren. "When you're calm. I think you haven't been sleeping, Aidan. I think you ought to go to bed for a while, and see how you feel after a few hours."

"She's not going to die." He said it loud enough for the whole house to hear. He wanted them to know it. "She's not going to die from this. I won't let her."

"No," said Townsend on the other side of him. "But you have to rest, for your wife's sake." He helped him up with Warren's assistance. "Rest here before the fire. We'll have the painting taken away."

"No!" It was all he had of her, the only likeness, aside from the sketch he'd made in the meadow. "Don't take it away. Put it up in my room."

"You've destroyed it, man."

"I don't care. I still want it." He made it to the sofa and lay down, then lurched up and grasped Warren's coat. "You come and get me if she needs me. Tell Mrs. Fleming. And wake me up in an hour."

"Yes. We certainly will. Sure you won't have a drink?"

Townsend held it out again and Aidan took a deep swig to mollify him. Beneath the burn of the brandy, he detected the sweetness of laudanum. Aidan glared at his friend, too furious to speak. "Just a little," Townsend said in apology. "The tiniest bit."

"I'll have you arrested," he said.

"Later. You can have me arrested later. For now, get some sleep."

Chapter Sixteen:
Love

Aidan woke in the dark, in the early morning hours. Someone had pulled the curtains and banked the fire, and piled him with blankets. The portrait was gone from the corner. He sat up with his wife's name on his lips.

His head spun at the movement, and his stomach lurched. A servant looked in on him from the door. "Water," he rasped. "And something to eat."

At once, the servants produced an ewer of fresh water and a basket of bread, cheese, and currant cake. The bland food settled his stomach while the water worked to clear his head. His friends were right, he had needed a rest, but now he needed to go back to his wife.

He climbed the stairs with nervous urgency. They would have woken him if she'd taken a bad turn. The whole house would not be abed, so silent, if Gwen was in crisis. He reached his rooms and went inside, and found Minette bathing Gwen's forehead and cheeks.

"Where is the housekeeper?" he asked. "You should be resting in your condition."

"I don't mind helping," said Minette with her typical cheer. "Your wife is better now. The fever has broken, but she's very tired."

"I must sit still, for Jack," Gwen whispered. Her eyes were closed, her head heavy upon the pillow. "I must be still."

Minette soothed her gently. "Of course you shall be still."

"Where is Jack?" Her eyes fluttered open but she didn't seem to see them. "I'm being still."

"That's good, darling. Rest a while, and then we shall have some tea." Minette looked over at Aidan. "Will you speak to her? I think she'd like to know you're near."

Aidan didn't think she would want him near. She wanted Jack, for all his poor behavior. She'd already fallen back into sleep, dreaming of the meadow, perhaps.

"I met Gwen two days before we were to marry," he said to Minette. "In a clearing, by a lake. I sketched her there. I was dressed in common clothes, and I told her my name was Jack."

Minette clutched her chest. "What a relief. She's been speaking of this fellow Jack ever since the fever broke. I didn't know what you would make of it." She wrung out the cloth and laid it over the edge of the bowl. "Would you care to sit with me a while?"

"You ought to be resting," he said again. "Have you had breakfast?"

"Yes, and I am in fine health. Women do not become weak and pitiful creatures just because they are with child." She patted Gwen's hand as Aidan took a seat on the other side of the bed. "As for your wife, I think she is on her way to recovery. She's very strong."

Aidan studied Gwen's face, her eyelids twitching in sleep. "She's strong enough to leave me," he said. "And almost die in the attempt."

Minette gave a subtle shake of her head. "I don't think she was leaving you. I think she only meant to get your attention."

"She has my attention. She's had my attention from the start. I've tried to be a good husband, but she's never liked me."

"She calls you 'Sir,'" said Minette quietly. "When she talks about you to others, she refers to you as 'the duke.'"

"Well, I am a duke, as much as she abhors me for it. I can't change who I am, or who she is, or where she came from. She is my wife now, and calls me 'Sir' as a measure of respect."

"And that is important to you?"

He gave her sharp look. "For her to respect me? You respect your husband. He surely requires it."

"I respect him and I love him. But I never call him 'Sir.'" She returned his look very directly. "Perhaps that is your way of distancing yourself from a wife whom you feel, perhaps, too far below you."

He had known Minette since she was a child—and he had never heard her speak so bluntly. Worse, her words had a ring of truth. Not just a ring, but many bells tolling.

"She believes I feel that way," he said. "But I only like to cleave to proprieties."

"You've always been a stickler for manners and such." She studied him a moment. "I wonder if you've been raised too properly, so now your marriage is too cold and proper. I wonder if you don't know how to be a simple man."

A simple man, like Jack, the man Gwen called for in her sleep.

"I'm not a simple man." It always came back to this. "I'm a duke, Minette. It's who I am. It's my duty, my purpose, my responsibility."

"Your title and responsibilities will always be part of your life. But Gwen and her needs must be part of your life now too."

He made a low, gruff sound. "That would be fine, except that I don't understand her needs, and she refuses to understand mine. I married her because the King of England told me to. I have an image to maintain. A sacred legacy."

"What image? What sacred legacy? That you're a greater fellow than her? That you're too lofty for such trifles as love and caring?"

He crossed his arms over his chest, defending himself from Minette's incisive words. "I care for her. I take exquisite care of her, for all the good it does me."

"Do you love her?"

Aidan leaned forward and put his head in his hands. He would have given anything for the Minette of his childhood, toddling around their ankles and eating cakes.

"I want to love her," he admitted between his fingers. "But there is this distance between us. Perhaps I've put it there. I only wished for her to respect me. I only wanted her to accept me as I am."

"As a duke? What about plain old Arlington? Or Aidan, if you will? The kind, caring friend we all know?"

"I've tried to be kind," he burst out, looking up at her. He lowered his voice as Gwen stirred in her sleep. "I've tried to be kind and caring, but she wants something more. She wants love, this sweet, romantic ideal that she dreamed of as a child. I don't know how to give it to her."

He was stunned to see tears in Minette's eyes. "Don't you remember?" she said. "Don't you remember how I wished for Barrymore to love me, and how much it hurt me when he refused to?"

Good Lord. All of them had suffered, watching that misery. It never occurred to him that he was doing the same to his wife.

"He thought he was doing what was best, and what was good," Minette continued. "He had his reasons, but it was the worst sort of torment, being denied love by my husband. All I wanted was a smile, a kiss. Some sign of true affection. When Barrymore wouldn't give himself to me, I thought I wouldn't survive."

"Our situations are not the same," Aidan said. "You loved him and you wanted him. Gwen doesn't want me."

"Do you think she would have ridden out into the icy night if she didn't want you? If she wasn't desperate for your love?" Minette clasped her hands so tightly together that her knuckles whitened. "I know a little of being a desperate woman, Arlington. I recognize myself in her."

Minette's throat worked as she fished out a handkerchief. Aidan bowed his head.

"So what do I do?" he asked, feeling more desperate by the moment. "Help me, Minette, since you've been there. What can I do to save us? How did you finally get through to Barrymore?"

"I threw a porcelain swan at him," she said, wiping her eyes. "It shattered everywhere." She fluttered the handkerchief with a tinkling laugh. "I don't imagine that is helpful advice. But I threw a swan at him and shrieked that he had to love me. I behaved like a madwoman." She gave him a pointed look. "Some might say Gwen behaved like a madwoman too."

Was it true? Had her flight not been an act of rebellion, but a cry for love?

"She knew she could not get to Wales," said Minette. "She is not an idiot. She was making a calculated move. Now, I suppose the next move is yours. And you know, I don't think you told me the truth earlier. I think you do love her. I think you love her as desperately as she loves you."

"Yes," he admitted. "I love her in a completely unreasonable way."

"Why unreasonable?" asked Minette.

"Because there is no basis for it. Only that she is mine, but you see..." He leaned forward again and rubbed his eyes. "I'm afraid that beneath all my richness and finery, and grand title, there is nothing to appeal to her, nothing I can give her. We are nothing alike."

"Oh, goodness." Minette chuckled and adjusted Gwen's blanket. "Barrymore and I are nothing alike, as you well know, but I love him with all my heart and soul. He puts up with my chattering, and I put up with his brooding. I appreciate the things that are special about him, even if he's nothing like me." She tucked away her handkerchief, her chin tilted in a thoughtful way. "Gwen has spoken of Jack on numerous occasions, even as she fought the fever. And Jack is you, without all your richness and finery, and grand title. Perhaps it would please her to wake to a husband more like Jack, and less like the Duke of Arlington."

"But I am the Duke of Arlington." He swallowed against the emotion in his throat. "That's always been all I am."

"If you truly believe that, dear friend, it makes me sad."

Minette stood and felt Gwen's forehead as Aidan fought to compose himself. Why was he so afraid to look beneath his riches and his titles? Who was he, truly?

He was a man who had behaved badly toward his wife, and was ashamed to admit it. He was a man who had made terrible mistakes.

He was a man who would have to start all over again, and try to make things right.

Minette reached for the wet towel, wrung it out and mopped gently at Gwen's forehead. "Is the fever coming back?" he asked.

"No. She'll be fine. I imagine the both of you will be perfectly fine."

He walked around to Minette's side. "Do you think it will bother her if I sit on the bed?"

The lady gestured for him to take a place beside his wife, and then handed him the toweling. "It might soothe her to sponge her arms, and her neck. It's calming for invalids to be touched."

He took her hand before she moved away. "Minette. I still remember you tripping about in short skirts, with your curls in tangles and your ragged dolly hanging from your fist. When did you get so grown up, and so wise?"

"I suppose it was when I married, and realized the sheer complexity of loving another person," she said. "It gives trouble to the best of us, but

I'm sure you'll be all right. Love is not an easy thing, but the struggles are worth it."

"Barrymore is lucky to have you."

She grinned at him. "And Gwen shall be lucky to have you too, once the both of you sort out your feelings." Her smile wobbled, turned into something more sad and sober. "Just love her, Arlington. Don't make her wonder and question. Don't make her suffer anymore."

Gwen opened her eyes and blinked into moonlit darkness. She felt as if she'd been sleeping a thousand years. She turned to her right and found her husband asleep beside her, still in his shirtsleeves, a blanket pulled up over his legs. Why was she in his room? Why did she feel so groggy? Her thoughts cleared as if from a fog, and she remembered. She had tried to run away from him, and as expected, he had brought her back.

She began to remember other things, like cold and numbness, and a fall from her horse. She remembered the ladies leaning over her, mopping her forehead, and a physician speaking to the duke in a hushed voice, and the duke yelling back at him.

He must be so angry. She feared to wake him and face the consequences of what she'd done. She'd run away in the middle of his party, doubtless ruining the whole affair and sparking a new spate of gossip. Now, afterward, she wished she had made a different choice.

She wouldn't wake him, that was for sure. She wouldn't hasten the reckoning between them. She slid from the bed, being careful to make no noise, and stood propped against the side of it until her legs were not so wobbly. She found a cold, weak pot of tea on the side table and drank the entire thing, staring out the window at the moon.

Why was she so thirsty? How long had she slept? Was Eira all right, and cozy in her stable stall? She seemed to remember one of the ladies assuring her some such thing. Gwen felt grimy, as if she needed washing. She crossed into the duke's bathing room and lit a lamp, and ran some lukewarm water into a basin.

Her flannel nightgown felt as grimy as her skin, so she cast it aside and stood naked, and washed herself all over with one of the duke's soft towels. Her hair was a tangled mess so she washed it too, undoing the snarls with scented water and a fine tortoiseshell comb.

It must be Arlington's comb, she thought, looking at it. He had uncommonly long hair for a man, and always kept it in decent order. She wrapped herself in a towel and sat on a bench near his other things, razors and brushes and bottles of cologne. He kept an army of valets for when he wished to look smart, but sometimes he dressed himself.

She couldn't stop thinking about the comb, or rather, how he would look standing there combing his hair, dealing with snarls and knots just as she did. His grooming tools were so practical, like any other man's, like her father's, or her brothers'.

She felt cold, and she didn't want to put the flannel gown back on, so she took the lamp into his dressing room and found a long row of linen shirts. Surely he wouldn't mind if she borrowed one. She squeezed the last of the moisture from her hair, set aside the towel, and pulled his shirt over her head. How soft it was. It smelled like him, like the fragrant herbs they used to launder it.

She knew the scent of him so readily. Why could she not know *him*, the man who combed his tangles out? The man who got dressed in this room, after putting on one of these shirts? She went to the next shelf, studying his shoes and coats, and hats, and cravats. There were drawers of gloves and stockings, all arranged in impeccable order, sorted by color. *Help me understand him*, she prayed to the heavens. *I don't want to run away. I want him to love me.*

She crept along the shelves, touching bits of lace and silver buckles, and velvet-covered buttons. She found the outfit he'd worn on their wedding day, the fine dark coat with glittering embroidery. How handsome she had thought him, and how horrible at the same time.

But had he really been horrible, or just unfamiliar? She had been so frightened to go to bed with him that first night, but he had taken the time to calm her. Told her silly tales of marauders and medieval maidens. The next morning, when everyone had come barging into the room, she had been clothed.

Somehow.

It could only have been by him.

She had never thought of it until now, that he had done those things for her when he barely knew her. And what had she done in return?

Cried, and reviled him, and caused him trouble at every turn. Perhaps he would have loved her if she had not been such an adversarial shrew from the outset. Now, since she had run away and humiliated him again, she feared he would never love her.

She wished she could start all over and do things differently. Perhaps when he woke and started shouting at her, she could appeal to him with those words. *Give me another chance.* Maybe she could appeal to his sensual side. Maybe that was all they would ever have, their lurid compatibility in bed. Maybe that was what she deserved, to be pleasured, but not to be loved.

She crossed to the other side of his dressing room, past a leather-covered bench and chest of drawers. There was a large, rectangular parcel propped against the chest, swathed in a cloth. She peeked beneath it, then pushed it back to reveal their formal painting. Tears rose in her eyes. Someone had savaged the thing, torn it to shreds.

"Gwen."

The deep voice startled her. She spun to find her husband watching her. His gaze traveled over her shirt, or rather *his* shirt, and returned to her face. She didn't know what to say. Nothing came to her lips. No excuses for her flight, no asking for another chance. Nothing came but anxiety.

"Someone has ruined it." She gestured to the torn canvas. "Someone destroyed our painting."

"I destroyed it," he said.

So it was *that* bad. Gwen shrank away, ducked behind the ruined painting as if it could protect her from this moment.

"You put my shift back on the morning after the wedding," she blurted from behind the frame. "It must have been you. And the night before, you told me those stories about wedding nights and marauders to distract me, so I wouldn't be afraid."

He said nothing as she reminded him of these things, only stood there looking at her with his hands open at his sides.

"And you tried to stop me running off on Eira that time, so I wouldn't be hurt," she said. "And you kept her for me, when you would rather have gotten rid of her. You loved me once. In the beginning, you loved me, at least a little."

His voice sounded soft after her panicked outburst. "I have always loved you, Guinevere. Not just a little."

"Then why...why did you rip up our painting?"

"Because I thought it was horrible." He held out a hand. "Come here, please. Come away from that wretched thing."

She crossed to him and he caught her up and sat with her on the bench, holding her in a smothering hug.

"I'm sorry," he said. "I'm sorry for all the ways I've hurt you. I tore the painting because I was cold and wrong, and I'd like to start over. I'd like another chance."

Gwen blinked at him. "I was going to ask you that same thing. For another chance. I'm so sorry I ran away and ruined your party."

"I don't care about the party, Gwen. I care about saving this marriage. I care about your happiness, because I believe it is inextricably tied up with mine."

His eyes were so sad. So deep and blue and *sad*.

"I want to make you happy," she said. "I want it more than anything. I just don't know how."

"Darling." His hand trailed up and down her arm, over the soft linen of his shirt. "If I've been unhappy, it's my own fault. There's nothing at all wrong with you. It was my loftiness, my pride."

"No, it wasn't all you. I asked you for love when I behaved so unlovably. You must admit it's true. I've been awful."

"Not awful," he said with a hint of a smile.

"Mostly awful. The way our marriage began... I was so confused by you, and so afraid."

"I was also confused by you, and afraid."

"You were afraid?" She couldn't imagine him afraid of anything.

"Yes. Afraid of going about everything the wrong way. Which I prevented by...well...going about everything the wrong way. I was so concerned with maintaining my authority over you. There you were, spirited and strong as anything, and I thought I'd better hold you down. I can only ask you to forgive me, and let me begin again, with less pomposity and hauteur this time. Less authoritative nonsense."

She blushed, and reached to trace the Viking lines of his jaw. "I like your authoritative nonsense at times," she admitted. "Goodness knows, I like it a great deal. But I miss having friendship in my life. Sweet words and soft touches, and affection."

He put his hand over hers. "Then I promise more sweetness and affection. On one condition."

"What condition?"

"That you call me Aidan instead of 'Sir,' and stop referring to me as 'the duke' in conversation. 'Arlington' or 'husband' will do in a pinch."

"All right," she agreed. "But will you do something for me?"

"What's that?"

"Don't call me Guinevere in that biting manner when you're scolding me. It always terrifies me."

"What if I generally try to scold you less?" A smile crinkled his deep blue eyes. "I'm going to try to scold you less and appreciate you more, for there are so many things I appreciate in you. Your spirit, your sensuality. Your beauty and determination, and appreciation for nature. The way you cared for my mother's garden in Oxfordshire, and the way you sailed with Eira over the fence. Your stubborn, peevish tirades, which I have always secretly admired." He took her hand. "And of course, your enduring belief in the necessity of love."

She saw some new softness in his regard, and curled her fingers about his. "Love is necessary, isn't it?"

"Unavoidable, with you around."

Goodness, he meant that he loved her. "You ought to kiss me now," she said. "This seems like the perfect moment for—"

His lips cut off her words. He kissed her gently at first, for this was a new beginning. She supposed they were both a little scared. She shifted closer, wrapping her arms about his neck to give him strength and encouragement. His kiss deepened and she responded with all the hope in her heart. *I love you.*

He said he had always loved her, and she had loved him too, this lofty duke who protected her and understood her, even if he had his own flaws. With love, they could work out their differences. Oh, she hoped...

But first, this warm and wonderful reconnection. As soon as one kiss ended, another began, until she was dizzy with his closeness. How had she ever left him to ride out into the icy night? And why? She drew away, battling a surge of nerves.

"What's the matter?" he asked, stroking his thumb along her lip.

"Are you not...the slightest bit...angry about what I did last night?"

"Last night?" He grimaced. "You mean three days ago?"

"Three days?"

"You've been in bed for three days, my love, and there were hours I feared you wouldn't wake again. And yes, I was angry, then panicked, then sad, and generally beside myself. But my friend told me your actions were a cry for love. And I should tell you that when I shouted at you to leave..."

"That was a cry for love too," she murmured, when he couldn't finish. "Perhaps we ought to develop more appropriate ways to talk to one another."

"I would like that," he said.

They sat in silence a while, in his dim dressing room with his arms around her. She could feel his warmth like a blanket, and his steady heartbeat made her drowsy. "I think I want to sleep again," she said.

"I think you are already halfway there." She clung to him as he picked her up. He carried her back to his bedroom and laid her in his bed, and crawled in beside her.

"I borrowed one of your shirts," she said, snuggling into his embrace.

"I noticed. It looks good on you, and is probably more comfortable than that matronly nightgown. You know, you had a fever for two days. I worried so much I couldn't sleep. The gents had to drug me to put me to bed."

"They drugged you?"

"Without remorse."

"I can hardly believe that."

"You may believe it." He sighed. "We've got the best friends in the world, you know. They were determined to save our marriage, but I think it's up to us now."

She buried her face beneath his chin. "For my part, I swear I'll never run away again. Especially in a freezing snowstorm."

He chuckled and dealt her bottom a half-hearted crack. "For my part, I swear I'll blister your arse if you ever so much as attempt it."

"We are in accord then," she giggled, fluttering her eyes closed. This felt so perfectly warm and cozy, the way a marriage should.

"Yes," he said, palming the sore spot on her bottom cheek. "At long last, we are in accord."

Chapter Seventeen: Right of Possession

Aidan woke before her, and saw the servants had been there. The fire was tended and the curtains closed against the daylight so they might sleep. Gwen sprawled beside him, still clad in his voluminous shirt. He couldn't help noticing that one side of the neckline gaped open, displaying an alluring expanse of breast.

He slid off the bed, taking care not to wake her, and went to his desk and dug out his sketch book and charcoal. He hadn't drawn a thing in months, but he wanted to draw her this morning. He wanted the memory of her sweet slumber, and the way she looked in his shirt. He wanted the memory of their new beginning, here in this quiet room with the fire crackling in the hearth.

He began the sketch with bold lines, black hair and white linen. Her arm rested against her waist, the other curved by her head. He took special care to form her delicate fingers, and then he started on her face. Dark lashes and a pert nose, and lips like an angel's. A smattering of freckles. He moved closer, thinking to count them, but there were too many, more than he thought.

He regarded the sketch. It was a very good likeness. He would show it to her later, perhaps even draw her again with her pretty eyes open, lounging about in his bed. Or perhaps tied to his bed.

Hmm. A compelling idea.

He put down his book when he heard a tap at the door. Mrs. Fleming peeked in.

"I've tea, Your Grace. Would you like some luncheon?"

Luncheon already? He nodded to the housekeeper as Gwen stirred. Two maids brought trays of buns, cakes, and sandwiches and set them on a table next to the tea. By the time they left, Gwen was awake, peering at him from her bundle of covers.

"My goodness," she said. "Is the bread still warm? It smells wonderful."

"Will you have some?"

"Yes, Sir...er...Aidan." She smiled sheepishly. "I promise I'll get better. It's something about the way you look sometimes."

He made her a cup of tea and handed it to her, and carried the food over to set it on the bed. "Do I look like a grand and haughty duke?" he asked, teasing.

"Yes, you do, even shirtless, in your breeches."

"I fear I've intentionally honed my aristocratic air of condescension over the last twenty years." He held out a bun slathered with preserves. "You must be patient with me, if I am still lofty sometimes."

She took a bite, and ended with a bit of blackberry on her lips. He could not resist kissing it away.

"I must try to accept you as you are," she said, looking at him from beneath her lashes. "You said something to me once. 'We deserve one another's kindness.' If only I'd listened to you then."

"If only I'd listened to myself. But as I recall, you were rather preoccupied with the horse I'd just shown you, and I was still fuming about that letter you wrote."

"Oh, that letter." She popped the rest of the bun in her mouth and shook her head. "That was an awful thing to do. You were right to punish me for it."

"I try to only punish when it's warranted. I try to be fair. That was not a fair letter, though it helped me understand how homesick and desperate you were."

She took a cucumber sandwich and added a slice of ham. She looked so pretty and fresh and rested. He desperately wanted to tumble her. He would, when she had eaten a little more.

"If things ever get that way again," he said, "perhaps you might address a letter to me. You may be as cruel as you like, provided you are honest."

"I don't want to write you any cruel letters," she said.

"You don't right now." He suppressed a smile. "But you may wish to in the future. Marriages have ups and downs. We can't expect everything to be perfect. We can only try to..."

"Be kind?"

"Yes. We must care for one another, as well as our future children. They will want to have parents who love one another."

"Our children." She put her hand to her waist. "I hope we'll have children soon, Aidan. I wonder if we will have boys or girls, and whether they will have your temperament or mine."

He laughed at that. "Sometimes I think we share the same temperament. We're both headstrong and stubborn."

Her green eyes glinted with humor as she bit into another bun. He fondled a lock of her ebony hair.

"Perhaps my fairy queen will give me a dark-haired fairy princess."

"Or perhaps we'll have a little boy who looks like a Viking," she said.

Aidan grimaced. "I think one Viking duke is enough."

She laughed, a beautiful sound. He looked down at the tray, which he had mostly ravaged. She had eaten a good amount too. "How are you feeling now?" he asked.

"Much better. Perfectly better."

Her gaze shone with contentedness. How long had he wished her to be content and happy? If only it had not taken a brush with death to snap him out of his idiotic behavior. He felt her forehead and cupped her face. "You are really better?"

She looked down, shy again. "I feel very well. I apologize for giving you such a scare. I suppose if I ever deserved punishment, it is now."

She peeked up again and met his gaze. Everything inside him clenched: his heart, his soul, his cock. He wanted her so badly.

"I suppose you do deserve some consequences for your actions," he agreed. He picked up the trays from the bed. "Go in my bathing room and take care of your necessities. I'll be waiting for you here."

Her eyes went wide. Well, she'd practically begged for it, hadn't she? She responded with equal parts dread and excitement, lovely girl, and scurried off to use the privy. When she returned, he was ready with four lengths of sturdy rope.

"Take off that shirt, darling, and lie back on my bed."

"What are you going to do?" Gwen asked, staring at the ropes and then back at his face.

"I'm going to tie you up for a little while," he replied. "It seems an appropriate consequence for someone who's run away."

"Oh."

There was a world of emotion in that "oh." Fear and reluctance and curiosity and longing, and the same lustful craving he felt. She draped his shirt over a chair and climbed onto the bed, and lay back upon it. Ah, those long legs, those supple breasts. His cock bucked within his tightening breeches.

"How long will you tie me up?" she asked as he gathered her arms and raised them over her head.

"As long as I wish. I fear I may still be a lofty and commanding master when it comes to your body." He made quick work of the knots, taking care not to bind her wrists too tightly. She might still be weak as a kitten, but he wanted her to feel tied down, conquered. He knew she loved that feeling.

And he, of course, loved conquering her. In this, there were no apologies to make, no pleas for second chances.

"Open your legs," he said.

She inched them apart. He made a soft sound of amusement and palmed her quim.

"Don't pretend to be a shrinking miss. I can feel how wet you are. Open your legs for your husband. Open them wide."

She made such a delectable picture, spreading her legs as he probed her slick, heated folds. She arched against his hand, still trying to be ladylike about it. He'd have her writhing and begging soon enough. For now, he applied himself to tying her ankles to the bedposts. When he was finished, she lay beautifully open to him.

"There," he said in a teasing voice. "That's what happens to young ladies who try to run away from their husbands. Are you sorry for what you did?"

She tugged at the ropes, until he could barely restrain himself from mounting her. *Soon. Don't rush through, when things have just begun again.* He wanted to play with her a while.

"Answer me," he prompted, putting a hand to the falls of his breeches. "Are you a sorry little duchess?"

She nodded, putting on an adorable show of dread. "Yes, Your Grace. I deserve to be punished."

"You certainly do," he agreed in all seriousness. "But you are still recovering, so I can't dole out the severe corporal punishment you so richly deserve."

"How unfortunate," she murmured, as he released his cock from its confinement. "About the punishment, not the recovery."

His organ sprang forward, fully aroused. "You shouldn't push your luck. Not in your position."

"Yes, Sir." She stared at his cock and tugged at the ropes again. "May I still call you Sir in these sorts of situations?"

"I would recommend doing so. But only in these situations, if you please." He crawled onto the bed, between the legs of his willing victim. He cupped her breasts and stroked her nipples, and ran his palms down over her hips, and thought how very beautiful they made women in Wales. Her shining black hair spread out, dark and wild, upon the pillow.

"Now, what shall I do with you?" he asked. He teased her pussy, entering it with his fingers to make her moan and arch. "How shall I make certain you never leave me again?"

"Goodness," she whispered. "You frighten me sometimes."

"Why?" He pressed his fingers deeper. The ropes creaked as she squirmed from the stimulation.

"Because of the way you make me feel."

He leaned down to place a kiss at the apex of her sex. "Don't be afraid. Just enjoy it."

He placed a palm on either side of her trembling thighs and explored her quim, teasing her with his lips and tongue. She groaned and arched her hips as he delved between her folds to her little thrusting pearl. He loved how her breathing sped up, and her movements intensified. She was so alive when he touched her. She opened herself to him as no other woman ever had.

"You like that?" he asked, looking up at her.

"Yes." She nodded and squirmed some more. "I like it. I do."

"I'm going to put my cock inside you next. I'm going to press inside you and make you mine."

"Like...a..."

"What?"

"Like a...marauder," she said breathlessly. "Claiming me."

He grinned, basking in the scent of her femininity. "Yes, an English duke marauding a Welsh stronghold. I shall take the baron's only daughter for my own." He ran his hands down her inner thighs, to the rope about her ankles. "I'll force her to my will, and once I've been inside her, no one will be able to deny my claim."

She trembled as he palmed his cock. "Perhaps a...Viking duke," she suggested. "You look more like a Viking than an Englishman."

He laughed. "Such imagination. A Viking duke then, with a fairy queen tied to my bed, completely at my mercy."

"A fairy queen? Not a baron's daughter?"

"I get to have my fantasies too." He laid over her, nudging against her entrance. She pretended to struggle, embroiled in their game.

"You can't escape me, my wild, exotic queen." He grasped her bound hands to settle her, and held her gaze. "And when I take you, then I shall be king by right of possession."

"Release me," she cried.

"Never."

He pressed inside her, arching over her with his best Viking-duke expression of carnal mayhem. "How does it feel to fall to your enemy?" he taunted. "I'm going to make a baby inside you. An Engli—er—Viking baby so that our family lines are linked forever. You'll never get away from me."

"Oh, please." Her hands fisted as she strained at her bonds. "How ruthless you are."

By now, his fairy queen had submitted completely to her Viking invader, arching her hips, squeezing upon his cock.

"You're mine now," he said as he drove repeatedly between her tied-open thighs. "Mine forever. How does that feel?"

"It feels very...very...wonderful," she gasped.

"Show me how wonderful." He kissed her neck and nipped at her nipples and breasts. His thrusts quickened, sending pleasure deeper and thicker within his body as she bucked to meet him. "Show me how fine it feels to be claimed by your Viking king."

She dissolved into ecstasy, and he felt a victorious sense of satisfaction, as if he really were a marauder, only his captive was willing, and the dynamic between them felt perfectly right. He came inside her, pure male contentment. His woman, his love, and eventually, the mother of his children, children who would be born of two very different parents who had finally discovered they belonged together after all.

Even if one of them occasionally needed to be tied down to the bed.

Gwen watched her husband with the usual mix of complicated feelings. Lust, embarrassment, pleasure, excitement. But mostly lust. Second chances felt very, very good.

He looked as satisfied as she. Rather than untie her right away, he touched various parts of her body, stroking, caressing, lingering over the curve of her hips. He brushed her hair back and leaned his forehead to hers.

"I love you," he said. "As a Viking and an Englishman."

She giggled at his seductive grin. "I love you, too."

Yes, love. That was the other part of what she felt, aside from the lust and embarrassment and excitement and all of that.

"You needn't untie me yet," she said as he reached for the ropes. "I mean, if you don't wish to."

His grin widened. "If I had my choice, my greedy wanton, I would never untie you. But we've a crowd of friends downstairs who are doubtless worried about your well-being, not to mention my state of mind. And my valet is surely beside himself, that I haven't called for his help in days."

She sat up as he freed her arms. "Does your hair need combing?"

He turned and gave her a quizzical look as he untied her right ankle. "I imagine it does."

"Because I can help you as well as your valet," she said. "I mean, I am exceedingly good at combing hair. I wouldn't pull your tangles or anything."

He set to work on her left ankle. "I suppose you may comb my hair if you like. If it would please you."

She was probably only imagining the color spreading across his cheeks. It was hard to tell with his tawny Viking complexion. He ran a great tub of warm water in his bathing room, and they sat in it together, and she did comb out his hair, all the long, wild glory of it, so different from her tame black locks.

He had commanded her, pleasured her, confounded her feelings, but in this simple, intimate act she finally began to feel like his wife. Not his duchess...she had always known she was his duchess. Goodness, it was an impossible fact to ignore.

No, she began to feel like his true wife, treasured and loved.

"I suppose I have made you more trouble these last few days," she said regretfully, as they rose from the tub to dry off. "With the gossips and such."

He gave her a wry glance. "I expect it's only the smallest fraction of trouble you shall cause me over our lifetimes. Don't fret about it. Everything will work out in time."

"I'll do what I can to fix things," she promised. "I'll be a perfect, obedient duchess."

They were both laughing before she could finish. "I've heard that before," he said. "But I would appreciate your best attempt. You needn't be perfect." He took her in his arms and gave her a noisy kiss. "Just love me. And stop hinting to the king that our marriage is forgettable and that you would rather be back in Wales."

"I'll try."

He gave her bottom a hearty smack. "Don't try. Do."

Gwen sobered as they crossed into his dressing room. The shredded portrait still drooped in the corner. "What will you do about that? Our painting?"

"I don't think it can be saved. Or should be saved." He stared at it a long moment. "We've given one another a second chance. I suppose we'll give the artist a second chance too, perhaps in the spring, if you don't mind a bare mantel until then."

"But in the spring..." She brushed a hand over her middle. "I might be expecting by then."

He winked at her as he pulled on a shirt. "I hope so. Then the following spring we can have a family portrait made, in Wales, in our meadow, to create new memories there. Do you think that would be all right?"

Sometimes her husband came up with the best ideas. Gwen felt a warmth of happiness spread through her entire body, even to her toes. "I think that sounds wonderful. Maybe we can have a portrait made every year, as our family changes and grows. We can commission portraits until we're wrinkled and old."

"Absolutely. Very wrinkled and very old."

Her husband was rapidly disappearing beneath layers of fine clothing, while she remained naked, wrapped in a towel.

"May I borrow your shirt again," she asked, "so I can return to my chambers and dress?"

He tugged away her towel and looked her up and down. Oh, that look...it made her feel hot and lustful all over again.

"I think I would rather watch you streak naked across the hallway," he said, pulling her closer to fondle her breasts.

In the end he didn't make her do any such thing, although it was nearly teatime before they finally managed to present themselves to their company in the front parlor. The children were there too, playing and crawling about, fresh from their afternoon naps.

"Look who it is," said Townsend brightly, as the ladies flocked over to Gwen.

"How are you, my dear?" asked Josephine.

"You look so well!" said Aurelia.

Gwen grinned at them. "I feel completely better." She reached to clasp her husband's hand. "Arlington has nursed me back to health."

"I bet he has," snorted Barrymore, who was promptly stifled by Minette.

"It's wonderful that Arlington has got you feeling better," said Minette, smiling between the two of them. "And Gwen, my goodness, your convalescence has suited you. You've got a glow."

"Indeed she has. We're overjoyed to see both of you in such fine spirits," said Warren. "We are all of us happier than you can believe. Won't you sit and have tea with us?"

They agreed that they would love to. Gwen turned to look at her husband, keeping hold of his hand. How pleased he looked, and how happy, just like a man in love. It seemed her maiden's prayers in the meadow were to be answered after all.

I wish...perhaps...someday he might come to love me, if he's the sort of duke who's not too lofty to fall in love.

As it turned out, he was not too lofty a duke at all.

Chapter Eighteen: Epilogue

Six Years Later

The afternoon was glorious, the sort of sunny, breezy day that made one want to take off hats, gloves, coats, and bonnets, and simply exist in the green surroundings. Aidan clasped his wife's hand in his lap. Now and again he turned to look at her, even though it made the artist pull a frown. They'd hired an Italian fellow this spring to paint them out in their garden, which was only appropriate. Their family was growing like flowers.

Gwen held the youngest, an infant cherub named Louisa Rose, who made his heart clench in paternal adoration each time she cooed or gripped one of his fingers in her little fist. Their dark-haired three-year-old, Gareth, cuddled between him and his wife on the picnicking blanket, content to play with his toy soldiers. Their oldest son squirmed with restlessness on his mama's other side. He had been made to comb back his mop of gold hair and wear a handsome coat and breeches like a big boy, when he would rather muck about and play.

The strapping child was formally titled John Daniel Worthington Drake, the Marquess of Wescott, and would one day be the next Duke of Arlington, but for now, he most often answered to Jack.

"When will they be here?" he asked his mama. "We've been sitting here for *hours and hours.*"

"Not hours," said Gwen, patting his hand. "Only a half hour or so. I know it's a trial, darling, but we want to remember this beautiful day, don't we? When we all sat together and picnicked by the flowers?"

"I don't care about flowers. I would rather George come and play dragon-slayers with me."

"That sounds like an apt game for the two of you." Aidan patted his son to sustain him in these "hours and hours" of filial duty. "Have you heard of St. George and the dragon?"

"My friend George is not a saint," said the boy.

"You can say that again," murmured Gwen under her breath.

It was true the Warren children had a tendency to wildness. George, the oldest, was even blonder than Jack and known for relentless activity. His younger sister Ella was a tomboy of the first degree; Aidan suspected the unconventional Josephine encouraged her in this. Ella would doubtless join the boys in their dragon-slaying, while the youngest, Dennis, toddled behind, dragging his favorite blanket.

"John Daniel," said Aidan, so his son would know he meant business. "You must sit straight and still beside your mama, or baby Louisa will fuss. You must set the example for Gareth too. We'll be done in another quarter hour."

"But I don't like posing for pictures, Papa."

"Sometimes you have to do things in life that aren't very fun. It's a nuisance, I know, but big boys learn to put up with things. You'll grow to be a grand duke someday, and people will want to know what you looked like when you were five years old. So you ought to put on your most handsome face and finest manners and sit as still as you can until George comes. It won't be long now."

Jack sighed, but stopped fidgeting. Aidan well remembered the burden of duty at that tender age. He protected Jack from it, to a point, but he would need self-discipline to succeed in his future endeavors, so Aidan occasionally put his foot down.

"Ba babba babba," chattered Louisa.

Gareth giggled. "Mama, is Louisa speaking Welsh?"

"Not yet," said Gwen with a smile. "But someday she will learn it, like you and Jack. How else could she speak with her Welsh cousins?"

Yes, all of them had learned Welsh, although the boys could speak circles around Aidan. When they went to Cairwyn to visit the Lisburne side of the family, there were chattering Welsh children all around, half of them with names impossible to pronounce. The proliferation of cousins astounded Aidan, as Gwen's seven brothers got an astonishing number of offspring on their wives. Of course, he and his friends had not done so badly. They all had at least three little ones, with the industrious Townsends having already reached four.

At long last, the artist left for the day, and the other families arrived at Arlington House to the picnic. Jack went running off with George and Ella, along with the Townsend boys, Edward and Will. The Townsends' oldest, Felicity, sat primly and played with baby Louisa and her own baby sister Belinda. Lady Felicity took her status as the oldest child of the bunch very seriously, and like her well-mannered mother Aurelia, displayed laudable breeding for a child her age.

Goodness, thought Aidan. That pretty little charmer would make some man a powerful wife someday. Jack, perhaps? It was tempting to match up their children, at least the ones not too closely related. Jack and Felicity would make a likely pair, although the Barrymores' curly-headed twins might take issue with that. The chattering mini-Minettes, Isabella and Constance, had taken a shine to Jack in the past year and followed him everywhere, so the dragon-slaying party grew to an unwieldy mob right away.

"Lord Augustine," said Gwen to Barrymore and Minette's oldest son. "Aren't you going to go off chasing dragons too?"

"Perhaps in a while," he replied, gravitating toward the dark-haired Felicity. They were both quieter sorts of children, not given to rambunctiousness. They both enjoyed music, and sometimes played duets on the piano when the families got together. If Aidan had to bet on any weddings, he would bet there.

But who could tell where their hearts would end up? He would never have thought he would find his legacy with a Welsh-hellion fairy queen, who grew more beautiful and compelling to him every year.

"What a magnificent day," said Josephine, lounging back on the grass.

"And Arlington has the most beautiful garden in the spring," said Aurelia. She turned to her husband. "Why, I remember when you courted me here just before we married. We took a walk about the garden, pretending to be in love."

"Yes, as you begged me to break our engagement. You also named me a blackguard, as I recall."

The rest of them feigned horror.

"Such vitriol, Aurelia," Josephine chided.

"It hurt my feelings," said Townsend, ducking as Aurelia tossed a bit of crumpet at him.

"You had no feelings back then," his wife teased. "None of you did. You all had to be rescued by good and patient women."

"I don't know who rescued whom," said Warren. "If not for me, Josephine would have been married to the Earl of Stafford. Her entire inheritance would have gone to financing his collection of obtrusive rings."

"Obtrusive is one name for them," said Barrymore.

"I won't argue that I was rescued," said Josephine, after the laughter died down. "Even if Warren's methods were somewhat questionable."

"If you want questionable methods, look right there," said Warren, gesturing to Barrymore, whose given name was Method.

"I can still beat you up," said Barrymore, rolling his eyes. "Although I won't, in front of the children."

The children took no notice of their parents' conversation as they ran past the picnic blankets, shouting and brandishing sticks.

"I don't doubt they've got that dragon on the run," said Gwen.

"When shall we call them to eat?" Minette asked.

Aidan reached for a cake, and handed one to his wife. "I suppose when they've slayed an adequate number of dragons, their hunger will get the better of them. It's a perfect day for playing. We ought to let them run."

"How serendipitous, that Arlington's garden harbors such a vast number of dragons," said Warren.

"At least it keeps them busy," said Josephine. She and Gwen pulled faces at baby Louisa as she began to fuss.

Aidan ran a hand up and down Gwen's arm. He loved his friends. They were like family. He'd never been that close to his own family, but now he had Gwen's prodigious Welsh clan, and of course, all these friends with their warmth and support. He stared at the back of his wife's neck, wishing he might lick it. Later. Time for that later.

For now, he enjoyed the food and camaraderie. The children made another pass, yelling and gesticulating with their imaginary swords. "It's hiding in the big marble cave," George shouted.

"Yes, in the big cave," the curly-headed twins echoed, dogging Jack's heels. "You must go and kill it for us, Jack."

"The big cave?" Minette looked at Arlington. "Have you a marble cave on your property? The wonders of this place never cease."

"We don't have a cave," said Gwen, laughing. "The only marble thing is—"

She locked eyes with Aidan. Warren sat up straighter, and Townsend jumped to his feet.

"Remember, you're not allowed in the temple," Aidan shouted to Jack. "Tell the other children not to go in the temple!"

"Is it locked?" asked Barrymore.

"Locked or not, if George wants to get in there, he'll find a way," said Warren. "My son can be devilishly clever when it comes to mischief."

"I'll go head them off," said Townsend, hurrying across the clearing.

Aidan hid a smile as a garish blush spread over his wife's cheeks.

"Well?" said Josephine. She studied them with a speculative look. "You must tell us now. What on earth is inside that temple?"

Barrymore chuckled and Warren burst into laughter. Gwen shook her head and spread her hands. Aidan rescued her by passing over a sandwich.

"I'll describe it to you later," said Warren under his breath. "It's too delightful to be believed. But not a place for children to go exploring."

"No, not a place for children," Barrymore echoed.

"Tell us," begged Minette. "Don't tease."

Barrymore turned and made sure young Felicity and Augustine weren't listening. "Let's just say it's on par with Townsend's illicit literature collection. Perhaps even better."

"Oh, my," said Josephine. Minette put her hand over her mouth and blushed. Aurelia raised a brow and grinned at Gwen.

"Have all your gentlemen friends been in there?" Gwen whispered to Aidan.

He made a helpless gesture of apology. "We threw some wild routs in our younger days. Aurelia was right. We needed rescuing. Some of us more than others, I'm the first to admit." Before she leaned away, he drew her closer and spoke in her ear. "You know, it's been a while since we visited the temple. Too long."

"I was just thinking that."

The children came running back in a chattering group, corralled by Lord Townsend. Adorable, all of them, with their smudged coats and disheveled curls. They joined the babies, and Felicity and Augustine, and sprawled on the blankets to devour what was left of the afternoon's repast. Aidan caught his wife's gaze as she hummed and rocked the baby. Later, he would take her to the temple and have her.

And she would go willingly, judging by the pleased flush lingering in her cheeks.

They set out after dark, when the children were sleeping soundly under their nurse's watchful eye. Gwen held Aidan's hand; he carried a lamp with the other. It was so dark in the garden at night. The flame threw shadows that heightened her excitement and nerves.

They nearly always came here under cover of darkness. Gwen felt freer at night, more capable of surrender, whether she was to be pleasured or hurt. Sometimes she was punished in the temple, generally after one of her "Welsh hellion fits," as Aidan called them. She didn't misbehave that often anymore, but when she did, she submitted to whatever consequences her husband deemed necessary. He was always fair, if strict, and she always felt better afterward, as if the tensions between them had been eased.

But tonight was not going to be about punishment. She had been very, very good of late, an estimable duchess who was finally earning the regard of the *ton*. She had even merited another audience with the crown, during which she had managed to be absolutely inoffensive, even charming. Aidan marveled about it afterward, but it was easy to be happy and charming when one was in love.

At last they reached their private temple of iniquity, and Aidan unlocked it with a key they kept hidden in a vase. He gestured her inside with a suggestive smile. Gwen turned about in the marble chamber while he hung the lamp in the corner. "It feels different to be in here, now that I know all your gentlemen friends have been here too."

"We didn't all crowd in together," he said. "I let them borrow it sometimes. At parties. And other times." He grinned at her dark look. "There were ladies before you, my darling, but none I remember by name." He gathered her close and kissed her, and began to work at her gown. "None of them even half so lovely and fascinating as you."

Gwen started undoing her husband's clothes, pushing back his coat and unbuttoning his waistcoat. All the garments were discarded posthaste, thrown into a careless pile. "Do you think your friends will want you to share it again?" Gwen asked.

"What?"

"I mean, when they tell their wives what sort of garden folly this is... Do you think they will all wish to try it out?"

Aidan chuckled. "Perhaps. It depends whether they are as depraved as you, my love."

"I am not depraved."

His chuckle transformed to a laugh. "Tell me that again in five minutes. We'll see if it's true." He led her toward the whipping post. "Raise your hands in surrender, my perfectly demure wife."

"I didn't say I was demure either."

He put a finger over her lips. "Enough chatter. While the cuffs are on, you're not to speak, do you understand? Not unless you're spoken to."

"Yes, Your Grace." The authority in his voice sparked an aching pulse between her legs.

A few years ago, her husband had commissioned some fine leather cuffs which were now affixed to the pole at her precise height. He still used rope sometimes, if he wanted to give her some leeway to pull and writhe about. He used the cuffs when he wanted her fixed and controlled. She studied his handsome features as he secured her wrists in the restraints. She still found him every bit as beautiful as Jack in the meadow. If anything, he'd improved with age.

He met her eyes when he finished, his lips curving up in a smile. He had a daunting ability to read her moods and thoughts. He kissed her, simultaneously pulling down on the cuffs to make sure she was secure. When he was satisfied, he smoothed his hands down her arms and to her nape. He took her hair down, pin by pin, until it cascaded down her back. Then he wrapped it around one hand and pushed the lot of it forward over her shoulder.

She shivered as he caressed her bare back. *Please, take me now,* she wanted to beg. How wise he was, not to let her speak, for she'd be babbling like a madwoman. *I love how you caress me. I love the heat of your body at my back.* How strong he seemed, how commanding when he explored her this way. His thick cock poked against her bottom, a delicious threat, although he rarely buggered her except after punishments. Disciplinary sodomizations, as he called them, for naughty wives.

He made a low sound as he nuzzled her nape. "How good you're being," he said. "Not a sound, although I can see you trying to rub your quim against the pole."

Oh, yes, she was, although her husband discouraged such lascivious lapses of discipline. He held her waist with one hand and palmed her pussy with the other, thrusting his middle finger deep inside. It slid within her moisture, betraying copious arousal.

"Not depraved, my sweet?" His laugh was rough and lewd as his touch. "You're hot enough to burst into flames."

She moaned as he stroked her, taking his time, bringing her closer to that peak but not allowing her to reach it. Oh, she wanted his cock inside her now, but she knew he would play with her first, play with her until she was reduced to a needy and desperate puddle of longing. It appealed to the tyrant and sadist in him, to make her wait. To even, occasionally, leave her unsatisfied.

Goodness, she hoped this wasn't to be one of those nights. She couldn't even beg for what she wanted, because he'd taken away her permission to speak.

And you love it, she thought. *His control excites you beyond bearing.*

She heard him rummage in one of the trunks, and shifted from foot to foot. The cool air had her nipples hard as pebbles. She felt his hand on her hair, and then soft fabric against her face. He looped a length of silk around her eyes and tightened it so she couldn't see. She made a soft pleading sound, wanting to be touched, stroked, anything. She heard rummaging again. No point in turning to look. Not that she ever turned to look, since that only made her more anxious.

Oh, hurt me, please.

She felt his palm against her arse. He smacked it a few times, readying her, she knew, for something harder. Then he stood back and dealt her a stinging blow that could only have come from the tawse.

She shrieked and danced on her toes. It hurt so badly, stung like spreading fire on her cheeks. He gave her four more blows in quick succession, so she thrilled and hurt and nearly jumped out of her skin. Heavy impact, heavy sting. She feared the tawse, for it could be such a brutal implement. She gritted her teeth so she wouldn't speak, wouldn't cry out loud for him to stop.

After the fifth blow, she felt his heat and presence behind her. His thick cock slid between her legs and then thrust strongly into her quim. She struggled in her dark world to reorient herself from pain to pleasure. Another thrust, and another, stretching her in ecstasy, and then he was gone, leaving her empty.

"No," she cried, even though he'd forbidden her to speak. Because she knew what was coming. Teasing, and more pain.

"Hush," he reminded her, and then the swish and thwack of impact echoed in the marble room. The heat was more intense now, coming on the heels of the too-short respite. Five blows again, as she cried and danced about, going nowhere. Then his cock drove inside her again. She used to be ashamed that such rough play excited her, but not anymore. *Oh, oh, oh...*

"You feel that?" he asked, pressing inside her. "Feel how hard I am for you. You want to be fucked, don't you? You want me to fuck you until you come."

"Yes, Sir," she answered, taking the opportunity to speak, even if she could barely form the words. "Please let me come."

"After you take your spanking," he said. "You know you come much harder and longer after you've been properly spanked."

She shook her head, and pulled at the cuffs in frustration as he left her again.

"Please," she cried out as the tawse resumed its stinging torture.

Rather than chide her for speaking out of turn, he put his hand over her mouth and gave her a good, steady volley of whacks. She protested against his palm, but oh, it felt so good. It felt intense and scary, and wonderfully liberating, because she was so completely under his control, unable to speak, unable to see. She lost track of how many times he spanked her and fucked her in alternation, never letting her get a foothold on her way to climax.

She would feel this tomorrow...even though it was play, this sort of spanking would leave bruises. She'd feel it when she walked, and when she sat to tend the children. Whenever she had time alone, she would pull up the back of her skirts and gain perverse pleasure from gazing at the marks in her looking glass. That was the type of duchess she was, for better or worse, and her husband rejoiced in it.

Especially at times like these.

"I want you to come now," he said at last. He placed his hands over the cuffs and thrust inside her, banging his hips against her tender arse. "Come for me, Guinevere. I want it."

Nothing triggered her pleasure more reliably than his gruff, insistent commands. Her pelvis contracted, her pussy clenching around his pounding shaft. He drew rigid behind her, with a jerk and a long groan. His final thrust nearly lifted her from the floor. The cuffs rattled on their chains as he held her close, sighing contentedly against her ear.

She didn't speak yet. She wished to be a good wife and obey his directions, so she waited until he removed her blindfold and released her from the cuffs. Then she turned to him and threw her arms around his neck.

"I love you," she said. "I love you. I love you. And that *really hurt*."

She reached one hand behind her to rub away the sting that remained, but of course, Aidan stopped her.

"You know better," he said, clasping her wrist. "Perhaps we ought to begin all over again with a real punishment, if you'll disregard my rules."

"Oh, no," she said. "I'll be good."

She put her arm back around his neck and hugged him, unwilling to break the connection that came from this intense sort of play. After a moment, he lifted her so she was eye-to-eye with him at his prodigious height.

"Say it again," he prompted. "I like those words."

"I'll be good?"

"No, the other words."

"I love you." She hugged him tighter, pressing a kiss against his ear. "I love you. I love you."

She drew back and gazed at him, the fairy queen and her king in their marble temple. His hands smoothed over her back and cupped her bottom with a tender grip.

"I love you too, Gwen," he whispered. "I'll love you forever."

And for that, she'd always be his perfect, obedient duchess.

Ask the heavens for what your heart wants. In her case, someone had answered. Someone tall and commanding, and sometimes a bit lofty, with a Viking marauder smile.

THE END

A Final Note

Endings are always bittersweet. I've had a blast writing about these four gentlemen in 1790's England, and if you've read all four of the Properly Spanked novels, thank you from the bottom of my heart for supporting the whole saga. I hope you found something in each novel to love.

But maybe this isn't the end. Wouldn't it be great if all those children in the Epilogue grew up and had adventures, and maybe even paired up romantically around 1820 or so? Hmm, that would be pretty fun. We'll see.

If you enjoyed *Training Lady Townsend, To Tame A Countess, My Naughty Minette*, and *Under A Duke's Hand*, I would be eternally grateful for a review or a recommendation to a naughty-minded friend. Your reviews and encouragement are so helpful, and keep me motivated to sit in the chair every day and give you my best work. I also love to hear from my readers at annabeljosephnovels@gmail.com.

Many thanks to my beta readers for this series: GC, Janine, Tiffany, Tasha L. Harrison, and Doris. Thanks also to my editors, Audrey K., and Lina Sacher of Lina Edits. Huge, huge thanks to Kate at Bad Star Media for designing a quartet of luscious historical covers.

In closing, I'd like to apologize for the fact that you will never look at ginger the same way again.

Coming Soon:

A new steamy bodyguard romance from Annabel's alter ego, Molly Joseph:

PAWN, book one in the Ironclad Bodyguards series

High stakes chess competition has always been a man's game—until Grace Ann Frasier topples some of the game's greatest champions and turns the chess world on its ear. Her prowess at the game is matched only by her rivals' desire to defeat her, or, worse, avenge their losses. When an international championship threatens Grace's safety, a bevy of security experts are hired to look after her, but only one is her personal, close-duty bodyguard, courtesy of Ironclad Solutions, Inc.

Sam Knight knows nothing about chess, but he knows Grace is working to achieve something important, and he vows to shelter her from those who mean her harm. In the course of his duties, he realizes there's more going on than a simple chess match between rivals, and his fragile client is all too aware of the stakes. When she leans on him for emotional support, attraction battles with professionalism and Sam finds his self-discipline wavering. Soon the complexity of their relationship resembles a chess board, where one questionable move can ruin everything—or win a game that could resonate around the world.

Other Historical Romance by Annabel Joseph

Disciplining the Duchess

Over five seasons, Miss Harmony Barrett has managed to repel every gentleman of consequence and engineer a debacle at Almack's so horrifying that her waltzing privileges are revoked. If she's not in the library reading about Mongol hordes, she's embarrassing her family or getting involved in impulsive scrapes.

Enter the Duke of Courtland, a man known for his love of duty and decorum. Through a vexing series of events, he finds himself shackled to Miss Barrett in matrimony. But all is not lost. The duke harbors a not-so-secret affinity for spanking and discipline…and his new wife is ever in need of it. Will the mismatched couple find their way to marital happiness? Or will the duke be forever *Disciplining the Duchess*?

Lily Mine

When Lily wends her way down the country lane to Lilyvale Manor, she hopes the coincidence of names bodes well, for she is in dire straits. She's been disowned by her London family and finds herself desperately in need of a job.

Lord Ashbourne is equally at ends, his fiancée having jilted him for a commoner and run off to the Continent. Her powerful society family is determined to delay the breaking scandal in order to save the younger sister's prospects. When a servant leads Lily to his parlor, James is astonished to discover how closely she resembles the missing lady of the manor.

He hatches a plan, convincing Lily to play his absent "wife" to keep the gossips at bay. He reassures her it will be in name only, but soon enough, playacting turns to real attraction, and friendship to aching, mounting desire. The strictures of society and unforeseen tragedy combine to test the pair's forbidden love, even as they are driven ever closer into one another's arms...

Cait and the Devil

The young maiden Cait has always lived a simple, secluded life in the Scottish woods. Then, in her eighteenth year, she is summoned to Aberdeen and informed with cruel disdain that she is the unwanted daughter of the king. To deal with this "problem," Cait is forced to marry a forbidding stranger, Duncan, the Devil of Inverness, who has already buried one wife.

She travels to the Devil's castle reluctantly, in dread, and Duncan is none too pleased to welcome the pale, dark-haired creature as his wife. But the two soon realize they are more perfectly matched than either suspected. His deep desire to dominate and discipline his new wife is matched only by her bravery and willingness to submit to his perverse demands and desires.

But a phantom threat stalks Cait, and Duncan is troubled by her secret and mysterious past. Can Duncan protect his vulnerable wife? Will their powerful and unusual brand of love prevail?

About the Author

Annabel Joseph is a multi-published, New York Times and USA Today Bestselling BDSM romance author. She writes mainly contemporary romance, although she has been known to dabble in the medieval and Regency eras. She is recognized for writing emotionally intense BDSM storylines, and strives to create characters that seem real—even flawed—so readers are better able to relate to them.

Annabel also writes vanilla (non-BDSM) erotic romance under the pen name Molly Joseph.

Annabel Joseph loves to hear from readers at annabeljosephnovels@gmail.com.

You can learn more about Annabel's books and sign up for her newsletter at annabeljoseph.com.